Not the head

No less than Si...
the despot of Po...
took a shot-gun to intruders...

But surely there was a mistake? This man seemed harmless and utterly charming. But then their eyes met once again, and Patti saw, hidden in their dark depths, a lurking intention of something that sent a shiver up her straight back.

Dear Reader

A Christmas treat from Paula Marshall, THE CYPRIAN'S SISTER is another sparkling Regency. In Christine Franklin's HEART OF A ROSE, Patti is convinced she has to right a wrong. From America we have SWEET JUSTICE by Jan McKee, and a look at Pennsylvania coalmining in 1870 by Doreen Ownes Malek. Quite a variety! Have a happy Christmas!

The Editor

Although born in Essex, **Christine Franklin** now lives in Devon. Since she has been an avid reader since childhood, it seemed only natural to write stories as she grew up, and in the late 1960s this urge to write became all-important.

Happily married, with a grown-up son, Christine is the author of several contemporary romances, children's books, and books of folklore and walks. She has an absorbing curiosity about the past, and enjoys researching and writing for Masquerade.

Recent titles by the same author:

A CERTAIN MAGIC

HEART OF A ROSE

Christine Franklin

MILLS & BOON

MILLS & BOON LIMITED
ETON HOUSE, 18–24 PARADISE ROAD
RICHMOND, SURREY, TW9 1SR

All the characters in this book have no existence outside the imagination of the Author, and have no relation whatsoever to anyone bearing the same name or names. They are not even distantly inspired by any individual known or unknown to the Author, and all the incidents are pure invention.

All Rights Reserved. The text of this publication or any part thereof may not be reproduced or transmitted in any form or by any means, electronic or mechanical, including photocopying, recording, storage in an information retrieval system, or otherwise, without the written permission of the publisher.

This book is sold subject to the condition that it shall not, by way of trade or otherwise, be lent, resold, hired out or otherwise circulated without the prior consent of the publisher in any form of binding or cover other than that in which it is published and without a similar condition including this condition being imposed on the subsequent purchaser.

*First published in Great Britain 1993
by Mills & Boon Limited*

© Christine Franklin 1993

*Australian copyright 1993
Philippine copyright 1993
This edition 1993*

ISBN 0 263 78241 7

*Set in 10 on 12 pt Linotron Times
04-9312-80839*

*Typeset in Great Britain by Centracet, Cambridge
Made and printed in Great Britain*

CHAPTER ONE

'NO ONE wants me! Professor Matthews says he considers me too young to be his wife's companion. . .'

Patricia Nevill's unhappy face stared across the breakfast-table as she dropped the letter she had just read. Then her dismay lifted slightly when her sister said fondly, 'Don't be downcast, dearest! I know you'll find a new situation soon—and in the meantime just enjoy being here with us. Why, it's like the old days—remember?—when James and I were first married and you lived with us, before you went to London to take up your post with poor Miss Clarke. You must stay with us as long as you like, my love.'

Patti looked across the rim of her coffee-cup into Beth's soft grey eyes and instantly felt comforted. Huskily, she murmured, 'Darling—how understanding you are.' Then, clearing her throat, she added more briskly, and with a tilt to her dimpled chin, 'But I don't intend to outstay my welcome. Just a week or so—until I find that situation.'

Beth's eyes twinkled. 'And remember, you're a very talented and efficient young woman; even if the professor considers you too young, dear Miss Clarke thought you a wonder!'

Patti laughed to hide her quick surge of feeling. 'Thank you. I only hope all the other would-be employers think so too!

'Of course they will. But cheer up; think of something else to concentrate on while you're writing away for posts.'

'I will, Beth—I really will. But—but I'm sure you and James can't truly want visitors—you're so completely happy as you are.'

Beth smiled reassuringly. 'You're not a visitor, Patti. You're one of the family.'

Breakfast continued in quiet content, but Patti mulled over these last words as she buttered her toast, experiencing a stab of pain as she thought about the family she did not have—except for elder sister Beth. Father and Mother had died within months of each other, making both girls orphans while only in their teens; and now her employer, kindly Miss Edith Clarke, had died after a long illness just ten days ago. Patti sniffed as the unhappiness of her situation revealed itself.

Memories came, unbidden. 'Miss Clarke was so kind,' she mused, letting the toast drop, forgotten, to her plate. 'She let me have the freedom of her entire library, you know. . .' Then, abruptly, an expression of excitement brought a new gleam to her tawny eyes. She relaxed in her chair, transported back to happier days. 'I read a lot about gardens—and flowers—and especially about roses. Oh, Beth——' she smiled infectiously '—do you remember how Grandfather used to talk about roses? Mysterious flowers from the past, he called them. Why, he once showed me a book—an old, heavy book made out of parchment—with wonderful pictures in it. And he said that the most beautiful rose of all—a Gallica, I think he called it—had an equally beautiful name. Madame Léonie de Sange. . .' Patti whispered the name softly, repeating it to herself before she noticed Beth's abruptly veiled eyes.

'Doesn't it sound lovely?' she asked, smiling. 'And he said it belonged to us, to our family. I remember him saying so. "Madame Léonie belongs to us Nevills". He was quite autocratic about it, wasn't he?'

A hush settled around the table, broken finally by James rising to his feet and folding his newspaper over the back of his vacated chair. He smiled down at both girls. 'Time for me to start work, my dears. Patti, I could do with some of your charming enthusiasm — to force into the unthinking heads of my village pupils!'

He bent to kiss Beth's cheek, looking fondly down into her smiling eyes. His voice deepened. 'Don't do too much, my love. Leave the rough work for Cissie. I'll be home for tea, as usual. Goodbye, Patti — I hope you enjoy your little holiday with us.'

'Goodbye, James. I certainly intend to, thank you.'

Patti was on her feet, running to the open window to watch James crossing the village green towards the long grey building of the school near the church. 'You're so lucky, Beth,' she said in a small voice. 'What a wonderful husband James is. . .'

Beth was beside her in a moment, an arm around her waist. 'He certainly is. But darling, one day you will find one just as nice.'

'Hmm — I wonder. . .' Patti forced a note of gaiety into her subdued voice. 'Sometimes I doubt it. I'm not nearly as sweet-natured as you, Beth. I've always been — well — naughty, haven't I?'

'A little wilful, perhaps. Rebellious. Only at times, of course — but——' Beth hugged Patti warmly, laughing as she went on '— but always full of life and idealism. You're not so bad! And anyway, stop fishing for compliments. . . Now——' her tone grew more brisk '—exactly what are your plans for today, Miss Nevill?'

'To do whatever I can to help you, of course.'

'Nonsense. Take no notice of James, he's a real fusspot. And Cissie will be up from the village in a few minutes. She'll do all the horrid jobs. All I have to do is tidy up the parlour and be a lady of leisure! Which reminds me, Patti, there's an employment agency advertising in yesterday's paper. What a blessing women are allowed to leave their homes and think about careers now...' Leaving the window, she went to James's desk beside the far wall and rummaged through a pile of old papers. 'I'll find it and then you can start writing some more letters of application. Not that I want you to go, dear, of course, but...'

'But I have to live, don't I?' Patti sighed, her thoughts focused again on reality. 'Father's money is nearly all gone, and my salary from dear Miss Clarke for last month won't last very long. So yes, I'll write lots of letters. But in the meantime....'

Her voice grew quick with renewed vitality. 'Do you know, Beth, I think I might treat myself to a little adventure! I want to find the garden of someone called Challoner—I read about him in one of Miss Clarke's horticultural magazines. It seems he's a very famous international rose grower. Now, if anyone might know where Grandfather's old rose has got to, surely it'll be him. I'll make enquiries in the village—perhaps at the post office... I'm almost sure I read that he lives somewhere in South Devon...'

She turned, and her voice died as she saw the look on Beth's startled face. 'What is it? Why do you look like that?'

'Challoner, did you say?' Beth's soft voice quivered. 'Oh, dear...'

'Why "Oh, dear"? You don't...?' Impulsively, Patti leaped across the room to tug at her sister's arm. 'You don't actually *know* him, do you?'

'No,' Beth replied very firmly. 'I certainly do not know him.'

'Then why are you keeping something from me?' asked Patti, her eyes wide and a note of rebuke in her voice. She smiled persuasively. 'Come on, now—tell me what it is. *Please*, Beth...' There was a world of charm in the last word, and reluctantly Beth's face eased into an answering smile.

'Oh, dear, I never could keep secrets, could I?' Abruptly her voice grew anxious. 'But Patti, I really don't think you should dig up all that old business about Grandfather and his rose. After all, he became very woolly-headed at the end... He probably made up all that he told you—the rose's name, his claim to its ownership...well, everything...' She looked at Patti severely. 'And I really do think you should do something far more practical than waste time talking about *roses*!'

'I'm not wasting time. Roses are very popular these days!' Patti's cheeks turned quite pink, and she looked at her sister with what Beth feared was crusading zeal. 'Perhaps you don't realise it,' she exploded, 'but Miss Clarke was helping bring old roses back into popularity in gardens! She wrote lots of newspaper articles saying that stuffy Victorian formal planting is long since finished and that big informal borders are in fashion now... I mean, that's where my interest in roses began, Beth.'

'I see.' Beth soothed, and was about to turn away when Patti said sharply,

'Oh, no, you don't! Don't try and sneak off without telling me whatever it was you didn't want to—if you know what I mean...!'

Their shared laughter filled the room and then Beth said gently, 'If I must, then I will. But one last word of warning, dearest—don't let your interest in roses lead you into the same sort of trouble that Grandfather got into. He was at loggerheads with his cousins, you know, and created quite a family feud—I would hate you to do anything to dig up all that past unhappiness...'

Patti caught her sister's hands as, anxiously, she locked them together. 'Darling Beth, don't worry! You sound so serious, but all I want to do is to cheer myself up with a diversion. I can't write letters of application all day, can I?' She laughed and saw Beth's face relax. 'Now—kindly tell me your big secret, Beth Mortimer!'

'Yes. Well, the big house on the far side of the green—Porphyry Court, it's called—is the home of the Challoner family. The son, Sir Robert, must be the man you spoke of. He's certainly a famous rose grower.'

'Wonderful!' Instantly Patti was cock-a-hoop. 'I'll go and call on him—this morning—now! Why not?'

Beth became very agitated. 'You must do nothing of the sort! Go and call there, on your own? Really, Patti, what an idea!'

Patti pouted. 'Don't be so stuffy! This is the twentieth century, you know—we're not repressed old Victorians any longer! And Miss Clarke chaperoned me so heavily in London that I simply *long* to come and go as I want now!' Then, as she saw the frown linger on her sister's face, her voice grew more persuasive. 'I only want to creep in and look at his gardens. I'm just interested in seeing what he grows. That's all—well, for a start, anyway. And no one will see me.'

'Out of the question. It's common knowledge that Sir Robert is an absolute despot when it comes to protecting his beloved garden. He's been known to take a shot-gun to intruders.'

Patti tried wheedling. 'But I'd only be half an hour or so. It depends on where the borders are—and the rosebeds, of course——'

'For goodness' sake, Patti—think again,' chided Beth despairingly. 'No one ever dares go into Porphyry Court without an invitation——'

Patti's lower lip pouted stubbornly. 'Then I'll make sure I'm not seen. And I'll manipulate a proper invitation later.' She paused, looking at Beth teasingly. 'If you like I'll leave my card under the rhubarb leaves...'

'You're impossible, Patti Nevill!' Beth shook her head, but now her eyes had begun to twinkle again. 'You know, those three years in London don't seem to have done you any good at all!'

'Yes, they have. I've learned to be an excellent companion—and if I didn't particularly enjoy life in town I do know a lot about gardens now. *And* old roses!'

'Maybe, but you're still as wayward and impulsive as you were as a child.' Beth's words were stern, but her smile gave the lie to real reproof.

She watched Patti wander slowly to the fireplace and look into the mirror hanging above the mantel. She twisted a drooping auburn ringlet around a small, strong finger, and then met Beth's watching eyes in the mirror. Smiling wickedly, she said softly, 'Darling Beth, don't worry so much. I'm not planning to break into this Challoner's high-powered glasshouses, or steal his exotic plants! I only want to inspect his rosebeds.'

'You're quite impossible!' Beth turned away to conceal her grudging laughter. 'And when do you propose to go?'

'Now! Straight away! Cissie will help you, won't she? And you did say I needed a rest. . . Oh, Beth, let me go—please?'

'How can I stop you?' Beth shrugged her shoulders, and then followed Patti as she skipped out into the passage, grabbing her cream leghorn straw hat from the rack and quickly trying to tie the pale chiffon veil that anchored it to her head.

'Here, let me do it. . .' Beth crossed the remaining space to her sister's side and expertly retied the rather untidy bow beneath the dimpled, strong jaw. 'Never could tie a bow properly, could you?' She looked keenly into her sister's glowing tawny eyes. 'Oh, bother that silly story of Grandfather's—I'm sure it's better to forget it.'

'But Beth, it's interesting! And I *do* need something to cheer me up today, after that letter from Professor Matthews, turning down my application. . .' Patti's enthusiasm was infectious and Beth had never been able to resist her sister's charm.

She sighed, turning away. 'And so you intend to go, uninvited, into the Challoners' garden, and——'

'And no one will see me. My dress is green. I'll fly like a lacewing from one bush to the next! And Beth. . .'

'Yes?' Reluctantly Beth halted at the door, waiting

for the inevitable favour that she guessed she was about to be asked.

'You're so clever with people — so loved in the village. And I know you'll be your usual, wonderful, organising dear self, and arrange for me to call on the Challoners, won't you? *Please*, darling Beth?'

'Patti, your determination has no bounds! I don't really see how I can — —'

'But of *course* you can! And you will!' There was a swirl of linen skirts, a few quick steps, and Patti threw her arms around her sister. 'I know I'm a wretch — selfish, impulsive, yes, all of that! But my heart's in the right place. And it would be such fun to slip into that wonderful garden and have a look around. . .' Patti's smile was radiant. 'I'll just take a quick peep at the rosebeds and then I'll come straight home and behave myself. And this very afternoon I'll start writing off to that other employment agency, if you can find the address.'

Beth, released from the suffocating hug, watched the trim, green-clad figure skip away down the passage and shook her head in a familiar helpless gesture. It was useless to try and resist that charm and overwhelming stubbornness. She knew Patti would get her own way. She always did.

But, as elder sister, Beth made sure she had the last word. 'Come back here, this instant,' she ordered sternly. 'At least you're not going without your gloves, Patti Nevill.'

Patti approached the vast garden of Porphyry Court from a sly angle. No good thinking she would get past the pompous old lodge keeper. But this way — crossing the meadow, skirting the brook, taking a short cut through the churchyard and then letting herself into the garden by the private church gateway—was a real brainwave.

But she held her breath, as carefully, she eased open the black wrought-iron gate, praying no one would hear the tell-tale squeal it gave before swinging back behind her.

Safe inside, she looked around. The house was invisible, concealed, she imagined, by a curving driveway softened with the immense, sun-touched foliage of flowering shrubs and heavily leafed trees. The May morning held a tremulous haziness and Patti felt as if the whole world—like herself—was holding its breath.

She should not be here. Oh, dear, but how right Beth was! Beth was always right, reflected Patti gloomily; it was irritating how right she could be. And what had she said about Sir Robert Challoner having been known to take a shot-gun to intruders?

Nervously Patti moved from one shady shrub to the next concealing tree, staring around and wondering where the rose garden might be. At the back of the house, she thought sagely, where the south aspect would be more open than this wooded drive.

And then a bird started to sing and she was lost in the sweetness of its music, touched by the morning sun's warmth and utterly enrapt by the beauty all around her. After those long years in London, her heart now felt as if it might burst open, so strong were the feelings of relief that asailed her. Gardens, indeed, were the most wonderfully lovesome things, thought Patti, a little wildly.

She had not expected to experience the return of this heady lack of self-control. As a child, of course, it had been only natural for her to love the beauty of nature without restraint, but three years with crotchety but beloved Miss Clarke had run a ring of uneasy conformity around her easily aroused emotions.

'I am a "young lady", as Miss Clarke kept telling me,' she reminded herself. 'Not an undisciplined country girl. . . Oh, but I do realise now how I hated London! And how much I adore the country. . . How hard it will be to take up another position and go back to the grime, and the crowds, and that awful lack of beauty. . .' Patti's thoughts ran riot as she fingered a deeply cleft green leaf, and then bent her head to smell the fragrance.

And then she saw the grotto and could no longer contain those surging, delirious emotions. . . 'Oh! But how wonderful. . .!' Leaving the shadow of the large rhododendron, with its budding scarlet flowers, she ran across velvety green sward towards the shell-encased grotto opposite. It was backed by a high, shadowed wall, down which dripped ferns and ivy and lichen, and innumerable small plants which caught the dappled sunlight and shone like tigers' eyes in deep undergrowth.

Captivated, Patti sank down on her knees beside the little pool which filled the grotto, and dabbled her fingers in the cool water. Sighing, she felt completely filled with happiness. Nothing could ever irritate her again. She would be good and dutiful to dear Beth; she would find herself a situation somewhere and lead a respectable, dull life — if only this sense of content and beauty could remain forever, locked inside her. . .

Then, abruptly, like the cold finger of fate, an enormous shadow fell upon the sun-touched water, covered the grotto, the pool — and her.

'Excuse me,' said a chillingly vibrant voice and, gasping, Patti turned, to find a man standing over her.

He wore a shabby lovat-green tweed suit. His boots were scuffed and had surely never been polished. Such clothes instantly conveyed his position as a gardener, and, despite her confusion, Patti found herself quickly trying to place him — perhaps the head gardener? He certainly had an air of imposing authority about him.

And he was decidedly unmannered, she thought, recovering swiftly from the shock of being found out. No servile removal of his battered hat, not even a touching of the forelock of thick black hair that fell across his wide brow. She rose somewhat clumsily, thankful that Miss Clarke was not there to witness this unseemly confrontation. Then she banished the thought with a snappy condemnation of the man for not having even offered her his hand to assist her to rise.

Standing very straight and refusing to allow herself to be intimidated by his height, Patti looked up into the dark eyes that watched her every movement without blinking.

'Now, my man. . .' With practised hauteur she allowed herself a slight smile. 'I can explain exactly what I am doing here.' Waiting for a softening of the hard expression, she paused — was that a glimmer of interest lighting the chocolate-brown gaze? Even a flicker of — could it be *amusement*? She put the uncomfortable idea out of her mind at once. This man was far too insensitive to find her of any interest. He merely wanted to get on with his gardening.

But the lean, angled face was watching warily, and so she continued, her assurance wilting as she spoke. 'Of course, as you seem to be a gardener here — head gardener, perhaps. . .?' Her most winsome smile had no more effect than to tighten the muscles around the straight mouth. She rushed on. 'I can quite appreciate your wondering whom I am. Well, I am Patricia Nevill—*Miss* Nevill—the sister of Mrs James Mortimer, who lives at Clematis Cottage. My brother-in-law, Mr Mortimer, runs the village school. . .'

Then her words petered out, for surely he *was* looking amused. . .intuition whispered he was also intrigued. Even—attracted? Patti gasped and banished her milling thoughts. No, no! Surely all she had seen on that handsome, lean face was an expression of impatience—wasn't it?

She drew in a deep, controlling breath. Drat the man! How did he manage to make her feel at such a disadvantage? After all, he was only a servant. 'Yes—well. . .' She pulled herself together. 'Having heard how splendid Sir Robert's garden is, I just slipped in—'

'And now, if you please, you will just slip out again. The church gate, as you have already discovered, is behind you. Good day, Miss Nevill.'

That voice again—resonant and full of music. It was doing something most strange to her senses. She gaped foolishly and wished he would continue speaking so that she could listen forever. And then, thankfully, she recovered her wits. What was she thinking of? Even if his voice was educated and attractive, he was still only the gardener. . .

Doggedly her self-control returned and she knew that she must do as he had ordered. Bowing her head, she turned away, walking slowly—he must not have the satisfaction of thinking he had browbeaten her, even if he had! But, at the last minute, she could not resist the awful need to turn and glance back over her shoulder. . .

He still stood there, watching her. And this time the expression in his deep eyes sent a prickle of some hitherto unknown sensation hurtling up and down her spine.

Patti decided against telling Beth. Why worry her with unimportant things? But it struck her, during the afternoon, that Beth looked as if she was already worrying about something. By teatime Patti had decided Beth should confess her problem, and so went to work on her sister with the usual persuasive charm.

'Darling, I do so hope you're not worrying about my future.'

Beth looked up from her sewing, meeting the bright gaze with some reluctance. 'Of course not. I'm sure you'll soon find a suitable position.'

'So — is it James you're anxious about?'

'Why should I? He's very well and loves his work here.' Beth pursed her lips and slowly squared her shoulders. 'Patti, I know where all this is leading,' she said accusingly. 'You're trying to get something out of me.'

Patti's soft chuckle held a ring of victory. 'That's right! So hurry up and tell me. You never could keep things to yourself, could you? Don't start now!'

'Well. . .' Beth avoided her sister's eyes. 'It's about the Challoners. They're — they're actually relatives of ours. . .'

'*Are* they? You never told me!'

'I wasn't sure. But while you were out this morning I looked at some of Grandfather's letters which Father kept, and the name cropped up in several of them. Apparently Enid, Lady Challoner and her only son

Robert, who grows roses, are very distant cousins. Well, it has to be the same family who lives at Porphyry Court. . .' Beth's words petered out, for Patti was suddenly dancing around the little room, her face alight with triumph.

'But how marvellous! So now, darling, you can write Lady Challoner a note and tell her that we're a distant connection and——'

'Only *very* distant, I'm sure——'

Patti ignored the interjection. 'And please may we call on her? And *him*. . .?'

'Patti, I really don't think——' began Beth weakly, but her sister's enthusiasm was too much for her.

'But I do, Beth! Now, come along, here's your notepaper and here's James's pen. . .quickly. . .' Patti struck a pose, head back, eyes concentrating. 'Dear Lady Challoner. . .' Then she relaxed again, smiling persuasively. 'Oh, you can put it better than I can! Hurry up, Beth—I can't *wait* to get into Porphyry Court and inspect those lovely gardens properly.'

'Are you ready, Patti? Hurry, or we shall be late. . .' Beth stood at the bottom of the cottage staircase, her voice only faintly reaching Patti as she put the final touches to her *toilette*.

Still in mourning for poor Miss Clarke, she had hummed and hawed frantically about what to wear for this important call upon the Challoners. The pale lavender day dress which she had bought so recently for the funeral, judging it not to be formal mourning, just a mark of the respect and love she had held for her late employer, seemed perhaps just a little too smart for country calling—but it was so pretty, and suited her so well.

Worn over a straight-fronted corset, which left her gasping for breath as she drew the laces tight, the dress pouched softly over her small bosom before falling in extravagant pleats from the tightly cinched waist. The gentle frou-frou of the frilled hem over the bare elm boards of her bedroom whispered to Patti of anticipation and restrained excitement.

Elbow-length gloves, reaching the gathered cuffs of enormous square-shouldered sleeves, completed her ensemble, together with her hat. The heavy cream straw, trimmed with ribbon exactly matching the colour of the braiding on the dress, was embellished with a huge plume of ostrich feathers, silvery white, that glistened as the sun touched it.

Patti fingered the curling tendrils of dark red hair that refused to be confined beneath the large hat, and wondered yet again if she was not over-dressed for a mere afternoon call upon a distant and so far unknown relative who lived in the depths of the Devonshire countryside. . .

'Patti!' Beth's sharp summons from below decided her. Too late now to remove her finery and change back into a simple cotton or flowered linen. Well, Lady Challoner would at least learn that her newly discovered kinswoman could look like a Bond Street fashion plate when she so wished.

'All right, all right, I'm coming. . .'

Gingerly Patti descended the steep stairs in her smart, high-heeled cream shoes, dark mauve parasol in one hand, small black leather handbag in the other.

'Oh, Patti—*no*!' There was a world of mingled reaction in Beth's gasp. 'What on earth are you all dressed up for? You look like a—like a. . .'

'Well?' asked Patti, dangerously polite.

Beth swallowed and then smiled resignedly. 'I mean, of course, that you look magnificent. Extremely elegant. Very. . .well—er—urban, I suppose. . .'

'Hardly surprising, as I've lived in London for a long time.' Patti swished the small train of her gown behind her and advanced resolutely to the doorway. 'I only hope I don't have to walk too far. This corset is killing me.'

'You won't. I've hired Peter Radway's dog-cart.'

'Dog-cart? How common!'

Beth flared instantly. 'It's what we're glad to use in the country. For goodness' sake, try and forget all your fine airs and graces—motor cars haven't reached Moorwood yet.'

'Well, I trust we can both get in it,' Patti grumbled, looking at Beth's plain yet pretty pink and white print dress, and then grudgingly adding, 'At least you won't take up as much room as I shall.'

'Come along. We mustn't keep Lady Challoner waiting.' Beth led the way out into the sunny garden and through the gateway to the waiting gig. 'It's so very good of her to invite us. Her note was most gracious.'

Patti's wide mouth became mutinous. 'What's especially gracious about meeting long-lost relatives? Don't be such a doormat, Beth!' Giving grinning Peter Radway a brief smile, she settled herself on one side of the little cart and, looking beneath her lashes at her sister, saw how anxious the grey eyes seemed, and then instantly berated herself for such a shrewish remark.

'I'm sorry,' she said softly. 'I keep forgetting I'm not a London young lady any more, but just Patti Nevill, trying to get her own way! Forgive me, darling? I promise I'll behave and be a credit to you—and to all the dead Nevills in that huge family tree that somehow links us with her ladyship. Truly, I won't say a word out of place!'

Beth's set mouth softened. 'I'll believe that when it happens,' she said wryly. 'When did you ever not say exactly what you felt? And always at the wrong moment. . .'

'This time it's a promise,' vowed Patti. And told herself sternly that she really did mean it.

But, as usual, Beth had the last word. Leaning forward so that her voice could not reach the driver's ears as he clucked encouragingly to the pony, she said tersely. 'And do try to appear ladylike, Patti—some of the old Victorian qualities still matter, you know; a marriageable girl without a dowry should always ensure that at least her reputation is intact. If Lady Challoner is to accept us as kin, she'll expect you to know how to behave.'

They were shown into the orangery, some fifty yards' distance from the front entrance of the house. Tall palm trees created welcome coolness and shadowed the cane tables and chairs set out beneath the glass windows, over which trailing, scented plants wound like great colourful serpents. The air was warm, the mixture of heavy fragrances slightly cloying, and Patti, recalling her corset, took a last huge breath of fresh air as she entered behind Beth.

Lady Challoner, dressed in an old-fashioned afternoon gown of soft pale grey wool, greeted them with the ease and graciousness of a practised hostess. If her fine blue-green eyes widened slightly at the sight of Patti's elegance, her composure remained quite unruffled.

'Come in, Mrs Mortimer! How delightful to meet you,' she drawled. 'Strange that we should live so near for the past few years and yet have never discovered our kinship—I was most intrigued to receive your note telling me about it. And this must be your sister? How-de-do, my dear?'

After they were invited to seat themselves, there was a moment of silence, through which dresses rustled and cane chairs creaked. Then Patti, hearing footsteps behind her, half turned, expecting to see the arrival of servants with tea trays.

But no—her mouth fell open, her eyes widened and, instantly forgetful of her recent promise to restrain herself, she said loudly, 'Good gracious! It's the head gardener!'

The atmosphere was immediately charged with confusion and slight embarrassment. Beth murmured, 'Oh, dear!' and put a hand to her face, while Lady Challoner, staring, said, 'How very odd,' in a pointed voice and Patti wished, with all her fast-beating heart, that the orangery floor would open up, wafting her down to the nether regions of the hell that she was sure she must deserve by committing such a *faux pas*.

But all that happened was that the head gardener—now unhatted, and far more conventionally dressed in a dark, checked suit, noticed Patti, even as she sat staring up at him—smiled, with a twist of his mouth, and held out a lean, powerful, earth-stained hand.

'Why, Miss Nevill!' His rich, deep voice was friendly, and full of something which she could not quite identify, and did not really wish to—again, it sounded like concealed amusement. 'But how delightful to meet you again—which way did you enter this time?'

Here Miss Clarke's rigorous training at last came to

Patti's rescue, and by the time he had released her hand she was her usual self once more, able to return his smile, while answering calmly, 'My sister and I arrived by dog-cart, through the main entrance, past the lodge. How beautifully neat the gravel drive is. It must take you hours to rake it. . .'

'Believe me, it does,' he replied very solemnly, but with the suspicion of a brief smile.

Their eyes caught and lingered, until Lady Challoner said curiously, 'Do I understand you have already met Miss Nevill, Robert? So introductions are not necessary. . .?'

The tall, dark-haired man moved away from Patti's side and stood next to Lady Challoner's chair. One hand slid gently around her shoulders, and his smile, as he looked down, made Patti's heart unexpectedly somersault. 'Miss Nevill and I have certainly met, Mother. But not this lady, I believe. . .' And he bowed very charmingly towards Beth, whose cheeks grew becomingly pink.

'My son, Robert. Mrs James Mortimer, the wife of our village schoolmaster.'

'Of course,' murmured the head gardener, with a brief glance in Patti's direction, before taking Beth's outstretched hand.

My son, Robert. . .

Patti was still gasping, but, as Beth looked nervously at her, recalled her promise to behave, and somehow kept silent.

Not the head gardener after all, then — no less than Sir Robert Challoner himself, the despot of Porphyry Court, the man who took a shot-gun to intruders. . .

But surely there was a mistake? This man seemed harmless and utterly charming. But then their eyes met once again, and she saw, hidden in their dark depths, a lurking intention of something that sent a shiver up her straight back.

Yes, he could be nice when it suited him, she knew it instinctively; but, oh, dear, how horrible he could be when things went wrong. . .

CHAPTER TWO

CONVERSATION flowed gently in the warm, airless glass orangery, and Patti sat on the edge of her cane chair, uncomfortably aware of her restricting corsets, but even more so of the presence of Sir Robert Challoner.

He sat quite close, a large, relaxed figure just a little too near for comfort. She responded politely to Lady Challoner's occasional questions, and half listened to what Beth was telling their hostess about family matters, but all the time it was the indolent man with the steady, dark gaze and the air of only just subdued vitality that filled her mind.

When he said, in a lull in the conversation, 'After tea, Miss Nevill, you must allow me to take you outside; from the terrace you can see several parts of the garden which you have not yet inspected,' she turned, with a rapid blush of colour, as she recognised the quiet irony in his words. His eyes met hers with such impact that for a moment she was unable to reply—she thought he looked amused, intrigued, and, in some horrible way, even a little suspicious, all at the same time.

It took a few moments to recover her poise. Then she inclined her head and murmured politely, 'That will be delightful, Sir Robert.' But unfortunately an imp of mischief arose from deep within her, making her add, 'If you are sure you can spare the time from your other duties. . .'

Fearfully, she glanced up at him, expecting a cold

reply. But now the dark eyes smiled at her — a brief, brilliant gleam of acknowledgement which was gone even before she was able to enjoy it. Again, his glance was veiled, and she had no idea what he might be thinking. 'No duty, but a pleasure, believe me, Miss Nevill,' he answered lazily, looking at her across big hands drawn up below his chin.

Deliberately, Patti took time to smooth her full skirt and fold her discarded gloves. She refused to let him intimidate her. Without doubt he was merely playing games with her — well, she would meet him on his own ground. She began to wonder what he had thought of Beth's note, suggesting that possibly they might be kinswomen of the Challoner family — did he approve of finding new cousins sprouting up right beneath his garden walls?

Without knowing she did so, Patti sighed. Robert Challoner was indeed immensely good-looking, personable, and full of some strange magnetism that made her catch her breath each time he looked at her, but she would definitely not allow him to dominate her. Somehow she must stand up to his devious and complicated personality.

And then, suddenly, he was bending towards her, saying with wry, gentle humour, under cover of Lady Challoner's continuing conversation with Beth, 'Don't tell my mother I was wearing gardening clothes last week, Miss Nevill — she considers it vastly beneath the family dignity to do such a thing!'

'And yet you are a family of gardeners. . .' Patti was interested enough to forget her recent thoughts. She looked into his surprised eyes with a sense of achievement.

'How do you know that?' he asked curiously.

Patti caught her breath. How should she treat this mercurial man? Would it be wiser to keep her family background to herself? Beth had advised not mentioning Grandfather's interest in old roses, so perhaps she should not—yet—ask him about Madame Léonie de Sange. Hastily she decided to tell him, instead, about her own experiences in the horticultural world.

'Until recently,' she said levelly, 'I have been the late Miss Edith Clarke's companion, in London. She was the well-known writer about gardens and plants, of course. . .'

Robert Challoner inclined his dark head, amusement lighting his dark eyes once more, and Patti was mortified. Of course he knew Miss Clarke! Everyone who was anyone in the gardening world knew her. Recovering speedily, she went on, 'A lot of Miss Clarke's work was concerned with trying to popularise some of the old, forgotten plants, to make people forget Victorian planting in gardens and create an easier, more relaxed look——'

'I am familiar with her work,' said Robert Challoner smoothly, and again Patti felt foolish. But she stuck to her guns, refusing to allow herself to be vanquished by that unblinking brown gaze, that deeply vibrant voice, and the aura of knowledge and experience that her companion wore on his shoulders.

'Yes. Well. . .' She took a deep breath. 'Working for her, naturally I read many books and articles. And I also read about your own work, Sir Robert, with gardens in general and the old roses in particular. . .'

She stopped abruptly and looked at him a little doubtfully She hadn't really intended to mention Madame Léonie. Not yet.

Robert Challoner's eyes held hers, but she had no

idea of what went on in his mind. She fancied he looked interested, perhaps slightly irritated... Opening her mouth to stumble on, to cover the awkward silence, with relief she heard Lady Challoner say, 'Robert, we are trying to establish which branch of the family tree may unite us. Could it be the Davison-Grant side, do you think? I seem to recall there was a Joshua who took his great-aunt's name when he inherited — wasn't she a Nevill?'

Robert Challoner smiled at his mother. 'I think it quite likely, Mother, dear,' he said gravely. 'When tea is over, why not take Mrs Mortimer into my study and show her the family tree hanging over my desk. She may recognise some of the names.'

When the Worcester bone-china cups were empty, and both guests had refused a second piece of seed cake, Beth and Lady Challoner disappeared into the house, busy in amicable conversation of nostalgia and the possibility of a new kinship. Patti watched them go, glad to see Beth's unforced smile, for, since her return from London three weeks ago, it seemed to her that Beth had grown a little irritable once or twice, despite her sweet disposition. Patti sighed. She guessed she was occasionally a difficult visitor.

Robert Challoner unfolded his great length from the chair beside her. 'Shall we step outside, Miss Nevill? There's a good view from the terrace.'

Patti arose. She felt more sure of herself now, and she placed a hand on his offered arm, allowing him to lead her out through the wide glass doorway.

'Wonderful!' Out in the blessed fresh air, she filled her lungs as full as the restricting corset would allow and leaned elegantly upon her parasol. Suddenly she started, dropping her hand from his arm; her fingers had briefly brushed against his, and the unexpected tingle of the contact had made the blood race through her body. To cover her confusion, she smiled up at him, flickering her lashes archly. 'I've been working in London for some years, but I'm really just a country girl at heart, you know,' she said, and then paused.

At Belmont House, in Miss Clarke's gloomy and darkly furnished drawing-room, this trick had never been known to fail. One flicker of her eyelashes, and visitors had appeared stricken by some strange disease; first they gasped, then they lost their tongues, and finally they had become as putty in her small, strong hands.

Expecting a similar result now, Patti waited. But Robert Challoner merely looked down at her, before saying, with a clear hint of unexpected exasperation putting an edge on his deep voice, 'For heaven's sake, girl, stop your play-acting! First the dress—oh, yes——' as Patti, instantly outraged, opened her mouth to argue '—very pretty, of course, but——'

She could not contain herself. 'Pretty? It's magnificent!'

'I said so, didn't I? Pretty. But not suitable, either to the place or the occasion. And as for that hat. . .!' Now a smile twisted the straight mouth into a lop-sided expression of amusement that made Patti's blood boil anew.

'It's a beautiful hat!' She put up both hands, as if to protect it.

'And you're a beautiful creature. You don't need to gild yourself with extravagant gowns, or to flutter your eyelashes. . .' The edge on the vibrant voice faded, taking on a more soothing note. 'Why couldn't you have worn that nice little dress you had on last week?' asked Sir Robert.

Patti was flabbergasted, insulted, struck dumb for once. And then her senses stilled, and she was able to appreciate the unsubtle compliment. All her outrage left her and she smiled, a little chuckle bubbling up, as she looked into his eyes and saw honesty reflected there.

'You're right, Sir Robert. I always loved dressing up as a child, and today I couldn't resist the opportunity to do so again. After all——' she smiled persuasively '—one doesn't meet long-lost relatives every day of the week, you know!'

He looked at her very shrewdly. 'You consider us related, then?'

'Only very distantly, of course.' Instinctively she fluttered her lashes again, and then stopped, sighing. 'No, I must *not* do that. All part of the dreadful play-acting, isn't it? But you see, I learned the trick in London, and it seemed to work so well that——'

'That you practise it upon every poor fellow you meet. Shame on you, Miss Nevill.' Now he was smiling again, as he offered his arm, to lead her down the long, sunlit terrace to the furthermost end, where an elegant wrought-iron seat stood by a lead cistern filled with a glorious display of petunias, dark lobelia and trailing ivy.

'I only do it when I want to get my own way—oh, dear, but I shouldn't have said that, either!' She seated herself carefully, arranging the pale lavender dress, very conscious of his presence as he joined her, sitting a little distance away and leaning against the end of the seat, so that he could see her without having to turn aside.

'I'm sorry about last week. It was wrong of me to creep in like that — extremely rude.' While apologising, Patti examined his features with growing approval.

Not a conventionally handsome face, but one with much character and evidence of living stamped upon it. A proud, almost dictatorial nose, dark chocolate-brown eyes, and a mouth which was straight and, she thought perceptively, perhaps just a touch too vulnerable for its owner's piece of mind.

Lost in the natural charm that radiated from the steady eyes, she was taken aback when their owner said quietly, 'But I'm not at all sorry.'

Patti blushed. That deep voice had a gently vibrant ring to it, which now echoed so deeply inside her that she felt she was being uncomfortably stirred up, chameleon-like, having to change with every word and intonation she heard. For once in her life she did not know what to say.

'Oh!' Foolish and inadequate, it was all she could manage.

Lazily Sir Robert leaned forward, took one hand from her lap, and looked down at it for a moment before tucking his fingers beneath her elbow and then placing his other hand on top of hers, prior to drawing her to her feet. 'No, not sorry at all,' he said briskly. 'It's not every day that one meets the unexpected.' He slid her a sideways glance, full of solemnity, but with a hint of amusement dancing through it. 'A nymph, dabbling her fingers in my pool. . .'

Patti felt the sudden pressure of his hand upon her already startled fingers, increasing her disturbance. 'I'm not a nymph!' she said quickly, uncertain whether he was making fun of her or not. 'In fact I'm just a working girl who's lost her post. I'm having a short holiday before looking for another situation.' She was gabbling wildly now, trying to regain her lost self-composure.

'So *that's* why you're here. . .' She heard a note of relief in his voice. 'What a pity,' he went on, more lightly. 'Anyone can work. It's only the exalted few who look right kneeling beside a grotto.' Smiling down into her surprised eyes, his voice changed, growing more businesslike. 'And what sort of position are you looking for, Miss Nevill?'

The sensation of her hand below his was far more important then discussing the tedium of her future career. Patti said dreamily, 'I can typewrite and answer the telephone. My spelling is slightly erratic, but—but I can arrange flowers and play the piano a little. I speak French quite well, as Miss Clarke had a French maid, and we used to talk together. But I don't suppose any of those qualities will be of much use to me now. You see, I want to stay in the country—I shall probably end up serving in a village shop.'

'Nonsense.' He was leading her back to the middle of the terrace, where wide brick-coloured stones descended to a gravel path. As she removed her tingling fingers from his arm, he watched her hand fall to her side. Then he said briskly, 'You are a lady and so must find a congenial position. It shouldn't be too difficult.' He paused, frowned thoughtfully, and then continued disarmingly, 'Now, Miss Nevill—tell me what you see.'

Patti tried very hard to concentrate. 'Er—in the distance, a pergola——'

'No, no that's the vine walk,' he interrupted impatiently. 'But a little nearer—in fact, at the bottom of these steps.'

'Oh! A sundial. And what a strange-coloured stone—I've never seen anything like it before.'

'Come and inspect it. It's the family's pride and joy.'

She went down the steps beside him, conscious only of her pleasure in his company. They stopped beside the sundial and Patti stared at the dark red-purple stone in which large crystals shone in the afternoon sunlight. 'How beautiful,' she said slowly, reaching out to touch it.

The stone was warm and smooth, containing within it all the history of ages past. It brought a smile to her face. 'Beautiful,' she said again, and heard her voice trail away into the quietness of the spring day.

'I thought you would like it.' Her companion stood watching, and the note of amusement in his voice made her glance up at him.

'Why?'

'Because I believe you have a deeply sensual nature, Miss Nevill.'

In spite of her smart London sophistication, Patti blushed. 'I don't know what you mean, Sir Robert.'

'Of course you do,' he retorted wryly. 'I said you were a nymph, loving the natural world around you— wanting only to breathe and feel and sense the beauty of it all; was I wrong?'

She caught her breath then and, startled, stared into his dark, full eyes. She could have sworn she saw unwilling admiration in them. Then, recalling the feel of his hand upon hers, suddenly her mind expanded, and honesty surfaced. 'No,' she said at last, her voice a mere whisper, as she looked back at the sundial. 'All you say is quite true. . .'

'Then look at this. I think it will give you even greater pleasure.'

Curiously she did as he said, letting her eyes slide down from the shining brass hand of the dial to the base of the darkly gleaming rock. Again she caught her breath and then, in the same instant, turned to meet his watchful eyes.

'A border of roses!' she cried, entranced. 'Sculpted in the rock!'

'The Porphyry Rose,' said Robert Challoner, and his answering smile died, leaving his face warily expressionless, as he added slowly, 'I believe it was copied a very long time ago from an old Gallica rose called Madame Léonie de Sange.'

'Madame Léonie? Oh, goodness!'

Instantly Patti's mind flew back into the past. She was a child again, sitting beside Granfather at the library table while he told her that Madame Léonie belonged to their family alone.

'Madame Léonie,' said Grandfather, in his rumbling, slow voice, 'was found by my own father, many years ago, in rural France. He brought her back to England and developed her into a commercial product. And that's when the trouble started—your great-uncle Archibald insisting that it was solely his hard work and expertise which had resulted in her popularity. Ah, but Patti, dear child——' he shook his head very sadly, and pointed at the picture of lovely scarlet Madame Léonie with a shaking finger '—never allow yourself to believe that your great-uncle told the truth. As I said, Madame Léonie belongs to us Nevills. Certainly not to those wretched cousins. . .'

Patti blinked as she returned to the present. She felt the magnetic presence of the tall, quiet man beside her very strongly, felt him reaching out, invisibly yet overwhelmingly, to somehow influence her very thoughts. While her mind raced and twisted in confusion, unable to decide whether to confide in him all that she knew about Madame Léonie, she kept silent. But the silence soon became awkward, and so, feebly, she said, 'What a pretty name. . .'

'You disappoint me, Miss Nevill,' said her companion crisply. Patti slid a hesitant glance towards his watchful face. A faint smile touched that attractive mouth, but the dark eyes, so deeply set beneath heavily arched brows, remained unfathomable.

She swallowed to relieve the dryness of her tight throat, telling herself sternly not to be a fool. Why did she keep allowing him to dominate her?

She lifted her head sharply and asked, 'Why, Sir Robert?' in a much steadier voice.

'Because pretty is an inadequate word,' he told her sardonically. 'Lovely, or even perhaps glorious, would be more apt. Gallica roses are, indeed, glorious. . . Surely such a word would express your true feelings better?'

Patti thought hard and fast. His last words hinted at the pride he felt in the famous Porphyry Rose—the descendant of Madame Léonie. Suddenly, what had been merely of casual interest to her—that was, Madame Léonie's place in family history—now was becoming far more important. Grandfather's sombre words, Beth's warning about stirring up old unhappiness, and now Robert Challoner's own very emphatic pride in the rose all strove to create an urgent feeling deep inside her. Perhaps she should try and discover what had actually happened to lovely Madame Léonie after Grandfather died. . .

Smiling blandly, she looked into Robert Challoner's veiled and wary eyes, and said easily, 'Why, I believe you know me better than I know myself! Certainly that sculpture is a thing of great beauty, and, I agree, far more than just pretty—a silly little word! But you have the advantage of me, Sir Robert. . .' For a second she held her breath, but then went on, quite calmly, 'Clearly your Madame Léonie has a charm I have not yet appreciated. Could you tell me all about her?'

His eyes held hers, and her heart began to race. The dark-chocolate gaze was stern and thoughtful, Robert Challoner's lean face setting in hard lines as he probed her eyes and remained silent. The moment seemed to go on forever and Patti wondered a little hazily what strange situation she had got herself into.

But then, abruptly, his face cleared and that devastating smile flashed out for a second or two, as he nodded at her with wry amusement. 'One day, perhaps, Miss Nevill,' he said in a slightly mocking tone, before turning to ascend the steps behind them. 'That is if you're sufficiently interested. . . But now, come with me, if you please.'

Annoyed at his autocratic direction, Patti could only follow where he led, and found herself again sitting on the iron seat, where he stood awaiting her.

'Old roses are mysterious, wonderful things,' he mused, and she was caught by the undeniable note of passion in his low voice. 'The names alone are full of beauty. Bourbon, damask, musk. . .'

Patti could not stop herself. 'The Gallicas. . .'

He stared. 'Indeed, the Gallicas. So you *do* know about old roses, Miss Nevill?'

'I told you I did,' she said quickly, averting her face from his frowning, suddenly suspicious eyes. 'But of course my knowledge is nothing compared with yours.' She paused, wondering how she could return the conversation to a more friendly level. Already she was a little afraid of Robert Challoner—all questions about Madame Léonie must be postponed until she was more sure of him. She smiled persuasively. 'But I do know that their perfume is quite beautiful. . .'

Robert Challoner nodded. 'Indeed. A perfume filled with echoes of the hazy past and its many unsolved mysteries. . .' He stopped, looking at her with a strange curiosity; and then quickly his mood changed, and he smiled that warm, friendly smile that already had the power to send tingles down her spine.

Gone was the intensity which had filled him just a minute ago. Now he was again the charming man whom she found so easily attractive. 'But Miss Nevill——' the smile grew even more beguiling '—I did not bring you out here to give you a lecture on old roses!'

Patti opened her mouth to affirm her interest, but, smiling masterfully, he shook his head at her, before gesturing widely towards the prospect of the garden, stretching away before them into the sun-filled distance. 'No, no,' he went on, 'I wanted you to see how beautiful the whole garden is, and, of course——' Patti thought his smile contained within it a hint of mischief that, for the second time that afternoon, managed to bring a flush of colour into her cheeks '—to show you, in particular, whatever it was you came to find last week. . .'

'I. . .' Patti had never before felt at such a disadvantage. Shamed, she wondered where her London polish had gone, and tried desperately to find an answer to the question lurking in the last, pointed remark. She did not understand why she was behaving like a gauche child—all she had to do was smile sweetly and say, How kind of you, Sir Robert. The truth is, I would dearly love to see the rose garden... And without doubt he would take her there.

But his dark, wary eyes, that inviting mouth, and, oh, dear, the very presence of him, so close beside her, proved too much. What she actually said, fast and incoherently, without thinking at all, was, 'I really think I should go back to my sister now...'

The pathetic words rang in her head like a knell of defeat, and she dropped her head so that she would not have to see the answering expression on his face. What a little goose he must think her! Surely no longer a nymph.

His quiet voice dropped, like a plummeting stone, into her pool of despond. 'By all means. You are quite right. I must not monopolise your charming company. Forgive me for keeping you out here so long.'

She looked with dismay into his eyes, wondering if he was just being polite, or if he really meant what he had said. One glance at his strong, angled face, and she realised that Sir Robert Challoner did *not* mean all he said. Outwardly open, he hid within that charming manner a wealth of unsaid thoughts, of secrets, of mysteries...

Suddenly Patti felt unable to deal with such a character, and so she rose, quickly walking away from the seat, down the length of the terrace, until she heard familiar voices close at hand.

Entering the open doorway leading into the house, she could not bring herself to look back and see if he followed. Half of her disturbed mind longed for him to do so, while the other half was grateful for the absence of his undoubtedly charismatic presence.

Never before had she experienced such bittersweet conflict, and the moment she saw Beth and Lady

Challoner bending over a large photograph album she felt once again very much the younger sister, needing the security of home and family. 'Beth! Surely it's time we left — James will be returning soon — and. . . and. . .'

The reassuring smile on her sister's face was like a warm hand, reaching out for hers. Very soon they would leave Porphyry Court, and Patti felt uncertain about whether she ever wanted to return. Even the possible family connection faded in importance when she recalled her mixed feelings about masterful Sir Robert Challoner.

Supper was over. Patti sat by the parlour hearth, where a small fire crackled. It had been a beautiful day, but the evening brought a hint of frost and so Beth had put a match to the fire. Sparks danced up the chimney as Patti poked restlessly at the bright coals.

She felt uncertain and a little morose, although she could not have said why. Her mind flew back to the visit to Porphyry Court, nearly a week ago. The afternoon had been pleasant, Lady Challoner bidding them goodbye with a warm invitation to come again.

'I intend to write to one or two of my cousins and see what I can discover about your Davison-Grant relatives. How exciting this is! Thank you, dear Mrs Mortimer, for bringing my attention to the possibility of our kinship.'

Patti frowned. If only she did not keep remembering Sir Robert's complex character, and his strange manner when he mentioned the rose. The Porphyry Rose. She heard his voice saying, 'Madame Léonie de Sange,' and her dismay broadened.

Images and words invaded her confusion now, and

she rose, going swiftly to the window, seeking action to stop herself remembering with such regret.

Beth and James stood at the end of the garden, and suddenly Patti was filled with a despairing need. Beth was lucky, having a husband to look after her; would she herself ever find one? There had been several admirers in London, but no one she really cared for...

And then Beth came down the path, leaving James with a smile on his face. There were footsteps on the threshold, in the hall, and Beth entered the parlour. But now her smile was gone and she pressed both hands to her chest.

Patti swung around. 'What it it?' The alarm in her voice brought a faint return of Beth's smile. 'Nothing at all,' she said, over-brightly. 'Just a touch of heartburn; the pork we ate hasn't agreed with me. I think I'll just go upstairs——'

'But it's only just after eight o'clock!' Patti had never known her sister to want to go to bed so early. Beth moved a little heavily, towards the staircase. 'We've had a few exciting days,' she murmured defensively. 'I feel quite tired. Goodnight, dearest. I hope you sleep well.'

Patti watched her sister's slow ascent of the stairs with a feeling of growing anxiety. The bedroom door closed and very soon all was silence. When James marched briskly down the path Patti met him at the front door.

'What is the matter with Beth? Pork, she said—but she's always eaten pork...'

James, removing his shoes, looked at her thoughtfully.

'And she's so tired, James! But Beth is *never* tired...' Patti followed her brother-in-law into the parlour, watching as he sat down in his wing chair before reaching for the slippers awaiting him in the hearth.

Taking off the gold-rimmed pince-nez spectacles which made him appear so academic, James looked at Patti sitting tensely on the edge of her chair opposite and smiled reassuringly, as is she were one of his not so clever pupils. He polished the lenses very carefully.

'My dear Patti, don't distress yourself,' he said serenely. 'Beth is merely suffering what I understand to be the usual symptoms.' Reaching forward, he shovelled more coal on to the fire and again the sparks danced upwards.

'Symptoms? Of what?' Patti's voice was shrill with apprehension. 'You mean Beth is — is *ill*?'

'Certainly not!' James returned the empty shovel to the coal scuttle, and then gave Patti all his attention. 'I mean that she is merely undergoing a little sickness, some weariness. . .' Then, frowning slightly, but with a smile on his lips, he looked at her with concern. 'My dear Patti, am I to understand that your sister has not told you?'

Patti discovered a sudden lump in her throat. She clasped her hands in a knot of anxiety. 'Told me what, James?'

To her amazement, his frown changed to an expansive smile. 'That she is to become a mother, of course! Why, bless me, but I was so sure she must have told you by now. . .'

Thankfully, Patti unlocked her hands and relaxed, returning his smile. She felt as if a great weight had been removed from her shoulders. Beth — having a child! What a wonderful piece of news, indeed. And what an excellent mother she would make.

James picked up his newspaper, glasses glinting in the firelight as he gave Patti a final, benevolent glance. 'As you may guess, we are both delighted. I hope you like the idea of being an aunt.'

'I do. Oh, yes. I do!'

'But I cannot, for the life of me, think why she has not told you. Ah, well, no matter. Tomorrow you can say you already know the good news. . .' The paper crackled and Patti knew that James would not converse any further that evening.

Warm and happy in her corner of the small, homely room, she sat thinking, a half-smile of contentment wreathing her still face. Until, abruptly, an intrusive thought came to spoil her joy.

She knew why Beth had not told her—because a baby needed a nursery, and she, the visitor, was already occupying the only spare room in Clematis Cottage.

Next morning Patti was up early, writing several letters, applying to the employment agency Beth had mentioned, as well as to two others whose addresses she found in last night's newspaper.

After breakfast Beth watched her continued activity with an approving smile. 'So many letters! Well done, dearest—but I do hope you won't have to move away too far when you find a new position; James and I would miss you so much.'

'Darling Beth! How funny you are—and silly, too. . .' Patti rose, letters in her hand, pausing to give her sister a hug as she moved towards the hall. 'With a baby in the house, you're not going to have room for me.' She looked into the loving grey eyes and added accusingly, 'Why didn't you tell me?'

Beth coloured. 'I was afraid you would run off at once, no position, no home... Patti, promise you won't do that? Don't leave us until you have found something suitable and congenial.'

'I promise.' Patti offered the chiffon veil for Beth to tie around the shady leghorn hat. 'And now I must go and post my letters. Don't tire yourself, darling. I'll be back very soon to help with the work.'

'Before you go——' Beth was looking down at a letter of her own, which she had already opened and read '—I must just tell you what Lady Challoner has discovered.' Looking up, she smiled warmly at Patti. 'One of her cousins has written to say she actually recalls a Davison-Grant distantly related to the family, who took the name of Nevill upon adoption—a first cousin twice removed. Well, isn't that wonderful, Patti? Just think, we and the Challoners really do share the same family!'

CHAPTER THREE

PATTI caught her breath. She was on the point of telling Beth the exciting fact that the proven family connection went a little further towards proving Grandfather's sad story about Madame Léonie, but then stopped herself. Beth must have no extra worries piled upon her at this difficult time.

So, smiling back at Beth, she said lightly, 'Marvellous! Now we can go there to tea every week — that seed cake was definitely good enough to warrant another visit! I must run, darling, or I shall miss the post. . .'

But as she walked down the lane, Patti considered the strange situation very deeply. In the first place, what did this newly established family connection actually mean? Would it make any difference to Robert Challoner? And should she tell him that she had discovered one more link in the chain to the resolution of Grandfather's mysterious story?

But this idea, in its many ramifications, was altogether too confusing to pursue, and instead she forced her thoughts back to the need to cherish Beth and find herself a suitable position not too far away from Moorwood — just in case Beth needed her support and assistance once the child was born.

The letters safely posted, Patti hurried back through the village, intent on keeping her promise to help on her return. Perhaps she could persuade Beth to rest after luncheon; while she still remained at Clematis Cottage she must be sure not to tire her sister with extra work.

With her head so full of good intentions, she did not at once hear the extraordinary noise that gradually threatened to overtake her. But when a motor horn hooted and a powerful engine, only feet away, squealed to a stop, causing her to shrink into the hedgerow, she turned angrily, ready to tell the thoughtless driver of the monstrous, new-fangled machine just what she thought of his lack of manners. She opened her mouth, gasped, and then shut it again.

'Good morning, Miss Nevill,' called a familiar, deep voice as the engine was switched off, and once the huge goggles and tweed cap were removed Patti found herself staring into Sir Robert Challoner's dark eyes.

'Oh!' she exploded, pulling her cotton skirt more closely around her to avoid the white dust thrown up by the gleaming machine. Green-painted carriage-work, black iron supports, enormous wheels and brilliant brass accessories all shone with a blinding dazzle in the morning sun. The car and its driver provided her with a shock — she had not expected to see either, here in this backwater of the quiet Devon village, and was not sure if the encounter was a pleasing one.

As usual, it was necessary to say something — anything — to conceal her uncertainty. 'Really!' she snapped. 'How thoughtless of you to drive so fast down this narrow lane — you could easily have run me over, you know. . .'

'Nonsense,' countered Sir Robert briskly, and with a disconcerting smile, as he leaned towards her from the height of the driving seat. 'I'm an expert driver. Believe me, I haven't run anyone over yet, let alone a personable young lady wearing such a charming dress.' His eyes danced, and Patti, abruptly recalling his far from complimentary comment on her Bond Street gown last week, instantly forgot her annoyance and indecision. Grudgingly, she smiled in reply, and her thoughts began to grow in another direction.

Here was Robert Challoner in a good mood. It was a beautiful morning—and now here, also, was this sophisticated beast of a heavenly, exciting motor car... She eyed its sleek paintwork more appreciatively.

'Allow me to drive you home,' invited Sir Robert, watching her closely as he got out and stood beside her, cap in hand.

'Oh, no, thank you. I couldn't possibly accept...' Miss Clarke would never have sanctioned such unchaperoned goings-on. Patti's smiling mouth set primly, but the imp of excitement within her struggled determinedly.

'Get in and don't be so silly,' ordered that arrogant but utterly charming voice, and at once Patti dithered. Just imagine driving back to Clematis Cottage, surprising Beth—and anyone else in the village they happened to pass! The idea was extremely seductive. 'Well...'

'I was coming to call upon you, anyway,' said Sir Robert, and now his gloved hand was extended, his gaze very authoritative.

'Oh, dear!' She had forgotten what his touch did to her. Her knees began to tremble and obediently she allowed him to help her step up into the shining monster.

'Good.' For a moment his eyes met hers. His smile was approving. She watched him crank the engine, then return to the driving seat. He pulled the goggles down and put the motor in gear. 'Hold on to that pretty hat, Miss Nevill; off we go. . .'

Outside Clematis Cottage, Sir Robert stood by the gate, very charmingly rejecting Patti's invitation to come in and take a glass of sherry.

He shook his head, but his smile made her heart flutter foolishly. 'My compliments to Mrs Mortimer, but I have an appointment at noon with my estate manager.'

Patti said curiously, 'But you said you were coming to call — I wonder what for?'

Sir Robert raised a teasing eyebrow. 'How could I have forgotten? But I must confess that meeting my nymph again has driven everything else out of my mind. . .' Laughing quietly, his face straightened. 'Miss Nevill, my mother would like you to come to tea and meet Faye. Unfortunately she was not well enough the other day to come downstairs, but this morning she seems much better.'

'Faye?' Without knowing she did so, Patti frowned. Strange thoughts began to ruin her enjoyment. Could Faye be his fiancée? His wife, even? But Beth had said nothing about a *wife*. . .

'My sister, Miss Nevill.' His tone softened, but Patti saw a hint of concern veil his eyes. 'She is — well — delicate, and only just recovering from a summer cold.'

Instinctively Patti sensed that there was more to be said about Faye, but clearly he did not wish to reveal anything further. Quietly she said, 'I shall be honoured to meet your sister, Sir Robert. How kind of Lady Challoner to suggest it. When am I to come?'

She saw an expression of — could it be? — pleasure

flood his lean face. 'Splendid! Would tomorrow afternoon suit you, Miss Nevill?'

'Thank you. I look forward to it.'

He took her hand, bowed briefly as his engaging smile flashed out, and then returned to the motor car. 'Kendrick will call for you at three o'clock.'

'But I can easily walk — it's no distance. . .'

He cranked the engine, leaped into the driving seat, and pulled down his concealing goggles. The machine quivered, as if intent on springing off without more delay, and Sir Robert's voice, raised above the roar of the motor, also seemed to Patti to hold a touch of impatience as he called back, 'Nonsense! It might be raining!'

Resentfully, feeling like a rebuked child, Patti frowned and shouted back, in a most unladylike manner, 'In which case I shall use my umbrella!' But she realised he could not have heard her, for he revved the engine most alarmingly, and then the great sleek, gleaming monster rattled off down the lane, raising a veil of dust, and he was gone.

Patti went indoors to tell Beth, feeling both excited and disturbed. Sir Robert Challoner was a decidedly complex man, she thought, frowning, as she stormed down the garden path.

In the shady drawing-room, oak-panelled and cool, slightly old-fashioned, but furnished with gleaming heirlooms and a wealth of potted plants, Lady Challoner smiled graciously.

'Miss Nevill, this is my daughter Faye. Faye, dear, I have already told you about your new-found relation, Miss Nevill, who is staying in the village with her sister and brother-in-law.'

Faye had an unhappy face, made plain by petulance and a sallow skin, an air of suppressed frustration resulting in restless fingers and narrowed eyes. Patti took the limp hand offered and smiled a little warily, as she summed up the impressions she was receiving of the young girl staring across the drawing-room. 'Good afternoon, Miss Challoner. I believe you have been unwell — I do hope you are better now.'

Faye Challoner's voice was dull, conveying no strength and even less interest. 'How-de-do, Miss Nevill? Thank you, but no, I'm never really well. How could I be? I lead such a tedious life.'

Patti's eyes widened at such unexpected directness, and Faye went on, a brittle note of cynicism entering her monotone voice, 'You see, I have a dictatorial brother who orders my very existence.'

'Come, dear child! How can you say such a thing? Robert is the absolute soul of loving kindness. . .'

Patti thought Lady Challoner sounded more resigned than shocked at her daughter's embarrassing revelation, and looked at Faye's tense face with closer interest. Was she really delicate, Patti wondered perceptively, or merely bored?

Faye frowned, and muttered snappily, 'Oh, yes, indeed! So kind that he refuses to allow me any friendships — '

Lady Challoner cut in instantly. 'Now that is untrue, Faye. Robert only has your interest at heart, and the fact that he is disinclined to consider an early engagement just yet is — well. . .' Then her gentle voice halted and she flashed a commanding glance across the room, plainly reminding Faye that such topics were not suitable for general discussion.

Patti felt distinctly awkward. What a prickly creature

Faye was! To be so obviously unappreciative of her brother's regard and loving care, when Robert was probably merely safeguarding his only sister's well-being. . . And then her thoughts see-sawed uncomfortably. Did she not herself know what an arrogant man he could be? Was it not possible that Faye had right on her side, after all?

Lady Challoner poured tea while giving Patti a determinedly cheerful smile. 'Faye is inclined to bouts of self-pity, Miss Nevill, and that is why I asked you to come today and meet her. My dear——' turning in her chair, she raised her voice, as if to force her sulky daughter into more polite manners '—surely a new-found cousin will bring you some pleasure?'

'I would much prefer a more interesting life, Mother—but of course I'm glad to meet our relative.' Faye sounded bored, but then, abruptly, she looked intently at Patti. 'Have you ever lived in London?' she asked quickly, and now her voice took on a richer timbre.

Patti glanced at Lady Challoner, saw her nodding encouragingly, and answered, 'Yes, I have. Just recently, in fact——'

'Splendid! You can tell me all about it! Robert keeps promising me I can go and stay with Aunt Estelle, but I never seem to get there. . . You must describe it to me instead!' Faye was actually smiling.

Patti nearly dropped her teacup, for the plainness vanished and even Faye's sallow complexion could not prevent an elusive charm lighting up her thin face.

'What is your name, cousin?' asked Faye, with a suspicion of a gleam of interest in her green cats' eyes.

'Patricia. But everyone calls me Patti. . .'

'Cousin Patti. Hmm. Well, thank heavens you're not old and feeble!'

'Faye, really!' Lady Challoner's squawk of outrage made Patti stifle a giggle.

'I apologise,' said Faye wryly, 'but this house does seem so awfully *old*. . .even brother Robert behaves like a greybeard when he orders us all about. . .'

There was a movement behind Patti's chair — a door opening, a presence entering — and then Sir Robert's deep voice filling her mind and disturbing her composure as he strode across the room.

'I take exception to that, Faye. Not only did I shave when I got up this morning, but I haven't actually ordered anyone about all day. Not even the garden boy. . .'

Patti looked up, met the intensity of a dark, appraising glance, and quickly bowed her head, but not before she had seen Faye smiling wickedly, as she threw a challenging reply up at her brother.

'Good gracious, Robert — can it be that you're so excited by our new cousin's arrival that you've actually forgotten to be horrid, for once?'

'Children! Stop it, please. . .' Lady Challoner's command brought a truce. Patti watched how Robert and Faye smiled dangerously at each other before Robert turned away, to fold himself into an empty chair. He looked fondly at Lady Challoner. 'A cup of tea would be very welcome, Mother, dear. It's a hot day and I've ridden at least twenty miles around the estate with Thomson. You know——' leaning forward, he helped himself to a slice of cake and took a large, hungry bite '— I really think I shall invest in one of those splendid motor bicycles, so suitable for the countryside and far less energetic than a horse. . .'

Dark eyes danced as they looked across at Patti. 'But we're not here to talk about new-fangled inventions, are we? So tell me, Miss Nevill, what do you think of our proposition?' Stretching out a powerful hand, he lifted a silver cake dish and offered it to her. 'I mean, of course, Cousin Patti. . .that is, if I'm not being too forward.'

Patti was flustered. She took a slice of seed cake, dropped it, blushed, bent to recover the crumbs, and accidentally brushed her fingers against his as they both sought to clear up the debris. Again, that tingle. That prickle, streaking down her spine. . .

Sir Robert looked amused. He deposited the fallen crumbs on to a spare plate, found a clean one, and cut Patti another slice of cake. 'You haven't answered me,' he censured her, as she whispered a confused thank-you.

'I don't quite understand what you mean, Sir Robert. . .' Nearly choking on her small mouthful of cake, she then had the added trauma of feeling his hand gently slapping her back. 'Oh, thank you. That's m-much better. . . Sir Robert. . .'

'If Faye and I can call you Cousin Patti, don't you think you might return the compliment and call me Robert?' Not waiting for her reply, he leaned back in his chair, caught his mother's offended eye staring at his riding boots, and smiled lovingly back at her. But, noticed Patti, slowly recovering from this last assault upon her inflamed sense, he made no effort to hide them. Indeed, he actually stretched them further, so that not only mud from the estate but some shreds of cut grass and a few horse hairs were deposited on the muted pattern of the Turkish carpet beneath them.

'Come, now. . .' Having devoured his own cake, he was returning to the attack.

Patti stiffened as he looked very directly at her. 'You haven't answered my question, Cousin Patti. But perhaps we are being too importunate? You may feel you need some time in which to consider the proposition.'

Patti's mouth opened helplessly, and her mind raced. What did he mean? *What* proposition? Dismayed, she wondered if she was going mad, or, perhaps, suffering from extreme deafness. 'I—I. . .'

'My dear.' Lady Challoner's sweet voice was sympathetic, and Patti turned to her gratefully. 'Robert is so dreadfully autocratic!' His mother smiled at him adoringly, before continuing, 'And always demands a yes or no immediately. But of course I quite understand—and so will he and Faye—if you wish to consult your delightful sister before committing yourself. Now, child, let me refill your cup. . .'

Patti watched the exquisitely hand-painted china cup tremble as she passed it over, and knew instinctively that Robert also watched it. Her hand steadied immediately. She tried to calm her mind, to concentrate her thoughts. They were all talking about something of which she knew nothing. In fact, the afternoon was becoming extremely complicated. . .

But she refused to allow him to think her a fool. 'Thank you, Lady Challoner.' She sipped the tea and felt her strength returning. Setting the cup firmly back in its saucer—no more trembling, she noted with satisfaction—she looked around the table.

Faye, silent and intense, was staring with eyes that had suddenly become alert. Lady Challoner's composed face was set in the usual serene lines, but her elegant and heavily be-ringed fingers tapped on the arm of her chair. And Robert. . .

Straightening her already tense back, and lifting her chin defiantly as she met his steady, unblinking gaze, Patti saw that Robert wore a mask on his face — the mask she had already glimpsed before: once at their initial meeting and secondly as he'd mentioned Madame Léonie de Sange.

She knew that the only way to find out what truly lay behind that indifferent expression was to cultivate his acquaintance boldly. So she smiled, and both Beth and the late Miss Clarke would have applauded her self-control. 'If only I knew what it is I should discuss with my sister, then I would be happy to do so,' she said at last, her voice pleasant, but slightly challenging. 'As it is, I fear I have not clearly understood what we are talking about. . .'

She looked at Robert for an answer, but it was Faye who gave the explanation. 'Well done, Cousin Patti!' she said with a suppressed chuckle. 'Don't ever allow yourself to be browbeaten — Robert tries to do it all the time, I warn you.'

'That's not true, Faye!'

A small flame flashed in the cats' eyes. 'Oh, yes, it is, brother mine; and one day you will learn you can't live life on *your* terms alone ——'

'Now, children, please don't start squabbling again. . .'

Patti hid the quick smile that Lady Challoner's weary plea engendered. Clearly, brother and sister had been at loggerheads since their days in the nursery. Thank goodness she ran no risk of becoming involved in their arguments!

But Faye's next words put that happy thought into a

new and hazardous context. 'What we all want to know, Cousin Patti——' Patti thought apprehensively that if Faye's eyes held any semblance to cats' eyes, certainly her voice now contained a purring note '—is whether you will come and be my companion. And if the answer is yes, then, please, how soon can you begin?'

'Your—*paid companion*?' Patti had been prepared for almost anything, having by now accepted the slight but undoubted eccentricity of the Challoner family, but this particular possibility had never entered her head.

She gaped foolishly, only regaining her composure when Robert said lightly, but with an edge to his voice that made her at once turn in his direction, 'You make the term sound out of the ordinary, Cousin Patti. Yet, if you think carefully, you must surely realise that it is a situation which would suit you very well.'

Before Patti could reply, Lady Challoner chimed in helpfully, 'Exactly! Robert is right, my dear. You have all the education and talent—as well as the breeding— necessary to help Faye widen her restricted experience of life. And I understand that you speak French? That will be an enormous asset, as we have connections in France. Robert is very nearly bilingual, but Faye is slothful in learning——'

'Yes! You can help me with my French conversation, Cousin Patti! What a splendid idea! Jules will be so pleased. . .'

Faye's face was unexpectedly vital, and Patti instinctively understood the situation. So Faye planned to marry a Frenchman—— Then her thoughts were interrupted abruptly as Robert's voice, suddenly thunderous, broke into them.

'You are being foolish again, Faye. I've already told

you that you're far too young to consider marriage. And I'm not at all sure that Jules Lacoste is the right man for you, anyway.'

'He's your business colleague, Robert.' Faye's tone had grown sharp. 'I see no reason for your doubts. And think how advantageous it would be to combine the two businesses. . .'

'Hmm. . .' Robert retreated into chilly silence, and Patti's whirling mind expanded as the facts revealed themselves: Faye loved her Jules, while Robert had something against him. Thank goodness Beth and James don't wrangle so, she thought gratefully, and then realised Robert was talking to her, with that remembered hint of impatience jarring the smooth velvet of his deep voice.

'Forgive our little arguments, Cousin Patti. All families have them, you know. . .' Smiling persuasively, his tone softened. 'Now if you will just give me your answer, it will help us to plan the immediate future a little more certainly. *Well*?'

'Robert, do give the poor child time——'

'My dear mother, she's had a good two minutes already! Surely that's enough for anyone?' Robert's explosive reply resulted in Patti leaping to her feet, unable to endure his arrogance any longer.

She felt her cheeks redden maddeningly as she said tartly, 'Kindly do not speak about me as if I am not here! I may be only a cousin, and a very distant one at that, and certainly not a true *Challoner*. . .' Staring irately at Robert, she saw answering sparks arise in his dark eyes, and was delighted to have scored a point by puncturing his ridiculous family pride. Confidence soared, and blithely she went on, 'But I am a human being and I resent being treated like a—like a. . .'

Sickenly, words failed then and she floundered, until Faye murmured mischievously,

'A *companion*?'

Patti turned her rage on the pale, watchful girl, sitting so demurely that one hardly registered she was there, until the flat voice threw up such provocative remarks. 'If *this* is how you all intend to treat me, then the answer is no. Thank you—but definitely *no*!'

Lady Challoner tut-tutted with quiet restraint and Faye had the grace to stare down at the carpet, but it was Robert who handled the situation in his own inimitable way.

Standing up, he put a hand on her shoulder, turning her gently but firmly around to face him. Patti stiffened miserably, wanting only to escape his disturbing touch. His fingers, gentle as they were, seemed to burn through the material of her dress, and despairingly she felt her cheeks flame in sympathy. Somehow she forced herself to meet his eyes, knowing her own were stormy and afraid. She fully expected to be ordered, yet again, to give her answer. When he said, very quietly, as if they were alone in the room, 'Please forgive me, Patti; I fear I often behave badly—do you think we could start all over again?' she let out her sobbing breath in a gasp, and could think of no reply.

Robert's eyes were almost unrecognisably tender. She thought she discerned a gleam of humour shining in their dark depths, and very slowly her distress began to fade. Still unable to find words she nodded.

Robert's hand left her shoulder, and one powerful finger tilted up her chin. 'You'll be one of the family,' he said quizzically, and, forced to look at him, she stared in astonishment. His eyes dazzled her, as did his friendliness, and his sheer magnetism. In her anger she had forgotten how charismatic he was—how infinitely pleasing. Now, lost in his almost brotherly smile, she felt her ruffled feathers being soothed and knew that she could no longer say no to the situation being offered her. To be part of the Challoner family? To live here at Porphyry Court among such splendour and the beauty of growing things? Rapidly recovering herself, Patti considered. Even though Faye was a complicated little puss, yet Lady Challoner was delightful. And—suddenly her heart felt too full for comfort— Robert would be here, seen and encountered every day... Indecision racked her.

And then, still looking into his eyes, she saw the return of the familiar impatience...and was catapulted into saying in a tiny voice, 'Perhaps you will let me talk over the matter with Beth. You see, I have just applied for several other positions...'

Robert's hand dropped restlessly. 'Cancel them!' he ordered irritably. 'You said the other day you did not expect to easily find a really congenial post——'

'And what makes you so sure that this one will be as congenial as you think?' Patti snapped back, every nerve in her body newly tightened by his fresh burst of arrogance.

As if in the distance, Lady Challoner's anxious voice reached her. 'Now, now, Robert—Patti, dear child, I beg you...' But neither Patti nor Robert was listening.

They stared at each other as if engaged in a private war, and Patti was thankful for the sudden surge of replenishing vitality which gradually but steadily filled her. How much easier it was to fight Robert Challoner than to fall under his undoubted spell!

'I am not fond of being ordered about,' she said haughtily, and added, with an enjoyable sense of having surprised him, 'I am a free woman, you see. Independence is important to me. And so are ideals——'

'Forget your ideals,' he growled. 'You need to find employment. And here is the best chance likely to be offered to you. Our terms will certainly exceed any others that may come your way, believe me.'

Patti watched his quick anger die, the famous charm reinstating itself almost at once. She felt acutely disturbed as she struggle against its calculated and powerful effect.

Then a slight but gentle smile sweetened his cross face, and the chocolate-brown eyes melted once more into warmth and incurable fascination. 'Just think, Patti. . .' Even his voice radiated enchantment, she thought helplessly. 'One of the family! To live here with Mother and myself, accepting Faye as your cousin, with whom you will share interests, educations, outings and social life—surely this will be an ideal position for you? One in which your own delightful personality can develop and flower. Where you will be secure and happy. . .'

She had no will left, it seemed. All she could do was gaze into his mesmeric eyes and let his honeyed voice heal her sense of outrage. As if he read her thoughts and was determined to take advantage of her weakness, Robert held out his hand towards her. 'And speaking of flowers, Cousin Patti—if you come to live here, you will have the freedom of the entire grounds of the estate. . .'

His smile held a glint of mockery, and even as she stretched out her fingers in a gesture of obedience Patti wondered exactly what he meant. It was almost, she thought hazily, as if he suspected her of having some ulterior motive in coming here, to Porphyry Court. But then her hand was quivering beneath his, and a pulse raced deep within her as he led her to the open French windows, where the afternoon sun shone invitingly, and the distant garden stretched away from the house in intangible temptation.

'There,' murmured Robert, looking down into her wide and suddenly pleasure-filled eyes, 'all for your delight. . .' A suspicion of amusement in the whispered words made her hastily withdraw her hand as she stared down the terrace towards the dark-stone sundial, bordered by the mysterious rose sculptures.

But Robert's deep voice continued its seductive persuasion. 'You may enjoy it all whenever you wish, you know. The nymph may return to her grotto, uninvited. Lawns, woodland, walled garden, riverbank and parkland—all yours to explore, Cousin Patti. You will be no longer that curious visitor, searching for something as yet unseen. . .'

A hint of darkness in the final words made her turn hastily to meet his eyes, but his smile was bland and non-committal. Patti let the promises echo in her mind, uncomfortably aware that she was being manipulated, even as the words excited her. Her heart was pounding now. She gave him a searching look, saw the wryly smiling charm, and immediately came to an irrevocable decision. Yes, she would take the situation. She would come here, to the Court—to be one of the family, as Robert had invited.

Turning away quickly, she glanced back into the drawing-room, to meet first Faye's and then Lady Challoner's questioning eyes. She smiled warmly, aware of the rush of pleasure that filled her and said rapidly, 'Thank you. And please forgive me for being so difficult. The truth is. . .'

She sensed a movement behind her, but discovered Robert's presence was no longer a barrier to her peace of mind. 'I shall be most honoured to accept the position you have so kindly offered me, Lady Challoner.'

Faye's smile flashed out, and Patti smiled more broadly. 'I hope you will not regret the decision, Cousin Faye.'

'And I was about to say the same thing, Cousin Patti!'

'Really, Faye. . .' Lady Challoner rose, rebuking her daughter and advancing towards Patti, her gracious smile full of obvious relief. 'We are *all* very glad, dear child,' she enthused, and even her brief frown over Patti's shoulder in Robert's direction could not mar Patti's enjoyment any further.

'So! Now let us have some fresh tea. Robert, ring for Dora, please.'

Again, they were sitting around the tea-table, but now the easy smiles spread from one to another and the atmosphere was pleasantly relaxed. When Faye said hopefully, 'How soon can you come, Patti?' Patti found it no hardship to answer, 'Tomorrow, Faye — if that will be convenient.'

She saw Faye's approving nod, and heard Lady Challoner say heartily, 'Splendid! Kendrick shall come to collect you in the trap — shall we say at eleven o'clock?'

But it was Robert's approval Patti waited for. She held her breath, expecting his approving smile to meet her expectant eyes. He glanced at her, nodding, and she realised with a shock that already he was putting her out of his mind. Other matters—clearly far more urgent—were now calling him. . .

'I hope you'll be happy here, Cousin Patti,' he managed to say briskly at last, after downing a fresh cup of tea in one large gulp, before rising and striding impatiently to the window. 'Excuse me, if you please, Mother—Faye—Cousin Patti. . .' I must get back to work. Jenkins is expecting me in the glasshouses—trouble with the radiators. . . The engineer was here this morning, but I must make quite sure they're working properly again. . .'

He disappeared instantly, and Patti, quite taken aback by his casual dismissal of her, thought the room seemed all the emptier for his absence.

CHAPTER FOUR

FOUR days later Patti knew that Porphyry Court had indeed become her home. Of course, Beth's and James's little cottage down the road would always be dear to her, but she had known that her stay there was only temporary.

In some strange way Porphyry Court, on the other hand, seemed to hold her future within its ancient and aristocratic walls, and she sensed that she expected to remain here, if not permanently, at least for a considerable time. Probably until Faye married her Frenchman, and then. . .

But she refused to think any further. A joyous contentment was already slowly filling her. Faye was friendly, Lady Challoner—now to be known as Cousin Enid—seemed likely to become a mother-figure of kindness and consideration; and Robert. . .

Inexplicably, she had no decisive opinion of Robert. He had not been at the house for the last few days, driving off in his monster motor car soon after she arrived, and she had been far too occupied settling in to miss him.

That was, until yesterday, when his continued absence had made her realise that he was, indeed, the patriarch of the family. 'Robert will do this'. 'We must ask Robert about that'. Lady Challoner could make no decision without consulting him, and even prickly Faye occasionally deferred an important point to his supposedly superior judgment.

'Robert has gone off to London to attend a meeting of professional rose growers,' Faye told Patti, with a scornful edge to the words. 'He will come back littered with papers and catalogues, his mind completely awash with new ideas. I fear Robert is utterly selfish and obsessed with his own life, Patti.'

The flat little voice stayed in Patti's thoughts long after she had diplomatically changed the subject to something more exciting, and she now realised, with a sting of hurt pride, that Faye was undoubtedly right. Robert, having engaged her as his sister's companion with all the charm at his disposal, had now quite forgotten she even existed.

But today, with an hour to herself, while Faye and Lady Challoner conferred over the invitations being sent out to the small house party arranged for Friday to Monday the week after next, Patti was being foolish enough to let herself think of her new employer.

In her mind's eye she recalled his height and the air of strength and volatile magnetism he radiated. His teasing, lazy smile. One dark brow swiftly rising in a mocking but friendly look that she had already learned to anticipate, if not quite to enjoy. Then she remembered his vast arrogance and frowned. He was a mercurial man, one who liked to order events and people. And yet there had been moments, even in her short acquaintance with him, when she sensed she had seen something vulnerable behind the hard mask he so often wore. A shiver ran down her spine, and quickly she turned her mind to more mundane matters. For instance, her position here. Effortlessly she had slipped into the accustomed habits of the household. Accepted at once, both by servants and by Lady Challoner and Faye, she felt, deep in her bones, that she was in the right place. Patti looked around the morning-room, with the sun glancing off the polished oak table and the mirror above the fireplace, and knew she was content.

The old house filled her with delight. It was comfortable, elegant and mysteriously evocative of its past, and she was happy to wander from room to room, sensing the serenity, and enjoying the contrast of heavy antique furnishings with the small, personal touches of flowers and plants, bric-à-brac, and pictures that brought the rooms newly alive, reflecting their present owners' likes and attitudes.

But more than that—her heart soared at the thought. There were the gardens, stretching away into the blue distance of fields, hills and unseen river. They held an untold fascination for her and, as yet, she had had no time in which to wander in them.

Out of the silence, Robert's remembered voice came to tease her anew. 'All yours to explore. You will be no longer that curious visitor, searching for something as yet unseen. . .'

With an enormous effort of will she blanked out the memory of that vibrant, forceful voice. Forget Robert. Instead, take advantage of his absence and find the rose garden.

A memory flew out of the past, kindling her forgotten interest. Perhaps, even, find Madame Léonie. Go *now*. . .

Ned Jenkins was hoeing the rosebeds. The slope of his shoulders beneath his worn dark serge jacket and the easy rhythm of his arm movement brought Patti to a stop as she rounded the entrance in the tall yew hedge, and saw the rose garden stretching ahead of her.

She had expected something special, of course, but the true glory had been beyond even her vivid imagination. Roses, roses all the way! Her smile was unbounded, and she ran forward, unable to stop herself expressing the delight that filled her.

'How beautiful! Oh, quite wonderful! And so finely laid out. . .'

She knew that old Miss Clarke would have rejoiced in Robert's exquisite rose garden. Within the dark yew hedge, a wonderland met Patti's gloating eyes. A formal arrangement of rosebeds nestled happily inside encircling gravel paths, laid to emphasise the beds they protected. The planting, Patti realised, as her gaze flew from one lovely bush to the next, was all in silver, white, pink and red. Low clumps of herbaceous shrubs and plants served their humble duty in providing a subtle background for the richer, prouder flowers — for the queens of the garden, the roses themselves.

Every rose bush was covered in swelling buds, some already showing a glimpse of flower, and so radiating the glow of pale colour that had already set Patti's senses singing. In June, she thought ecstatically, they'll all be in full bloom. . .

In the centre of the garden her eyes halted at the focus point of the small lake filled with budding waterlilies. Around it a stone kerb gleamed, and Patti had an instinctive knowledge of what her fingers might feel once they touched those dark stones.

Surely the same sculptor who had fashioned Madame Léonie's likeness on the sundial had not been able to resist this wonderful place for his art?

She stared around, wondering which rose was Madame Léonie. . . But Ned Jenkins was watching her. She went to the bed where he worked. He had a gentle smile on his lined, weather-beaten face.

'Mornin', miss.'

Patti, touched by the timeless salute of gnarled hand to curly-brimmed bowler, smiled glowingly. 'Good day, Mr Jenkins.'

'Ned, miss. If you please.' He resumed hoeing, but still gave her his polite attention.

'Ned. Of course.' Patti admired the dignity of a servant who knew his place, and responded humbly, 'Please tell me about the roses, Ned. I know they won't flower until next month, but I'm interested to learn about the different sorts——'

'Species, miss. And then the hybrids.'

'Yes, Ned. There's a lot to know, I'm sure.'

'And the best one to ask is Sir Robert himself, miss. He be the expert, not me.'

'Oh, but. . .' Patti moved along the path in time with Ned's slow but thorough work. She watched the gleaming hoe dip, slice and lift again, realising something of the age-old serenity of mind engendered by working with the earth. 'Do you like working here, Ned?' she asked impulsively, without considering the etiquette of such a question.

Ned's faded eyes glanced up briefly. 'I do, miss. Man 'n' boy, I've bin here since Sir Robert's father were living. 'Tis my life, miss.'

Patti was almost mesmerised by the shining blade, the warmth of the sun of her back, and by the gentle rise and fall of Ned's soft Devonshire voice. Her thoughts slid backwards, to Grandfather and his story about Madame Léonie.

'Ned,' she said quickly, 'can you tell me about the old shrub roses? The Bourbons, the musks. . .' She paused for a second. 'The *Gallicas*?' She stared hard, willing the man to stop his work and tell her all she needed so badly to know. But Ned proceeded in his slow, rhythmic and obstinate way. 'You'm come to the wrong man, miss. Like I said, Sir Robert do know. Not me.'

'But you must know *something*!' Her agitation grew. She wished she could shake the information from the old man. 'Surely some of Sir Robert's knowledge has become yours, too?'

Ned at last stopped his interminable hoeing. He stood a little straighter, grunting as he eased his bent shoulders backwards, and his gaze moved far beyond Patti. She saw his eyes narrow against the noonday sun. He appeared to be frowning. But his voice, when he spoke was unexpectedly warm and full of pleasure.

'Like I said, miss, it's Sir Robert you must speak to on that partic'ler subject — an' here he is now!'

Patti whirled around, too startled even to try and hide her surprise. She stiffened at the appearance of Robert Challoner, dressed in an exceedingly smart dark pin-striped suit, with a gleaming white shirt and wing collar that emphasised the tan of his lean face. He looked a city gentleman, not at all the slightly shabby head gardener of their recent acquaintance.

He was not alone. Beside him stood a smaller, more slightly built young man, whose easy smile was directed at her, and whose twinkling blue eyes seemed full of something she instantly recognised as admiration. . .

'Patti! What on earth are you doing here? Oh, of course — the curious visitor is exercising her curious rights!' Robert's voice was light, but edged with a hint of mockery that caused Patti's susceptible emotions to misbehave. If Miss Clarke, in the past, had not told her that stamping her foot was childish, she would have stamped it now. How dared he be so chilling and almost offensive, when she had been about to warmly welcome him home?

'Good day, Sir Robert.' Dismissing his remark with the scorn it deserved, she looked directly into the stranger's smiling eyes.

Robert Challoner made a sound which resembled a stifled chuckle, and then made the necessary introductions. 'Patti, this is Jules Lacoste, my business colleague, who has come to stay for a few days. Jules, Miss Patricia Nevill is a cousin—a *distant* cousin—of my family.'

Again Patti's irritation flared, hearing his emphasis on the adjective, and she smiled more charmingly than was necessary at the French visitor. 'How do you do, Monsieur Lacoste?' She spoke in rapid French and then changed back to English. 'Are you a rose grower, too?'

'I am indeed, Miss Nevill.' His voice was husky, the English attractively accented. 'Although, of course, not so expert as your cousin—he is a veritable *professeur* of roses, as you must know.'

Jules Lacoste seemed friendly and unassuming, Patti thought—how different from his companion, often too autocratic for comfort. Instinctively she fluttered her eyelashes and then became flustered, knowing, too late, what Robert's reaction would be.

Sure enough, he said cynically, 'You will be at home with Monsier Lacoste, Cousin Patti. Another admirer to add to your list of conquests.'

Patti bit her lip, but kept herself under control. She smiled at the watchful Jules, saying pointedly, 'How ridiculous you are, Cousin Robert! I realise, of course, that Monsieur Lacoste has really come to see Faye.'

She watched the smile on the sallow, boyish face grow deeper, and congratulated herself on scoring a point on Faye's behalf. 'And Cousin Enid and Faye will be wondering where I am — so forgive me, please, if I leave you now. . .'

Giving Robert a disapproving frown, she bowed prettily as she passed Jules. Quickly she went down the path towards the archway in the yew hedge, very aware of the eyes watching her departure. And if her cheeks were red and her head held defiantly high beneath the open parasol, she told herself Robert deserved to be treated coolly. He was too arrogant for words!

Entering the house, she was at once confronted by Faye, in whose unexpected agitation and uncertainty she sensed a resemblance to her own unsettled emotions, which was even further disturbing.

'Where on earth have you been?' cried Faye excitedly. 'Robert and Jules have arrived, but where are they? Dora said Kendrick went to meet them at the station. The motor is in the courtyard and she thought she saw them going into the garden. . . *The garden*! Really, what rude creatures men are — why could Robert not bring Jules in to say hello before inspecting the wretched roses?'

Patti allowed the petulent tirade to die down before answering. She watched Faye flounce into a chair by the open French window, and then asked quietly, 'You have known Monsieur Lacoste very long, Faye?'

'Since we were children. Our parents met through the Rose Growers' Association, and then began to do business together. He and I — well — I mean. . .' Faye's voice died. Her hands pleated her skirt restlessly and she would not meet Patti's curious eyes.

'You love him? Oh, but forgive me, such a personal question. . .' Ashamed of her impulsive impertinence, Patti would have changed the subject, but Faye surprised her by lifting her head and said, in a resolute tone of voice, 'I think I do, Patti. And I believe he loves me. And what could be better than a marriage which will bring the two businesses together? Oh! Just think what an exciting life I will have, living in France! I've told Robert he *must* agree to our engagement — I could easily persuade Mother to do so, you know. . .' Faye's cheeks had grown a becoming pink, and she looked more alive than Patti had yet seen her. Then a wilful note came into her voice, and she frowned. 'But Robert is so masterful! So dictatorial! It's as if he holds something against Jules, but he won't speak of it. I do wish he would try and understand how important it is for me to marry and get away from this dull hole — to start really living my life. . .'

Staring at Patti, she added darkly, 'But of course, he can't understand about *love*. Not after that business of being jilted a couple of years ago. He turned into a veritable old curmudgeon once that had happened. But if I can understand him, why can't he do the same with me? He treats me like a child. . .' Abruptly Faye's voice had become flat and dispirited, and suddenly Patti realised why Faye was called 'delicate' by her suffering family. No doubt but that her frailty was actually rebellion against her brother's forceful will — headaches, sudden stomach upsets, whenever things went wrong and she felt sorry for herself. . .

'Oh, Faye,' cried Patti warmly, compassion wringing

the words from her. 'I am so sorry! If I can do anything to help you and your Jules, you have only to ask.'

For a moment they looked at each other in silence. Then Faye's smile flashed out, and she nodded. 'I knew you would be my friend. I'm so glad you're here, Patti—you can't imagine how lonely and frustrated I've been.'

'Things are different now. Please cheer up, Faye, dear. . .'

'I feel better already!' Faye leapt from the chair. 'I must go and change my dress before luncheon—before Jules comes in. Help me choose, will you? Quickly! I don't want him to see me in this dull old pink thing!'

As they ran across the hall, heading for the sweeping oak staircase, footsteps sounded on the parquet floor, and around the corner came Robert and Jules. Faye stopped in her flight, saying unsteadily, 'Oh! Hello, Jules—excuse me, I'll see you at luncheon. . .' She coloured, smiled, and bolted upstairs out of sight.

Robert's eyes held Patti's. 'Are you running off, too?' he asked sardonically.

She hesitated at the foot of the stairs, uncertain what to do or say, then glanced towards Jules, discreetly strolling away towards the drawing-room. 'I am Faye's companion,' she said at last, her voice doubtful, but standing still, aware that Robert was looking at her with a wry smile lifting his lips. 'She has asked me to go up with her and find a dress. . .'

'And I must not keep you from your duties.' The casual words seemed inappropriate, the way he was regarding her. Patti's heart slipped into its irregular routine and her bewilderment grew. Why did she have to react so strangely almost every time she encountered

Robert? Rather unsteadily, she said, 'I really should go. . .'

'If you wish.' But he continued to look down into her eyes. Suddenly he smiled, a great glow of friendship that nearly bowled her over. 'Come, Patti, stop all this companion nonsense,' he said briskly, with a laugh in his deep voice. 'We're cousins! Friends — aren't we?'

The idea was frightening, but quite impossible to resist. 'I hope so, Robert. . .'

'Very well, then. Go and offer Faye some smelling-salts and tell her what dress to wear, and then this afternoon you must come out into the garden with me, and we'll discuss the planting. . .'

Abruptly his voice dropped even lower, and Patti watched his smile fade slightly. 'We might even look at the roses,' he suggested, and she felt him watching her response.

'Thank you — that. . .that will be lovely. . .' Unable to face him any longer, or try to unravel the mystery that she felt had forced his last words, Patti tore herself away from his compelling eyes, and ran upstairs, feeling his gaze follow her every stumbling step.

'You have changed your dress,' said Robert approvingly as she joined him on the terrace some half hour after luncheon had ended.

'Yes,' Patti agreed, smiling blandly back at him. 'And so have you!' She was nervous about this unexpected and unchaperoned rendezvous in the garden; the word 'clandestine' hung uncomfortably in her mind. Quickly she added, 'I hardly recognised you in that dark suit this morning. You seem to have worn your nice lovat-green tweed jacket ever since we first met.'

Robert adapted his customary long stride to her smaller one. 'You're very profficient in fighting off compliments, Cousin Patti,' he said teasingly. 'I was about to say how much I like that cream blouse you're wearing — it makes you hair appear even redder. Oh, but forgive me — I believe the correct term is Titian. . .'

She threw him an uncertain glance. 'Do you expect me to thank you for such an ambiguous remark?' she asked bluntly. 'Really Cousin Robert, you are a most provocative man!'

'And you, dear Cousin Patti, are also highly provocative.' His voice was smooth, but something warned Patti of inner tension beneath the harmless words. 'Provocative in a different sense, that is — didn't one of those admiring city gents you met in London ever tell you?' He held her elbow lightly as they went down the terrace steps, and the clarity of her mind was instantly blurred. How could she rebuke him for flirting when his touch caused her such chaos?

'Don't bother to reply,' he murmured with amusement as she made no attempt to do so. 'Your silence speaks for itself.'

Patti jerked her arm away in a most unladylike manner. 'I was about to remind you exactly why I am here, Cousin Robert.' Passing the sundial, she could not help pausing for a moment to stroke the warm, dark stone. The porphyry seemed to offer some of its ancient, mysterious strength, and as they continued walking towards the distant yew hedge she was able to add more confidently, 'Remember, it was your promise to show me the roses that has made me come!'

'And not just for the pleasure of my company? Shame on you, Cousin Patti!'

Within the shadowy arch of the hedge he slowed his steps, and Patti was forced to do the same.

'I've been away for four days,' he said quietly, his voice full of deep music. 'Surely you've missed me?' Stopping, he turned to face her, his smile beguilingly innocent, but touched by some concealed undercurrent that made Patti tremble.

Faye had said Robert was an old curmudgeon — yet here he was, flirting with her. What was she to make of such a situation? Her growing nervousness suggested that it would be easier to cope with anger than the threatening feeling of enchantment. . .

Gladly, she allowed herself to become annoyed. Just because they were alone and half hidden by the thick foliage of the dark hedge he thought he could flirt with her! Breathing very fast, she stared up at him, feeling the colour rush to her cheeks, and hating the fact that he must notice it. 'I am Faye's paid companion, Robert — I would be grateful if you will please remember that.' Her voice shook, but the urgent need of self-preservation gave her a false strength.

She heard the rasping edge on her voice and instantly regretted it. Robert's benign smile had faded, and he was looking at her with a different expression — as if, she thought wretchedly, she was an unusual species of gallfly put beneath his microscope.

'Forgive me,' said Robert politely, but with a veneer of ice that chilled her through. 'I had thought you to be a sophisticated young lady, quite used to compliments and admiration. Obviously I was wrong. . .' His eyes deepened and he moved away from her. 'You are still only a child. Well, shall we go on to the glasshouses?'

Patti realised he had again become the autocratic head gardener, and knew the blame was hers. He had said—done—nothing wrong, so why had she been so rude? So—afraid. . .?

'Robert,' she ventured quickly, feeling guilty, apologetic and confused all at the same time, 'please forgive me. I'm sorry. I had no reason to be so—unfriendly.'

'The blame is all mine,' said Robert airily. 'I'll keep my distance in future; clearly, that is what you would prefer. . .'

Again his hand was beneath her elbow, his presence at her side a paradox of consternation and delight. But now, as they left the hedge behind and proceeded down the gravel path into the rose garden, she knew she had given herself away. He had thought her to be worldly, and, clearly, she had disappointed him. He wanted a nymph who knew about sensual, sophisticated things, and she was just a wayward, inexperienced creature. . .

'Here are the rosebeds,' said Robert, in the cool voice that always made her feel inferior. 'But you have already discovered them—no need for me to explain anything to you. . .'

Spontaneously Patti said, 'Oh, but please do! I really know very little about roses, and Ned wouldn't tell me anything this morning. . .'

Robert stopped so abruptly that she bumped into his side. 'So you talked to Ned—what did you ask him?' His voice was unaccountably sharp, and Patti, trying desperately to control, yet again, the effect of his nearness, stuttered foolishly, 'I—c-can't remember. Nothing much. . .'

The stern look on his face frightened her. She thought she had offended him again, but how? Merely by talking to the gardener? Dismay flooded through her, but even as her thoughts jostled so painfully she saw his sternness had gone and that he was smiling down at her, a more gentle being altogether, a man who loved roses...

'Well?' asked Robert again, but now he smiled good-humouredly at her. 'What did you ask Ned?'

Suddenly Patti was able to return his smile as she realised the bond of their shared interest. Abruptly her nervousness and inhibition were swept away. Words tumbled into her mouth. 'I was going to ask about Madame Léonie,' she whispered, 'but then you and Monsier Lacoste arrived, so I didn't.'

'Madame Léonie, eh?' Robert's eyes were deep and unfathomable. He lifted a hand, paused, and then smiled wryly as his fingers hovered delicately around her mouth. 'You have rosebud lips, Cousin Patti,' he murmured quizzically. 'Extremely seductive to a rose grower.'

Patti's confusion flowered yet again, but she returned his smile. Robert in such a good mood was far nicer than when deep in his pigheadedness. Her eyelashes fluttered, but only for a second.

Robert smiled appreciatively at her. 'Don't do that,' he said lazily. 'Keep it for your smart city gents, if you must...'

'I don't want to, Robert. And anyway — they were never mine...'

'I'm glad to hear it, Patti. The idea of your going off and marrying some tedious fool of a London businessman is entirely repulsive. Especially as I'm just getting used to having you here at Porphyry Court.' The moment was delectable, and Patti wished it would last forever, but she knew Robert well enough by now to realise that this was merely a particularly good-humoured occasion; the sun was out, he had just finished a pleasant luncheon, and now he was about to show off his famous roses. . . If she hadn't been here, any other girl would have done equally well.

So she returned his smile and together they sauntered towards the first of the glasshouses that stretched down the red-brick wall bordering the rose garden. A companionable silence linked them, until he said, 'In here, Patti. . .'

Entering the glasshouse, shimmering and dazzling in the afternoon sun, she was quite unprepared for the heat from the huge pipes, and immediately shrank backwards, as if to ward it off. Behind her, Robert's arms opened, and briefly she was caught in them.

Turning, trying to free herself, she stared up into his abruptly fierce eyes. They were as startled as she knew her own must be, and for a long moment they looked at each other in astonishment.

'Patti. . .?' His low voice was unsteady, and she heard in the word a question she knew she was not yet ready to answer.

All her youthful insecurity flared again then, and she wanted only to turn and run. But Robert stood in the doorway, and she could not free herself from those powerful yet gentle arms. His very nearness terrified her, even as his attraction called out to her.

Thoughts crowded in. He was aware of her undoubtedly sensual nature — indeed, he had commented on it. So he knew what she was feeling — how much she wanted to stay in his arms, to surrender herself. . .

But her fear of her own nature was even greater

than that primeval need, and it seemed that all she had left as a weapon was her temper, so quick to call upon, so easy to arouse. Pushing him away with unexpected strength, she said unsteadily, 'Please leave me alone! I didn't come here because I wanted you to—to. . .' Then shame made her unable to end the sentence, but, watching his eyes, she saw the damage was done.

Instantly he released her, standing aside, unsmiling now, with the mask once more in place, and Patti wished, with every ounce of her being, that she could recall the unkind words, but it was too late. He had turned back into that other Robert—arrogant, distant and too hard to reach. And, as he began to speak, she knew, dismayed, that she had been cruel to repulse him, for instinct told her that Robert, in his own way, was as vulnerable as she was.

'I apologise,' he said, in a cool, brusque voice. 'The heat of a glasshouse on a summer afternoon, and the presence of a pretty girl, is, of course, disastrous for any hot-blooded man. But you've made your preference quite clear. I won't bother you again.'

His glance left her then, seeking the rows of potted plants that lined the shelves on both sides of the duck-boarded walkway. 'Now, Cousin Patti. . .'

She thought he had entirely forgotten the way he had looked at her only seconds ago. His eyes glowed now with a different sort of passion as he explored the sides of the glasshouse. 'Back to business. You want to know about Madam Léonie de Sange. . .well, here she is. Or, at least, some of her progeny. Look. . .'

Speechless, Patti followed him down the glasshouse, stopping when he did, and staring down at the plants he indicated. She expected to see the glorious, familiar shape of the old Gallica rose, but instead she beheld a few miserable-looking stumps of stems, out of which grew very small buds.

Disappointment flooded her. Surely these wretched plants had nothing to do with Grandfather's beautiful picture? Piteously she turned to Robert. 'But—they're so small! Just stems—not even a leaf, let alone a flower bud. Are you *sure* this is Madame Léonie?'

'My dear child!' Abruptly, Robert had become the hard-faced connoisseur, who clearly found it impossible to be tolerant of ignorance. 'Am I likely to lie about such a matter?'

Foolishly, Patti feared she might dissolve into tears of dismay if he went on looking at her like that. Clasping her hands together in a tight knot, she turned her head away and sniffed hard. It would never do to make another scene. . .

And then a large white handkerchief was unobtrusively passed to her. Robert's voice changed dramatically, the hint of mockery almost affectionate, and not at all hurtful, as he said quietly, 'What a romantic child you are, Cousin Patti. How long have you been hoping to see a glorious red rose in full bloom? Since you first heard the name Madame Léonie, I shouldn't wonder, whenever that was. . .' He paused. 'And all that unfettered imagination and love of beauty has led you into the sad trap of expecting more than what is actually here.'

She turned, surprised at his intuition. 'But I've seen a picture of how lovely it is! And the sculptures on the sundial. . .' Her voice trailed away as a new, terrible thought darted into her confused mind. 'Oh, Robert! Are you telling me it's all just pretend?' she whispered. 'That Madame Léonie doesn't exist, after all? That— that Grandfather's story was—just made up?'

Robert's smile died and his face grew stony. 'And exactly what did your grandfather tell you?' he demanded bluntly, watching her closely.

Out of the blue, memories clamoured within Patti. Softly, she said, 'That Madame Léonie was a very beautiful, rare old rose.' Her face fell. 'But then Beth said he was woolly-minded. And old. . .' She looked at Robert uncertainly. 'Don't say it was all just a—a fantasy. Surely not. Oh, could it have been, do you think?'

'If only you will give me the chance to get a word in edgeways,' said Robert with a trace of irritation, 'I will answer as many of those questions as I can.'

Patti hung her head. 'I'm sorry,' she muttered. 'I know I'm over-emotional, but. . .but Madame Léonie meant so much to Grandfather. . .'

Robert's heavy arm touched her shoulder very gently, propelling her out of the glasshouse. 'Come and sit down,' he said, gruffly. 'I think we both need to cool off. . .'

She did not completely miss the irony of his words as they walked towards a nearby stone seat covered with a living green cushion, although she knew, quite plainly, that she was truly the overwrought one. But his expression gave nothing away. He sat beside her on the camomile-covered seat, yet not too close. Gratefully Patti inhaled the subtle fragrance that arose from the disturbance of the stubby leaves, and waited. She appreciated that he was being thoughtful, careful not to offend or scare her again. At this moment she was no longer afraid of his physical presence, nor of her reaction to it.

With his eyes studying the fair vista before him, Robert began to speak. 'First of all,' he said slowly, turning to watch her, 'I can't help wondering exactly what your grandfather——' his eyes deepened, and, without knowing why, she tensed '—a relative of mine, too, remember, told you about Madame Léonie...' He paused, then continued with a harder note in his voice. 'You know, of course, about the old family feud between him and his cousin, my uncle?' Again he hesitated, as if expecting an answer, and uneasily Patti looked away from his searching eyes.

'Yes,' she admitted unwillingly. 'Beth hinted that it caused great unhappiness...' Sighing, she recalled thoughts of Grandfather and his beloved rose. Then she added, 'Perhaps I've always attached too much importance to what Grandfather told me. Beth said he became...well, "woolly-headed" is the way she put it ...in his later years.'

Looking back at Robert, she discovered he was smiling at her approvingly. When he spoke, there was a suspicion of relief in his deep voice. 'Very delicate. I understand. So we'll leave it at that, shall we? At least——' his tone sharpened '—for the present.'

A sense of uneasiness arose inside Patti, spoiling the feeling of companionship she had thought to be growing between them. Then Robert was smiling, and telling her something that instantly restored her spirits.

'I can assure you that Madame Léonie really does exist, Patti. You've seen the plants—and I promise, with plenty of professional care——'

'And love?' She couldn't help herself, although she bit her lip as his austere smile twitched at his lips.

Gravely he nodded. 'Of course. And with love. They will grow into bigger and better Madame Léonies. Now does that make you feel happier, Patti?'

'Oh, it does, Robert!' Patti filled her lungs again

with the camomile's restorative fragrance and smiled radiantly into his dark eyes.

He was looking at her very intently, and she saw that his face was more relaxed than usual. 'Dreams seldom come true,' he warned her wryly. 'I wonder if we can make yours do so, Patti. . .'

CHAPTER FIVE

PATTI cheered up a little, reassured by this new gentleness. Her curiosity grew, and with it the courage came to talk about Madame Léonie. 'Was Madame Léonie some sort of seedling, I wonder? Is that how you grew all those little plants?'

To her surprise, Robert's smile developed into a laugh, and he shifted his large body an inch or two nearer hers. Again, the fragrance from the camomile cushion wafted upwards, and now, as she became aware of his closeness, she felt no alarm, just a growing pleasure, for surely he was enjoying her company as much as she enjoyed his. . .

'A rose lover you clearly are, Patti,' he said softly, turning sideways a little to look at her. 'But equally clearly you don't know a seedling from a graft or a bud!'

'A bud? A—graft?'

Laughing again, he reached for her hand, folding it warmly and authoritatively within his own. 'And I thought you knew it all!' he teased.

'How could I? I may be part of your family, but I've never professed to be a rose grower.' Her lightness of heart had returned, even though his touch was having its usual shattering effect. 'I only know what I've read, and what Grandfather and Miss Clarke told me,' she said, slightly defiant, fearful that he would be irritated, once more, by her ignorance.

But he laughed no longer. Looking at her thoughtfully, he pressed her fingers as if with a last touch of reassurance, before setting her hand back on her lap. 'What *did* the old man tell you?'

His tone was casual, but Patti's heart lurched. The all-important question again — so he was not content to let the matter drop. . . Instinctively she strengthened her defences. Robert was being exceptionally patient and understanding now, but he was still arrogant by nature. She decided to tell the truth — or, at least, some of it.

She took a deep breath. 'He said that Madame Léonie was a — a sport.' She faltered. 'Is that the right term?'

Robert nodded. 'Quite right. It means a bud variation. Some sports are very beautiful and have become famous.' His eyes narrowed in the way that made her uneasy about his unsaid thoughts. 'So he told you that Madame Léonie is a sport, Anything else?'

Patti's throat had grown dry. She sensed a hint of recurring impatience in the quiet, deep voice.

'Not — really. . .' Oh, dear — how much should she reveal? All the unpleasantness that Grandfather had told her about? The warning Beth had given her not to stir up any more unhappiness? Swallowing, she tried to clear her confusion and come to a decision, but how hard it was. What if all Grandfather's judgemental words *had* been mere fantasy?

'Well?' insisted that resonant voice, right beside her, and Patti turned her head to meet Robert's compelling gaze.

In desperation she clung to the innocent part of the old story. 'He said,' she muttered weakly, 'that Madame Léonie was a throwback to one of the roses in the garden at the Château de la Malmaison, where the Empress Josephine lived...' She paused, feeling ridiculous, unable to look at him, then added, even more foolishly, 'You know, Napoleon's wife — the one who loved roses so much...'

'Indeed I do,' said Robert. 'I have a Redouté picture of one of the Empress's roses in my study.' Instinctively she glanced at him. The sternness she had fancied she heard was now replaced by a gentleness that confounded her fears.

'Oh, how lovely! May I see it?' She caught her breath; why must she always let her feelings run away so? 'I mean, perhaps one day...'

He made no answer, merely nodded, and she felt a sudden stab of chilling caution as she realised how keenly he watched her. Turning away, she went on ingenuously, 'Yes — well, once I realised that Madame Léonie was so old and so important, I longed to see the real flower, not merely a print in an old book. And I had read in one of Miss Clarke's magazines that you were a rose grower who loved the old shrubs, so I imagined you might well have Madame Léonie in your garden — and that's why I came in, that day you found me by the grotto.' Now she dared to meet his eyes. 'I was only trying to find Grandfather's rose...' she whispered, her voice tailing off then, for the severity had returned to those steady, dark-chocolate eyes.

'I see.'

Again, Patti sensed that air of mystery.

Nervously she went on. 'So, Robert, will you please explain to me why those poor little plants in your glasshouse are so small and — well, really rather pathetic? Are they truly some of Madame Léonie's seedlings?'

Robert's gaze appeared to return from far away. He

smiled wryly at her. 'Not seedlings, Patti—grafted buds. And yes, if I'm lucky, they are direct descendants of your precious old rose. The first, after very many years of having thought she was completely lost to the world.'

'How exciting! But Robert—you said if you were lucky; I don't understand. Why lucky?' Curiosity replaced Patti's former nervousness.

'Budding is a tricky business,' said Robert patiently, and Patti realised what pains he was taking to explain things simply to her. 'Not all buds take—that is, grow into the rootstock. You see. . .'

She felt his enthusiasm grow and her own pleasure increased as he continued. 'You see, Patti, for many years we thought Madame Léonie lost. Then, only last autumn, Jules Lacoste's father found a bush growing wild in a ruined château garden. He took some scions. . .' The smile deepened and one eyebrow flicked up. 'A scion is a cutting, from which one takes a bud. . .'

'Thank you,' said Patti humbly. 'Growing wild in a ruined château! Oh, Robert, but how romantic!'

Robert's lips twitched, and he straightened his face. 'Yes, indeed. Romantic, as you say—but also extremely exciting for professional rose growers. Well, between Lacoste and myself, we have budded Madame Léonie into fresh rootstock, and now only time will tell if she has decided to grow for us.'

At last Patti understood. Her face lit up. 'And so those poor little stems in the glasshouse are actually terribly important and rare? How wonderful! So we just have to wait for them to grow?'

'Exactly that, Patti. We must be patient. Both of us. . .'

For a delightful moment she thought he was about to add something; his face warmed in a half-smile and his eyes grew soft. The extraordinary idea that he might confide in her filled Patti, and she waited, holding her breath.

But even as his glance caught and held hers, they both heard steps approaching down the path, and the moment had gone. Jules Lacoste appeared, happily unaware of his inopportune arrival, swinging his panama hat and smiling easily at them. Patti lowered her head in the hope that her uncharitable thoughts would not be read. . .

Jules bowed elegantly. 'Ah! So there you are, *cher ami* Robert. Enjoying your roses in the company of a charming lady — how admirable! But I fear I intrude. . .'

'I was just enlightening Cousin Patti on the process of creating new roses from old.' Although Robert's words were amiable enough, Patti, knowing him better with every shared conversation, realised he was annoyed at Jules's appearance. She took his hand as he helped her up from the stone seat.

'A miracle, that process,' Jules said quickly, and Patti, still watching Robert, saw how his eyes suddenly narrowed, but only for a second. Then again he was polite and bland, replying that if Jules thought him a miracle worker he should think again. 'It's a technique easily learned, as well you know, Jules. I recall showing you the way of it last time I visited your father's rosery.'

'Indeed you did, *cher* Robert. And we argued about the method I was using at the time — the new American process — but alas, I am still — what is your amusing saying? — all fingers and thumbs!' Jules's apologetic smile was charmingly self-deprecating and Patti thought warmly of Faye's feelings for this good-humoured, attractive young man. Until Robert's cool voice entered her mind with abrupt clarity, causing a new wave of uneasiness to surge through her. 'So you are still unlucky with your grafting, Jules?'

She heard a hint of something she could not identify—was it suspicion? Surely not! Then anxiety grew; why did Robert have this concealed feeling of distrust within him? First about Grandfather and the story of Madame Léonie, then with Faye's hopes of marrying Jules, and now with Jules himself, who clearly was a charming and amenable colleague.

Jules's answer was easy, his manner plain proof of her own good impression of him. 'It is early to say, Robert, and of course we still hope, but. . .' She watched him shake his handsome blond head, still smiling, the blue eyes wide and seemingly apologetic for the possible failure of the all-important budding process.

Robert's frown creased his deep brow, and his voice was clipped. 'I see. So it would appear that *my* Madame Léonie—if she grows, along with the hundred other buds I grafted—will be the only one surviving in today's world. And I had thought you to be as successful in France as I hope to be here. . .' Robert stared at Jules most strangely, thought Patti, feeling her unease grow.

An uncomfortable feeling came to her then—she had entered a world of which she knew nothing. A world which was filled with beautiful roses, but also with men who were naturally in competition with one another. Businessmen who made money from their roses and sought unlimited power.

She looked from Robert to Jules, and back again to

Robert, and childishly wanted to run away, for there was definitely a sense of something not quite right; of distrust on Robert's part, certainly. And what about Jules? Surely he was altogether too open and transparent to be anything but what he seemed? Yet the feeling of apprehension persisted. And she had never yet known it to be wrong. . .

Quickly she said, 'I expect Faye will be wanting me now. Please excuse me if I leave you. . .' And, without waiting to see what reactions her words caused, she fled down the gravel path, not stopping until the momentary shadow of the yew arch touched her, and she realised she was almost out of their sight.

Only then did she walk a little slower, leaving the hedge behind her, loitering when she reached the sundial, running her fingers around the warmth of the old stone, imagining the many secrets it must hold.

'If only I knew whether Grandfather made it all up,' she mused unhappily. 'And if only I could understand what is wrong between Robert and Jules. . .'

But no immediate resolution came to her and so, briskly, she left the sundial, realising that Faye would, indeed, be awaiting her back at the house. And from now on, she thought fervently, she must keep close to Faye and not ever again be tempted out into the rose garden, either by dreams of Madame Léonie or by the honey-sweet voice and capricious smile of Robert Challoner.

For she sensed with certainty, and growing dismay, that it was here in the gardens of Porphyry Court that Madame Léonie's secret hid itself. She would do well, in future, to keep away from both Robert and his glasshouses.

* * *

The weekend dawned misty and beautiful, with an early suggestion of the heat that was to come. Faye surprised both Patti and Lady Challoner by announcing firmly that today they must go to the river.

'To that pretty little sandy beach where we used to play as children. I shall paddle. Indeed, I might even put on my bathing-dress and go into the water!'

Anxiously, Lady Challoner asked, 'But is it warm enough, dear child? And have you really recovered from your cough? Do consider your delicate constitution, Faye, my love.'

Patti watched Faye turn from the open window in the morning-room to smile back at her mother, and was amazed to see the new vitality that now filled her thin face. 'I prefer to think of other, more enjoyable things today, Mother,' said Faye, with a richer note in her voice. 'Of course I'm stronger! And it's going to be very hot...and Jules and I could—well, be together, for a little while...' With a mischievous glance at Patti she added, 'Patti will be there to look after me! Don't worry, Mother.'

Patti smiled encouragingly, meeting the bright eyes with a reassuring nod. Of course she would look after Faye—it was fast becoming a most enjoyable habit. Every day her duties as companion were shifting, from merely cutting the pages of the latest novel, to telling Faye about London life and watching her slowly throw aside her old sense of inferiority and helplessness. Indeed, since Jules Lacoste's arrival yesterday, Faye had been increasingly demanding, and not merely in the cultivation of a better French accent. It was as if the presence of the man she loved was helping her slough off the skin of the old Faye and become the young woman she longed to be — charming, interesting and lovable.

Lady Enid's sigh broke into Patti's thoughts as Faye left the room in search of her bathing-dress. 'So wilful. Just like her brother. . .'

Amused, they exchanged understanding glances, and then Lady Challoner expression lightened. 'But of course, no doubt she and Jules have much to say to each other.' She paused, and then added confidentially, 'The engagement will not be announced yet because, for some reason, Robert is not in favour of it; but I see no reason why they should not be allowed to spend some time together — and, of course, you will be there to chaperon them. I'm sure the afternoon outing will be a great success.'

Lady Challoner's smile broadened as she went on, 'Faye has been so much brighter since she has been sharing your company, Patti.'

'And I am delighted to be with her, Cousin Enid,' Patti replied honestly. It was quite true — she liked Faye a little more each day, respected her kindly mother, and already loved the house and gardens.

And Robert? Sternly she told herself that her feelings about him were merely those of interest and occasional slight disturbance. Nothing more. Even Madame Léonie seemed to have faded into the background of her mind these days.

Languidly, Lady Challoner arose, heading for her boudoir. 'Splendid, dear child. Everything is going along so well. Now I really must attend to my correspondence before luncheon.'

* * *

Patti joined Faye in her bedroom, to find her watching Elsie, the lady's maid, rummaging through the drawers of the oak tallboy.

'You can wear this, Patti. . .' She handed over a cherry-printed bathing-dress with matching hat. 'It might be a little large, but you're not going to swim the Channel in it, are you?'

Faye was bright and happy, and Patti felt some of that happiness soaking into herself. She looked forward to an entertaining afternoon, chaperoning Faye and Jules — but she would not be too conscientious a chaperon, she thought, smiling; she would make a point of letting them wander off if they wished to do so.

But such plans were quickly disrupted by Robert's decision to accompany them on the outing. 'It's high time I had an hour or two's respite from work,' he said genially, as Faye prattled on about the river trip over luncheon. 'I haven't swum down there since I was a boy.'

'Last time we went you pushed me in,' said Faye accusingly.

Robert frowned. 'I did no such thing! You were in the middle of that broken-down little bridge and happened to get in my way as I crossed it. . .' His frown disappeared and he looked down the table at Patti, who was wondering how she could allow Faye and Jules to be alone if Robert was also there. 'How about you, cousin? Are you a swimmer? Or merely, like Faye, a dabbler of toes with accompanying shrieks of horror?'

His unexpected friendliness cut across her worries and she smiled at him as she remembered her childhood. 'At home in Somerset,' she said dreamily, 'we had a river, too. Beth and I both learned to swim. Oh, such happy days. Father and Mother liked picnics. And Grandfather came before he grew too crippled. He used to fish while we splashed, and — and. . .' The memories came easily, and suddenly she was too full of dreams to consider the wisdom of saying what she did. 'But of course Grandfather never left the house for too long,' she prattled on. 'He was always busy writing letters, trying to prove that Madame Léonie was — was. . .'

And then, abruptly, she felt the steel of Robert's gaze probing her mind. She bit her tongue, dismay crowding in as she saw the darkness of his thunderous frown. 'I mean — I mean. . .' Flushing deeply, she looked down at her plate, quite expecting him to question her about what she had left unsaid.

But, although his voice was cold, his words were unexpectedly casual as he remarked, 'I said you were a nymph, didn't I? So you'll be in your element this afternoon.'

And, although he bestowed a frosty, rather mocking smile upon her, she sensed his mind still mulling over her thoughtless words as the meal continued.

They drove down to the river with the reins of the fat little cob in Robert's strong hands, the dog-cart creaking and swaying as it rattled along the rough track beneath tall elms and thick hedgerows of wild rose, budding bramble and elder. Seated at one side, with her back to Jules, and Faye perched beside Robert's tall figure in front, Patti was content to close her eyes beneath the burning afternoon sun and inhale the various fragrances drifting up to her. Faintly she heard Faye chattering on to Robert, but the words eluded her. It was enough to relax and enjoy the moment, for she had an uneasy premonition that the afternoon was bound to be a difficult one.

When the dog-cart stopped, Faye jumped down excitedly, eager to explore. Robert carried the picnic hamper and Jules brought the bundle of bathing-dresses, parasols and towels. Faye pulled Patti along with her towards a fisherman's hut, just beyond the little scallop of sandy beach that the meandering river had deposited, beneath a small wooden footbridge. 'We can change here,' she called merrily. 'The men always go behind the bushes! Come along, Patti — hurry up! I do hope the water won't be too cold. . .'

She was the first one out of the hut, more alive than Patti could ever have imagined her to be, a vital figure dancing down the riverbank in a bright striped bathing-dress, her toes bare, busily in search of Jules.

'Jules!' she called. 'Where are you? I want to show you the old quarry before we go into the water. . .'

Patti, following more sedately, watched them, hand in hand, disappear discreetly into the tangle of saplings and scrubby bushes that wandered along beside the bank. Dismay struck her; now she was left alone with Robert, who would, of course, object to his sister being unchaperoned with the man he did not like. . .

Robert strode out from behind the bushes while she stood uncertainly on the sandy beach, hands busy with the errant curls which refused to be tucked into her saucy cherry-printed little hat. He looked bigger than ever, she thought, startled. The black bathing-suit emphasised his enormous shoulders and wide chest. A fringe of dark hair delicately arose from beneath its neckline, and strode up his bare arms. Patti's heart was beating too fast, and she felt foolish. Again, nervousness at his physical presence invaded her.

'Where's Faye?' he asked sharply, looking around him, but as Patti did not reply his eyes turned towards her, and he came to her side, unexpectedly smiling. She stood in awkward silence while he inspected her, from her bare toes to the top of the little hat. 'Most elegant!' he remarked in a teasing voice. 'Not exactly what I would expect a nymph to wear — but I suppose convention must be appeased. . .'

Unsure if he was laughing at her, Patti said stiffly, forcing herself to put a toe into the lapping water, 'I hope it's safe to swim here.'

'I can guarantee there are no jellyfish.' Robert's legs were near hers, one foot lifting and feeling the water.

'I — I. . .' Stricken with something she did not wish to identify, Patti gasped. This was ridiculous! She must get away from him — quickly. He had the most amazing effect on her, and she was not ready to — to. . . To what? Oh, never mind! Dismissing such disturbing thoughts, she took the plunge.

'Oh! It's *cold*. . .!' Her startled cry rang through the quiet woodland, alarming the doves that cooed nearby and setting them into flight, wings clapping as they flew away.

Silently the water closed around her and for a second she thought she must scramble out immediately. But then the long-forgotten pleasure of swimming returned, and, with it, a new warmth was forged in her body. She began to breathe more deeply, relaxed her mind, and thrust out from the little beach to explore the depths of the river as it flowed on downstream.

She had always loved swimming and today it was especially enjoyable. Out here she could get away from her worries and fears. Here, in the middle of this cold, green, implacable yet benign force that bore her up so carefully, she could forget Faye and Jules, let thoughts of Grandfather and his old rose fade away, even forget Robert and the terrifying effect he had on her. . .

Something slimy touched her foot — grabbed at it, caught it, and was joined by another. At first, Patti did no more than try to kick herself free. She reminded herself bravely that there were always reeds in rivers. Then she tried to find a rock she could cling to, but the current, seemingly so slight, had already carried her out of sight of the sandy beach, and now she was in mid-stream, and the water was deep — deeper than she had realised. And the weeds had her by the legs.

She could not get free. She sank and took a mouthful of water, returned to the surface, panicked, tried to scream, and swallowed another mouthful. Then she went down, down, the slimy thongs holding her legs more firmly. . . Her lungs were bursting, her mind full of disbelieving horrors.

And then hands found her, bore her up, and she came out, like a cork, breaking the surface of the water so fast that it exploded in a cloud of spray. Robert's face was close to hers, his thick hair slicked back to his head, those dark eyes wide and fierce and the strength of his body making her realise that she was still alive after all.

'Patti! Dear God! Try and breathe slowly. You're all right now, I've got you — slowly now, my love. . .'

Gasping, she experienced enormous relief until again a slimy reed touched her legs. Screaming, she took in a mouthful of water yet again. Wildly, arms and legs threshed, and it was only when Robert pulled her to his breast that she quietened.

His voice was authoritative. 'Stop it, Patti. Keep your mouth shut. You're safe. Just let yourself go limp—I'll take you to the bank. . .'

He swam on his back, arms around her shoulders, towing her swiftly out of reach of the racing current, and the searching tendrils of reeds, and at last she found the courage to relax. But still she trembled, and her teeth chattered as, picking her up in his arms, he waded ashore, to lay her on the warm, sandy earth, beneath a canopy of sun-dappled willow leaves.

His hands clutched hers as he knelt by her side. Looking into her stricken eyes, he smiled, but his voice was unsteady. 'I won't let any harm come to you—it's all right, you're safe, Patti. . .'

But the horror still within her was forcing its way out; tears streamed down her cheeks. She moaned, turned her head from him, and sobbed wildly until the spasm of fear passed. When it was over, she discovered she was sitting up, with Robert's arms about her, his damp body so close that she could hear the even thump of his heart. And her fear of him had gone. . . Fear had been there in the clinging weeds, in the lack of breath and the nearness of death by drowning in the freezing water. Fear could no longer possibly be where Robert was. . . Patti nestled into his body, letting his warmth soak into her, tasting the river's tangy drops as he pressed her close to him.

He bent his head, and his voice was in her ear, its deep music trembling through her agitated mind. 'God, but how could I ever have let you go into that deep pool? I'll never forgive myself, never. . .'

It seemed that he had to keep talking. Vaguely Patti wondered if Robert, too, had a need to exorcise fear, and this was his way of doing it. She closed her eyes and pressed closer to him.

'I was so busy watching you. You swim like a fish — I was admiring you. I didn't think about those damned weeds. That damned pool where the current flows so fast. . . Patti, are you *sure* you're all right?' Abruptly he put her from him, strong arms holding her away, and she saw his face contorted with anxiety, deep eyes pleading with her for reassurance.

She was limp in his arms, her mind a blur of already half-forgotten shock, replaced now by this wonderful new sensation. She wanted nothing but to stay where she was — so close to Robert's strong, exciting body. . .

But he did not allow her to. Slowly his arms relaxed about her, and his large right hand came up to gently encircle her throat, lifting her dripping face until it was only inches away from his.

'Patti, my precious little nymph. . .' he whispered huskily, one dark brow raising in the familiar mockery. 'Don't ever give me such a fright again — please!'

And then, to her intense surprise and delight, his lips moved, delicately wandering over her cold, wet face, warming her, pleasing her, proving with infinite sensuality that the magic she had felt sparking between them on that first meeting was now, indeed, in full force.

He kissed her brow, her nose, her temples, her chin — and then, at long last, found her parted lips, already waiting for him. After a moment of thoughtless bliss, Patti pulled away as reality returned to her. She gasped, despairingly. What must he think of her? To give herself to him like this, with such shameful abandon.

Perhaps he shared those thoughts, for suddenly he

leaped to his feet. 'Good God, what am I thinking of? You're freezing! You need dry towels and some brandy—wait here, Patti, don't move. . . I'll be back in a minute. . .'

She lay on her back, staring at the serenity of the untroubled hyacinth sky above. Shivering and trembling, she knew dully that she was not suffering from her dousing in the river—but instead from the far more potent effect of Robert's kisses.

And then, abruptly, the spell was broken. Footsteps came rushing down the bank; Faye threw herself on her knees, saying frantically, 'Oh, Patti! How terrible! How absolutely awful! Are you sure you're safe? Oh, Patti, dear Patti. . .'

Robert loomed up, his shadow falling over her like a warm, thick blanket. 'Stop having hysterics, Faye,' he ordered. 'Give Patti some of this.' A brandy flask was handed over and Patti gulped as the liquid fire trickled down her throat. 'Where's Jules?' demanded Robert sharply. 'And where the hell were you, too, little sister? Amusing yourself with that damned Frenchman somewhere out of sight, of course. Well, never mind, we'll talk about that later. Now go and get the picnic hamper. Patti needs dry clothes and a hot drink. I'll carry her to the hut and you can help her dress.'

Again, Patti was swept up in strong arms, and taken into the privacy of the hut, where Faye wrapped towels around her, and kept saying how ghastly it would have been if she had drowned. . .

Despite her sense of shame and shock, Patti discovered she wanted to laugh. 'Stop it, Faye,' she implored weakly. 'Don't keep reminding me! Just help me get warm — and what did Robert say about tea? A cup would be just wo-w-wonderful!'

Once she was dressed she felt better. Out in the sunshine again, she sat in the dog-cart drinking the strong tea that Robert gave her, trying to avoid looking at him, but fully aware of the concern that still burned in his dark eyes. Jules came to the side of the gig. 'You are safe, then, Mademoiselle Patti? *Quelle horreur*! I could not believe it when I heard — ah, you English are *tres sportif*, with your swimming and your love of exercise. But I am, as you say, a landlubber. I do not care for the water — I prefer to watch while others swim!'

'Such a fuss about a little cold water,' Faye interrupted, and Patti, sitting back, watching, thought she heard a hint of sharpness in the voice, which had suddenly reverted to its old flat monotony. Briefly she wondered what had happened between them to change Faye, and then hoped she was only imagining things.

Then Robert reappeared, clothed once more, and put his jacket around her shoulders. He ordered everyone into the dog-cart, carefully keeping his distance from her. 'We must get Patti into bed as soon as possible. I don't intend her to catch a cold. Hurry up, Jules, you're keeping us waiting. . .'

His abrupt voice put a damper on the journey, and wretchedly Patti recalled her premonition. Even Robert's next words, thrown autocratically over his shoulder as he guided the cob back along the woodland track, did no more than briefly rally her fading strength. 'You'll go straight to bed and stay there, Patti.'

'Oh, no! Not to bed. . .' she murmured faintly, and he turned, frowning so sternly that she blanched.

'Certainly to bed. You've had a severe shock and it'll be a miracle if you don't catch cold from such a dousing. You'll go to bed and do exactly as I tell you, Patti.'

She had no heart, nor the will, to argue. Was this the same Robert who had just held her to his breast and said she was his precious little nymph? 'Very well, Robert.' Her voice was low and defeated. She guessed that he was wishing he had never kissed her — never felt her cold, wet body trembling against his. . . Clearly he was regretting his moment of impulsive sensuality. And of course he must be thinking her no more than a fast woman — perhaps a similar one to the love who had jilted him in the past, as Faye had told her. Traitorous tears oozed from beneath Patti's closed lids, and the dog-cart jolted her painfully as Robert urged the cob into a trot. What a dreadful ending to the day. And how could she ever face him again, remembering his kisses and her shameful, all too wanton surrender?

Patti recovered speedily, despite her shocking experience. By the early evening she was sitting up in bed, wanting to get dressed, but not quite daring to do so without Robert's permission. She told herself crossly that it was absurd to have to wait until he said she could resume her life — but she was unwilling to risk his displeasure by defying those wishes.

Her thoughts during that long, quiet afternoon were legion. Robert's hands about her shaking body, his kisses raining on her face and throat. . . And then, in a wild attempt to stem the shame of such memories, she recalled Grandfather and his stories about Madame Léonie. It seemed that thinking of the past was the only way to exorcise the burning sensation of Robert's remembered touch. . .

With closed eyes, she ordered herself back into her childhood. And, as the hours slid away, she thought, drowsily, she could hear Grandfather's rumbling voice going on about his beloved old rose.

'What a colour she is! See how gracefully her petals lie. And, Patti, what a perfume!' Grandfather was leaning a little nearer to the small girl sitting at the big library table. 'And in her golden heart lies a secret — one we all long to learn; the mystery of life itself. . .'

Secrets. Mysteries. Grandfather beside her. . . Patti opened her eyes and discovered she was in the present again. But his message filled her mind. In Madame Léonie's heart is the secret of life itself. . . What could that secret be? Suddenly a glad fact presented itself to her. She needed to find out Grandfather's mysterious secret — and the answer must surely lie somewhere here, in Porphyry Court. She knew, instinctively and certainly, that it was guarded by Robert Challoner himself. . .

Patti wriggled restlessly in her bed. She longed to get up and start searching — oh, but what a muddle everything was today. If only Robert would come and sit on her bed, smiling in that teasing way, and say that she must get up at once, that the house wasn't the same without her. . . Her face fell. Robert would never come alone into her bedroom.

Even so, when a knock sounded at the door, her heart leaped. 'Come in!' The anticipation in her voice died. 'Oh, it's you, Faye. . .'

'How are you, Patti? You look better. More colour. Mother wanted to send for Dr Brent but Robert said no — he said you'd be all right again very soon.'

'Did he, indeed?' Patti was hurt. She might have caught a most dreadful cold for all Robert knew or cared.

'Is there anything you want, Patti? Books, or your embroidery?'

Patti lowered her tell-tale eyes. She knew that Faye was quite perceptive, and she didn't want Robert's sister reading her present thoughts. 'No, thank you. I hope to get up very soon. There's nothing wrong with me. . .'

'Robert said tomorrow. Breakfast in bed, he said, and then you may come down.'

Patti swallowed her annoyance. 'I see,' she muttered.

Faye wandered around the room, touching the curtains, staring out of the window. She turned quickly, looking back at Patti with sudden plain affection. 'It's not the same without you downstairs, Patti. . .' Patti was taken aback at the unexpected note of friendship in her voice.

'You mean you miss me?'

'Of course. I've never had anyone like you to talk to before — about life, about women. . . oh, you know! All the things we've discussed. I've almost forgotten what it was like before you came — when I used to get headaches and things. . .' A mischievous smile slid across Faye's face. 'I haven't had a headache in weeks!'

Patti said brightly, 'I should hope not! Not now that you've got Jules here. . . By the way. . .' Suddenly she recalled how Faye and Jules had slid away into the woods down by the river. 'Did you have a nice walk? *Alone?*' She whispered the last word and smiled broadly, but unexpectedly Faye turned away.

She looked back over her shoulder, her face abruptly

bleak. 'Yes. Well, I'll tell you about it later—Robert said I mustn't stay too long and tire you. Goodnight, Patti, sleep soundly...' Quickly she left the room and Patti was left with an image of disappointment filling her unhappy face.

Lying in the security of her quiet bedroom, Patti reflected sombrely on the uncertainties of life. Things happened so quickly, changing the course of one's existence as if in a flash. Faye had been so happy this morning, but no longer. She had been, so she said, in love with Jules; could love, then, come and go so speedily? Love—whatever it was...

Patti's heart pulsed, recalling Robert's strength and his caresses, but she had the honesty to face the fact that the passion they had forged so briefly had been caused only by the magic of the moment. Not by mutual love.

Patti managed a croaky little chuckle as the emotive word stuck in her throat. What, love Robert, her distant cousin, her arrogant employer? The enigmatic, chilling man who so irritatingly ordered her life? Robert, who was part of Madame Léonie's secret? Who had loved and lost, according to Faye, and so clearly thought himself immune to any further commitment to love? Love *him*?

Certainly not! The fact should have cheered her, but suddenly she was in tears, huddling back into her pillow, sniffing and sulking like a spoilt child. Until, unbidden, came the bleak knowledge that the kisses she and Robert had shared, their intimate and lovely appreciation of each other's bodies, had made her into a woman...

She dried her eyes then, resolutely telling herself she was a fool. She must forget Cousin Robert and his sensuous, forbidden attraction, and instead think of Madame Léonie and the exciting possibility of discovering Grandfather's golden secret. . . Patti's blood began to sing happily, and she felt almost recovered. Sitting up, she punched the pillow hard.

A tap at the door. Her stupid heart soared. 'Come in.' Again her voice was full of anticipation; again she was disappointed.

Elsie entered, holding a small bowl filled with flowers. She smiled as she approached the bedside table. 'Sir Robert said to bring you these, Miss Nevill.' Bobbing a curtsy, she handed Patti an envelope before leaving the room.

Patti's fingers closed around the long white envelope, but her eyes were held fast by the melancholy beauty of the cluster of lilies of the valley, floating in the little crystal bowl. Their bell-like heads held a perfection that enchanted her, and the lingering perfume made her senses tingle with delight.

Flowers, from Robert's garden. . . Deep inside her, warmth glowed like a hidden fire. It was some minutes before she recalled the envelope she held. Black and sturdily upright, Robert's writing was an impression of his dominant personality. Patti read the few words, unaware that she was holding her breath.

> For my waterlogged, precious nymph, in the hope that these few flowers will fill her mind with beauty and peace, thereby erasing this afternoon's unpleasantness. Robert.

Very slowly she let out the pent-up breath, savouring each word and hearing in her mind his voice — quietly vibrant, music that thrilled and excited, even as it struck harmonious chords within her, full of his own especial brand of affectionate teasing.

My waterlogged, precious nymph. Patti slid down the bed, smiling at the ridiculous phrase; but slowly her face tensed. She had wanted Robert to forgive her for such terrible behaviour there on the riverbank — but she had never expected a message of this kind. What did it mean? What *could* it mean? Flowers, and a loving expression that reminded her of the magical chemistry they had both felt. . .

What a complex, fascinating — infuriating! — man he was, to be sure. Patti's face slowly relaxed. Of course, he was just being nice to her, writing things that he found hard to say. Yes, that was it — clearly Robert had a problem with communication. Well, she would meet him tomorrow morning with a clear conscience, after all. The note meant he had entirely forgiven her and considered the whole episode little more than a rather disastrous joke. . .his precious nymph, indeed!

And then, on the threshold of sleep, she remembered what he had called her as he'd swept her into safety in that terrible moment when she thought she was drowning.

Was it really — could it have been — or was she only imagining that he had called her 'my love'?

CHAPTER SIX

NEXT morning Patti decided to brave Robert's displeasure by presenting herself at the breakfast-table. Nervously she ran downstairs, pausing in the doorway, ready to meet his eyes, eager to know his reaction to seeing her again.

But the big chair at the head of the table was empty. Her smile died, and she went slowly to her seat beside Faye, who was complaining to Lady Challoner about Robert's reproving remarks last night.

'He really is too much, Mother! He said Jules and I had no right to go for a walk alone.' Faye snorted. 'What an old Barratt of Wimpole Street he is! Has he no feelings at all? But I suppose that business of being jilted two years ago has turned him into a sour old man. . . Well, he's in the garden with Jules now, giving the day's orders to the gardeners. Let's hope he stays there!'

A chill fell on Patti's spirits as she realised Robert was too busy even to think about her being still stuck up in her bedroom, and she could hardly eat her breakfast. She knew she must seek him out to thank him for the flowers — and also, more importantly, to discover if he had truly decided to forget her indiscretion. . .

So self-occupied was she that she scarcely noticed her companions at the table, once their kindly enquiries as to her health had been answered. If Faye wrangled irritably with her Mother, Patti heard little of it. All she could think of was Robert and her need to see him.

When she slipped out, unnoticed, at the end of the meal, the garden, with its early morning haze, seemed to embrace her with an almost tangible welcome. It was June, and all the fragrances, all the beauties of springtime nature, were laid before and around her.

She lingered by the grotto, smiling with pleasure. In the vine-walk she admired the growing leaves and tiny budding flowers. She stroked the sundial's friendly warmth and then, heading towards the yew hedge, she tensed, anticipating Robert's reaction to her appearance in the rose garden.

But it was Jules she encountered first, emerging from the shade of the arch in the circular hedge. He frowned, running a hand through his mop of blond hair and clenching his panama as if seized by a grand passion. But the moment he saw her he seemed to change — Patti, newly aware of moods and unpredictability, noticed how he switched on the bright smile she had until now thought natural and friendly. Now she saw that, although his lips curved, the smile did not reach his eyes. Blue and calculating, they looked her up and down, and nervously she had an impulse to run.

Too late. He was at her side, taking her hand, kissing the back of her reluctant fingers. 'Mademoiselle Patti! Ah, *comme tu es belle*. What a delight to see you safe and sound. You have made my day happy.'

Patti backed away as far as she could, but he held on to her hand, relentlessly drawing her towards him. 'Such a lovely sight yesterday *chérie*, in your little bathing-dress.' His voice was low, his smile suggestive, and his fingers pressed hers fervently.

Patti froze. Someone was coming through the yew hedge, as yet unseen, but whose presence she recognised immediately. *Robert*.

Dismayed, she snapped at Jules, 'Stop it, please! There's no need to hold my hand any longer,' and saw the light in his eyes change as he, too, sensed Robert's approach. But to her fury he took no notice of her words; instead, he quickly pulled her closer, slipping his free arm around her waist.

By the time Robert had entered the arch and was through it, Patti was free again. Jules was laughing, as if at a good joke, smiling at her and saying, more loudly that was necessary, 'Ah, Mademoiselle Patti, but I think you are a naughty girl—beautiful, yes, but truly *méchante*, eh?'

And then, as if he had only just realised Robert was near, he turned, a look of assumed surprise covering his face. 'Well, this will get no work done—and I must see the catalogues you spoke of, *mon ami*. So I leave your pretty little cousin to you, eh?'

Nodding, he strolled off, putting on his hat and nonchalantly gazing around him as he went. Patti's anger had grown to hatred. How dared he? To flirt with her, when he was almost engaged to Faye—and to do so at a time when he knew Robert was bound to see. . .

'Good morning, Patti.' Robert's cool words burst into her rebellious mind like a bucket of icy water. Her rage melted. She felt exhilarated, but distinctly nervous.

'Good morning, Robert.' Her voice was a little higher than usual, not quite under control.

'So you're better?' He sounded polite but impersonal. Not waiting for an answer, he went on briskly.

'Are you sure you're well enough to be up? I told you to breakfast in bed.'

Such arrogance helped Patti's floundering self-control. Her head tilted an inch higher and her lips tightened dangerously. 'But I decided to get up.' Her slight emphasis on the pronoun made Robert's expression sharpen.

'I see. Well, it's nice to have you about again.'

What a grudging compliment! thought Patti, with a flare of stabbing disappointment. Somehow she forced a smile of artificial sweetness to her stiff lips. 'Thank you. But I didn't imagine you would have missed me.'

Robert's eyes narrowed, and Patti recognised the familiar glint of suspicion as he said curtly, 'Perhaps not quite as much as our French guest obviously did.' And at once she was filled with a terrible sense of shame and hurt.

But to explain Jules's unpleasant actions would attach far too much importance to them. Patti lifted her chin defiantly, determined to let Robert see that she did not care about his unfair assertions. She decided to ignore the comment.

Aware that he was following her as she walked briskly towards the first glasshouse, she said, with a touch of hauteur, over her shoulder, 'And what news of darling Madame Léonie's babies? Are they growing well? May I see them?'

Robert growled. 'If you wish. But I fear you will be disappointed, for they grow very slowly.' He sounded very cross and the fact was an added challenge to Patti. What *was* she to think of this sometimes charming, always prickly man, who saved her life one day, sent her flowers and a fond message, and then became barely polite?

Flowers. The word flicked across her mind. She hadn't thanked him for the lilies... Catching her breath, halfway down the misty-windowed glasshouse, she whirled around, words of simple pleasure on her lips, but Robert's attention was already elsewhere.

His profile was turned to her, and for the moment he ignored her, busily concentrating on the plants filling the slatted shelves. His big hands fingered, pinched and caressed; Patti's throat went dry, recalling those same hands on her wet body only yesterday afternoon. She could hardly breathe, and an urgent longing grew within her.

And then, as she continued to watch him, slowly all her pain and frustration faded, and in its wake came a gentle warmth of surprising serenity. There was no need to say anything. Occupied as he was with his roses, he was allowing the true, untroubled Robert to appear. She could stay here quietly and go on watching him — enjoy the sheer pleasure of being near, without the danger of saying the wrong thing, of creating more misunderstandings, more conflict.

Sometimes, thought Patti with amazement, silence could say far more than mere words... So she remained at the end of the glasshouse, rejoicing in the earthy fragrance of growing things, knowing that he was too deeply concentrating to be aware of her scrutiny.

He wore a slightly threadbare checked linen shirt, with a button missing at the neck, so that his faded varsity tie barely masked the space through which his strong, tanned throat showed. The old lovat-green jacket hung on a peg on the door, and his sleeves were roughly pulled up to the elbows. Again, she saw that dark fringe of thick hair, rising from strong, busy arms.

If she had not known that he was a famous international rose grower, thought Patti, a smile touching her mouth, she would again have taken him for a gardener. Memory chivvied her thoughts mischievously. Very much the head gardener, of course!

And yet, for all his casual appearance, there was a presence about him. That military stance. The poise of his well-shaped head, bent now as he studied his plants. Indeed, his very stillness, like a spring tightly wound, conveyed a composure which could, very easily, become dramatic action.

And she had not realised before what an unusually handsome man Robert was. Perhaps good looks were only really appreciated when seen against unobtrusive clothes, she thought sagely. That old shirt, the faded tie, dun-coloured breeches and leather boots that had surely not been polished for many years — they were all just a frame to the man they clothed.

She saw small beads of perspiration gleam beneath the falling straight hair on his forehead and, fascinated, watched him impatiently wipe them away with long, earth-stained fingers. He seemed completely unaware of her presence. She was still looking at him, discovering such exciting new attractions as the sunburned pillar of throat, the curved scar that swept down one leanly angled cheek, and the suspicion of unshaven stubble darkening his strong jawline, when abruptly she realised that he had felt her gaze upon him. He had turned away from the shelves and was looking at her.

Blushing, she met his gaze, uncertain whether to smile, whether to speak.

Walking towards her, Robert said, quite matter-of-factly, and in the teasing voice which she now knew masked deeper feelings, 'And how is my nymph today? As vital as ever, I see. *And* as beautiful — but of course, Jules has already told you that.'

The brittle compliment, with its accompanying tart comment, hung on the scented, warm air, and Patti's smile died. All her innocent feelings were being cut down. Her face grew taut and nervous. She was not sure what she had been hoping he might say, but the superficial rebuke had hit deep.

She tried to turn away, but the lack of space prevented it. Robert was beside her. He put out a hand to touch her arm, and for a soaring moment she thought he must be going to say he had only been teasing. Until she saw the hurt suspicion in his deep eyes.

Starting back impulsively, she retreated into fantasy. So much easier to be Patti, the play-acting London career woman, than Patti, the adorable nymph. . . Brightly she smiled up at him, trying to disguise the emptiness which she feared was etched on her face.

'What a tease you are, Robert! I'm no nymph, and well you know it! I'd much rather be thought of as one of those fascinating new independent women the newspapers tell us about. . . a modern emancipated twentieth-century woman! I've been telling Faye how I actually saw the Pankhursts in London — such wonderful idealists, don't you think? Just imagine! We shall all be getting the vote before long!'

She fluttered her hands in exaggerated gestures, and a finger brushed the small posy of lilies which was pinned to her breast with the cameo brooch which Miss Clarke had given her. Suddenly she remembered the flowers. 'So sweet of you to send me these,' she gushed, looking at them and so avoiding Robert's grim gaze. 'Such a wonderful scent. They cheered me up no end. Thank you, Robert.'

And then, without knowing why, she stopped. He was staring down at her with with such a fierce, incredulous expression that all her brave chatter dissolved in the knowledge of what he was thinking that she was doing it again — play-acting. They both knew it. Hated it.

It was a moment of revelation. Patti gasped anxiously. Was he angry, about to rebuke her further? To say, with searing scorn, even dislike, that she was behaving like the child she so surely was? Oh, but why had she tried to hide like that? Surely she knew, deep within her, that there was no need to play-act with Robert, this quiet, passionate, complicated man who, at times, hid behind his own mask?

They stood close, unashamedly aware of each other's inner feelings, and it was with no sense of surprise that Patti felt his arms slowly, tenderly, reach out to touch her, to draw her close and return her to that place of forbidden joy against his steadily beating heart.

'Patti,' he said, almost inaudibly, and then again, as if, she thought, he was trying to pull out words which refused to be said. 'Patti. . .' And then his embrace crushed her, hugged her; his fingers gently became entwined in her hair, and he leaned his face against the side of her head. 'I can't — resist you.' Just a whisper, but it filled her heart with exquisite joy.

Closing her eyes, she lay against him, until the courage came to look up, to move away enough to stretch out her hands and lock them around his neck. To pull his face down to hers. To kiss him with what she rejoiced in knowing was utter abandon. . .

Robert broke the embrace after the first few heady

moments of rapture. He held her away from him, examining her glowing face.

'Patti, forgive me.'

Very slowly, her joy faded. She drew back. 'For-*forgive* you?'

He nodded, stepping backwards, hands now clenched deep in his breeches pockets. He tried to smile, and Patti thought she had never seen such a failure. That expression of guilt and pain could never be called a smile. . .

'I told you before.' He cleared his throat and his voice grew stronger. He looked at her very directly and now there was a glint of armour safely guarding his eyes. Now he could actually grin mockingly at her. 'I told you before, didn't I? The temptation of a pretty girl in a glasshouse. And a girl like you, in particular. . .'

She saw the grin disappear, saw how the pain replaced it, and knew how he must feel, for she too was aching. 'A girl like *me*, Robert?' Quickly she jumped into the numbing silence. 'What sort of a girl am I then?'

It was impossible to remain silent with this brooding pain building up between them. Gasping, she forced herself to speak. 'Of course! You mean you saw Jules and me, just now. . .but that was just a mistake. It was nothing to do with me, Robert — truly. . .'

Staring at his grim face, she felt desperation spread. 'It was Jules!' she said wildly. 'He took my hand, he. . .he. . .k-k-kissed it. . .and then. . .and then. . .' Words petered out, because, quite obviously, they were having no effect whatsoever. Robert did not believe her.

She tried once more, smiling, as if the very idea of

his disbelief was itself ridiculous. 'How silly you are, Robert! I don't even — *like* — Jules. . .'

No good. His eyes were profound, as cold as the river in which she had so nearly drowned yesterday. The aching memory of his arms around her, his warmth, giving her new life, created new havoc in Patti's whirling mind. She turned away, but found herself facing the end of the glasshouse. To leave it she must pass Robert, but that was impossible. She couldn't go near him. Not now. Now now that her body longed for him with such urgency.

A shocking thought struck her, and she cried aloud, 'You think I'm just a silly child who flirts with every man I meet. But it's not true. . . Oh, Robert, surely you don't think that of me? But you do — is that what you meant? "A girl like me. . ."'

Sobs were working their way up through her chest, and to prevent them breaking out and utterly shaming her she said hoarsely, 'I'm sorry — but I couldn't. . .couldn't help myself. . .'

Robert's hands were on her arms again, their warmth and strength almost more than she could bear. He looked down at her, and she thought how deep and remote his dark eyes were, like desolate lakes in a wilderness. 'It's not your fault, Patti,' he said harshly, 'My fault. All mine — and I apologise.' His voice was low, unsteady and quite frightening in its depth of feeling. 'I had no right to. . .' She watched him bite off the words.

Robert stepped away from her, fiercely concentrating on the plants at his side. He touched a sprouting bud with a forefinger and thumb and scowled down at it. 'No right at all,' he growled again. Then, turning, he stared at her defensively. 'I fear you're the sort of child men take advantage of. First Jules—oh, yes, don't try and excuse him; I know the sort of chap Jules is!' Pausing, his face grew guilty. 'And now—me. You see?'

Patti leaned against the shelf, her mind swimming hazily. She thought he was trying to excuse her own shameful behaviour by taking the blame upon himself. Robert was always such a gentleman. . .

And then his voice penetrated her reeling thoughts. 'You see, Patti, you're beautiful. And desirable.' He cleared his husky throat and now the words became full of common sense, all emotion banished. 'But you're not at all experienced with men, so you have no idea how to handle our wickedly quick longings and desires! As your cousin, I feel it my duty to protect you and cherish you in future. You see——' Briefly he laughed, a hard, mocking sound that seared Patti's tense body. 'You're very definitely a temptation, my dear. . .'

'*Temptation?*' She choked, unable to accept the careless, deprecating term. Then she stormed past him, running out of the glasshouse like a miniature whirlwind, no longer concerned that in doing so she brushed Robert's stiff body, unaware that as she left he put out despairing hands to stop her flight; and then, alone, he turned back to Madame Léonie's grafted buds, his face as hard as the porphyry stone itself.

Beset by Robert's shockingly dismissive last words, haunted by the fragrance of the lilies at her breast, Patti flew into the wilderness, the stretch of garden which Robert, in his wisdom, had allowed to return to nature. Among concealing hazel bushes and dancing-leaved tall silver birch saplings, she sank down on the carpet of bluebells, and gave her explosive feelings full rein.

She wept noisily. He thought her fast. A sensual child with no control over her feelings. *A temptation*! And he considered he should become her guardian, her protector...

As the tears ceased, so her self-righteous anger grew. Her protector, indeed! No doubt that would make him feel a lot better. From showering her with urgent kisses, he would now become an anonymous official, merely doing his duty by keeping his cousinly eye upon her.

Very well, if that was what he wanted, then she would not hinder him. Life would be much less complicated if she thought of him simply as a *guardian*. As guardian and ward they could safely inhabit the same house. There would be no more ridiculously emotional scenes between them.

Again, Madame Léonie flew into her mind, a wholesome panacea. From now on she would completely ignore Robert's presence and devote her attention to discovering what it was about Madame Léonie that he so obviously chose to hide. Patti dried her eyes and went resolutely back to the house. The remainder of the day unfolded before her, dreary and full of the dangers of chance encounters with Robert or Jules. She persuaded Faye to remain in the morning-room reading the newspaper and working at French conversation until luncheon, which was a strained meal. No one seemed inclined to converse, and even Lady Challoner was slient.

Afterwards Faye hovered in the hall while her mother said fondly, 'I'm going to rest now, dearest — I feel rather tired. Why don't you and Patti do the same? It's extremely hot today.'

Faye turned to Patti as Lady Challoner went up the staircase. 'Come outside,' she said shortly. 'We'll rest in the hammocks. I need to talk to you. . .'

Disquieted by the thought that possibly Faye had seen Jules accosting her in the garden earlier, Patti unwillingly followed. Settling herself in the first crimson hammock, which swung gently beneath the huge cedar on the lawn, Faye smiled pensively at Patti as she carefully tucked in her linen skirt, making sure that not an inch of stockinged ankle might be visible as she lay down on the other hammock, in case Jules—or Robert—should appear. *Temptation*. The word was impossible to forget.

'Patti,' said Faye, hands behind her head, staring up into the swaying branches, 'I have discovered two upsetting things. One is truly awful—Jules is a flirt.'

Patti held her breath but said nothing. No doubt Faye would elaborate. She waited uncertainly.

'Yesterday,' said Faye bitterly, 'when we went off into the woods, down by the river, I thought Jules was following me. But. . .' She sat up and the hammock tilted dangerously. She lay down again. 'But he wasn't. Patti——' there was an urgency in the name and Patti turned to look at Faye's pained face '—he was watching *you*! Yes, he was! I caught him, peeping through the branches as you put your toe into the water. Oh, the wretch! I gave him a piece of my mind, I can tell you—I mean, we're as good as engaged, or nearly—but now. . .' Faye's dull voice subsided, and there was silence.

A breeze stirred the topmost branches of the cedar, and a few silvery-blue leaves floated down on to the shining, sunlit lawn. A blackcap in the nearby shrubbery burbled a golden thread of song through the quietness of the drowsing afternoon. Faye's next words came as bluntly as a nail being hammered into a piece of wood, and with just as much force. 'Don't fall in love with Robert, Patti—that's the second thing I want to say.'

Patti sat up and the hammock wobbled beneath her. 'I'm not!' she cried sharply. 'What a ridiculous thing to imagine—of course I'm not!' She looked into Faye's perceptive eyes and saw a knowledge there that startled her, sending extraordinary thoughts and images flashing through her mind. *Was* it love she felt for Robert, then—this longing to be with him, to understand all the hidden feelings and needs he so harshly concealed from her? But she had imagined that all she felt was a shameful physical attraction. . .

Slowly lying back on the hammock, she let the whirlwind mishmash of emotions inside her settle as she tried to discover the truth.

Faye was speaking again, her voice a little wry as she said, 'Well, if you are in love with him—and I can't believe you could ever really care for such a monster!—at least you know he isn't the terrible flirt that Jules has turned out to be. Oh, Patti—aren't men too awful for words? I don't think I can be bothered with them any more. . .'

The same conclusion had occurred to Patti, and now she nodded wretchedly. How simple life had been before coming to Porphyry Court. Her mind ran the gamut of all the feelings she had experienced since arriving here—and through them all Robert remained as the touchstone of every incident, every emotion she had suffered. She could not banish him, try as she did.

He was there, in the forefront of her churning mind, a force that somehow she must deal with. . .

'Men are natural flirts, Patti.'

Faye was still wallowing in her own misery, and Patti said, with a sudden explosion of determination, 'But we mustn't let them get the better of us. . .'

'Hmm. Perhaps not. . .' Faye was silent for a few moments, then abruptly the hammock tipped and she was on her feet, green eyes laughing into Patti's, a hand pulling her roughly up beside her. 'Come on, don't let's give in! I refuse to let Jules get away. I'll look so wonderful tonight that he'll quite forget he ever saw you in your bathing-dress—you see if I don't!'

And Patti thought that Faye's efforts had been worth while. She was resplendent in a shimmering eau-de-Nil silk dinner dress which emphasised her green eyes and made her sallow skin shine, as if newly polished with olive oil. Her hair, thanks to Patti's hard work, was washed and curled, the soft length framing her face like a gilt halo. No wonder Robert looked at her thoughtfully as they gathered in the drawing-room for sherry before dinner.

'You look very splendid,' he remarked. 'What's it all in aid of?'

Faye chuckled. 'That's my business, Robert.' She flounced off towards Jules.

Patti moved away to the bay window, out of range of Robert's all-seeing eyes. She felt quite unable to cope with him this evening, after Faye's shocking remark.

Dinner seemed never-ending. Jules sent sly smiles across the table in her direction, while Robert, on the contrary, appeared to have decided to ignore her.

Until after the meal, when she and Lady Challoner

and Faye had returned to the drawing-room. Patti was playing the piano, as she regularly did each evening now. In the middle of a Beethoven bagatelle, she sensed Robert's approach. Her fingers stumbled over the notes and she stopped, just as he opened the door to enter the room. Their eyes met, caught, and held for a moment which seemed timeless.

'My fault,' said Robert, so low that she only just heard. He stood in the bow of the piano, leaning his folded arms upon it and watching her intently. 'Always my fault, it seems. . .'

Patti held her breath. His coldness had thawed, and he was almost smiling. . . His next words enabled her to let out her breath in a long, slow sigh. 'Can you forgive me, Patti?'

Her reply was instantaneous. 'Of course! I mean—it isn't always. . .' Stammering foolishly, she was able to return his rueful smile. Then she looked back at her motionless fingers, wondering exactly what it was he apologised for. 'They don't always do what I want them to. . .' she murmured uncertainly.

'I understand. My feelings are the same.'

Another long, searching look, then a silence grew between them, with Faye's and her mother's distant conversation concealing their private moment. Robert's smile broadened, and Patti thought he had never looked so relaxed. 'Go on playing—please. I want to listen. You play so beautifully. I'm going to sit in the corner with my brandy—how about some Chopin? The mazurka you played the first evening you came?'

'But you didn't hear—you weren't listening. . .' She had thought him busy in his study, not interested enough to stay in the drawing-room, not aware of the new, childish little cousin who would, alas, prove to be just another temptation.

'You don't know everything, do you, little nymph?' There was so much good humour, so much unexpected friendliness in his quiet response, that Patti's amazement grew. Even if this happy moment did not last longer than the time it took to play a Chopin mazurka, she thought, bewildered, it was still something to be prized and remembered. Robert, listening to her, smiling at her with a peaceful expression in his melting eyes. . . A shutter in her confused mind abruptly clicked open. Did she love him? Certainly her feelings at this moment were of glad content, no longer full of mere physical longing — could it possibly mean. . .?

She gave him one last glance as he settled in the far corner of the room in a comfortable wing chair, before making herself forget everything save the discipline and passion of the music she loved.

There were plaudits when she finished, and her face glowed as she joined the little group beside the window for fresh coffee. Faye was openly envious. 'Why can't I play like Patti does?'

Robert grinned wickedly. 'No talent, sister mine — as simple as that.' He drained his brandy glass and stood up, tall, powerful and infinitely disturbing in his well-cut dinner-jacket and startlingly white linen. His dark hair was cut in an elegant line at the back of his suntanned neck, and his hands, Patti noticed, helplessly sipping her coffee, eyes riveted to him, were well scrubbed, but still slightly earth-coloured.

'Where's Jules?' asked Robert crisply, looking about him. 'Not here for a night-cap?'

'Packing, I expect.' Faye's eyes dulled for a moment, her mouth falling into a disconsolate pout. Patti wondered if her evening had been a disappointing one; certainly Jules had passed no compliments about the becoming new hairstyle, or the beautiful gown.

'I'll go and find him. Excuse me, Mother, Faye, Patti. . .' Robert's eyes lingered on hers for a second longer than was necessary, and she wondered if they held a secret message. Or was she just imagining it?

The room seemed lonely after he had gone. Patti wandered to the window and watched the slip of silver moon riding high in the June sky. The hushed garden would smell marvellous at this time of night, she thought; and it wasn't even properly dark. How she would love to slip out for a breath of air before bedtime. . .

Impulsively, she turned. 'I've forgotten my handkerchief, Cousin Enid. Excuse me, please.' It was half true: she knew she had dropped it when she had risen from the hammock this afternoon. She would go and find it, and then take a turn down by the border. The lupins and paeonies were out now. The silvers and whites of the underplanting would glow luminously in the moonlight. And then she would visit the rose garden. . . Perhaps there she could sort out the confused feelings that had her in thrall.

The garden was warm and enticing, and a delightful sense of tranquillity slowly invaded Patti, easing her mind as she wandered down the shadowy paths, skirted looming shrubs, and passed a myriad drowsing flowerheads. She drew in great restorative breaths of the balmy night air and felt herself grow calmer. Nature managed to put everything into perspective. It was so wonderful to be here alone; alone but never lonely

Yet not quite alone. Footsteps approached and she

slid behind a huge clump of rambling rose that climbed a stone pillar. Suddenly her anxiety returned. She knew that the gardens held secrets — perhaps she was a fool to be here, among them... She wanted no company tonight, not even Robert; holding her breath, she waited for the footsteps to pass.

Jules walked down the path, inches away from her. His eyes were pale in the moonlight, and Patti thought they reflected a glittering intensity. Her heart started to race, and she watched him, walking rapidly, heading for the glasshouses. Once he looked behind him, and once he exchanged the small bag he carried from his left to his right hand.

Patti's mind swam with confusing images and ideas, and for a few moments she could not believe what her inner voice told her was happening. It couldn't be so surely! Jules, going to the glasshouse to take some of Robert's grafted buds? Actually *stealing* rare, beautiful Madame Léonie?

Her immediate reaction was to run, to tell Robert, to alert him to the sly action of his trusted colleague; but then she stopped. Robert might think she had followed Jules out here. Even — she swallowed a hard lump in her dry throat — that she had made a *rendezvous* on Jules's last evening...

A temptation.

She shook her head, told herself to stop being afraid, and to deal with the matter herself. She could not risk Robert ever saying that hateful word again. Slowly, stiffly, and with infinite stealth, she went forward to the first glasshouse, where Jules's blurred figure could clearly be seen as the moonlight etched the shape of the building against the indigo shadows of the wall surrounding it.

CHAPTER SEVEN

AT THE glasshouse doorway Patti stopped, staring fearfully at Jules, inside. Despite her suspicions, she could not believe what he was doing. Suddenly hesitant, fearful of declaring her presence, she hovered uncertainly; but her steps, light as they were in evening slippers, had been heard.

Jules straightened up, turned, and came towards her, a menacing figure looming up out of the twilit shadows. 'Ah! The little cousin. . .' His voice was light but dropped to a threatening depth as he added, 'You come to spy, I think. Yes?'

'No!' She was afraid; his eyes were so cold and hostile in the filtered moonlight. 'I didn't know who it was. . .'

'But you know now, *ma petite*.' He put a hand on her arm, pulling her into the glasshouse. 'Why are you here?'

'I was just—out—in the garden. I heard footsteps. . .'

He exclaimed contemptuously, 'You expect me to believe that? *Mais non*! You plan to catch me with the roses.'

Patti's shocked brain did not instantly understand. 'Catch you?'

An unpleasant smile spread over Jules's thin face. 'Such innocence! Come, do not pretend! I take a few buds, you see? Like this. Robert has so many he will not miss these few.' His hand left her arm and she followed his gaze as he pointed to the shelves below. Four of Robert's expertly grafted buds, now growing so well in individual flowerpots, had been removed from their earthenware saucers and put into a small Gladstone bag.

Aghast at finding her suspicions confirmed, she snatched at her breath. 'You're stealing them. Jules, you're a thief! But why?'

He grinned. 'You wish to know?' His blue eyes were coldly amused. 'I tell you. The grafting, you see, Patti, is an art. One that I have still not perfected. But your Sir Robert, now, he does it with his eyes closed, I think. What did he tell me? A team of his three men, working all day, can bud up to fifteen hundred plants!' Jules's voice rose. '*Incroyable*! But at home, in my father's rosery, we cannot do any such thing. And even the American method, which I learned last year, is not reliable. And so, *voilà*, we do not have enough plants to sell the next year. So I just take a few of these. . . My gardeners will see how the expert performed. They will examine, understand and copy. They will take fresh cuttings, so next year we have even more Madame Léonie than Robert himself. Simple, eh?'

'You're wicked!' Patti could not control her rage. She longed to hit out, to punish Jules for his slyness, his dishonour, his infidelity. . . but she had the sense to contain her anger. Jules, she sensed fearfully, would take pleasure in punishing her if the need arose. She must be clever, escape somehow, raise the alarm before it was too late. . .

His hands were about her, drawing her close. He stroked her arms, pressed her hands, grinned into her repulsed eyes, and then returned to his packing. The precious plants went into the bag, and although Jules no longer looked at her he still exercised a threatening force which kept Patti motionless at his side.

'*Voilà*!' He closed the bag and snapped the clasp. 'It is done. Now we return to the house and tomorrow I go home.' Turning, he smiled unpleasantly. 'First, I go and kiss little Faye goodnight—it is good that she still loves me, eh? We will marry one day and then I shall have no more need to envy Robert's expertise, for he will share it all with me. But until then. . .' His voice dropped again. 'You, *chérie*, are far more attractive than the plain, dull sister. . .' He gave her an assessing look and one hand lifted to tilt her chin towards him.

Patti watched the pupils of his pale eyes contract. He said rapidly, 'You will tell no one of this. No one, I say. . .'

'Indeed I will!' Rage overcame her fear. 'I shall go and tell Robert now—this instant—'

The grip on her chin was suddenly painful. 'You will *not*,' muttered Jules threateningly. 'For if so, I merely get rid of the plants—hide them, destroy them, it matters not—and I say the pretty little cousin, she is a liar, as so many women are.' His hand eased, and one finger stroked her chin, but in a way that made her flinch. 'I tell your good Sir Robert that you are cross, for you have been playing with me, leading me on. . . and I have not responded.' Jules's voice bubbled with cynical amusement. 'Am I not unofficially engaged to his sister? And there is a saying, I think—something about the fury of a woman scorned. Yes?'

Patti's rage dissolved into despair. 'But Robert would never believe such a pack of lies!' Her voice trailed away, as doubt grew. *Would* he believe such a distasteful story? Past incidents crowded her mind, taking on new, fateful meanings. The way she loved to play-act. His view of her as a temptation, at every man's disposal. To say nothing of his knowledge of her abandoned response to his own kisses. . .

Then the present moment reasserted itself, frightening, fearful, with Jules laughing softly as he watched the play of emotions ride across her face. The sound of his voice galvanised her into panic-stricken action. How she hated him! The devious, scheming wretch. . .! With clenched fists she threw herself against his chest and heard the laughter grow deeper, tinged now with an excitement that made her hit him all the harder.

'But how fierce, my little hellcat! What pleasure you can give. . .' He pulled her so close that she could no longer fight him and was forced to stand, tense but hatefully submissive, within the circle of his restraining arms. His accent thickened. 'I teach you a lesson, I think, Mademoiselle Patti. . .'

His lips were bruising hers when a glimmer of approaching light forced him to raise his head, staring into the darkness outside the glasshouse. Abruptly he let her go and Patti, pulling away at once, heard the welcome sounds of footsteps on the gravel path near by.

A second later she saw the light being lifted high, illuminating the looming shape of a large body. Shocked, she stared up into Robert's grimly questioning eyes and felt her heart miss a beat.

'What on earth are you two doing out here?' he demanded truculently, and then said no more, for the answer was immediately plain: Jules had grabbed Patti and was kissing her with ever growing abandon.

With a great strength born of utter desperation, Patti somehow managed to twist herself out of Jules's embrace, turning her head as she did so in Robert's direction. Instinctively she knew that, unless she could convey all her fear and repulsion in one swift glance, he would withdraw. He would think she was enjoying these vile kisses, that she was a flirt, the temptation of his own words. . .

'*Robert*!' Her shrill voice screamed through the still night as he began to turn away, and she sensed the rapid leap of his feelings towards her. Knew that he now understood the situation and would save her. . .

As Jules's arms dropped, Patti saw the expression on Robert's face. She watched how, with a fierce grin of relief and sheer pleasure, he dumped the lantern on the ground, before striding uncompromisingly into the glasshouse, big hands clenching into fists as he came.

She felt as if a war had broken out all around her, and a despairing conviction that she was the sole cause of it became the only coherent thought in her swimming mind.

Then, roughly, she was thrown aside as Robert fell upon Jules, his powerful arms elbowing her out of the way as if he was also angry with *her*. There were hateful grunts and thuds, some French obscenities, and finally the shattering of glass, making her turn aside, trembling, hands covering her ashen face.

She stood by the wall behind the glasshouse, cowering in the shadows and longing to fly, but knowing that she must wait and explain her presence here to Robert — once the war was over.

Peace came very rapidly. Jules, limping, black-eyed and cradling his right arm, soon beat a swift retreat. He said nothing and passed Patti without appearing to see her, spitting out a bloodied tooth as he went. Then Robert's huge body loomed up beside her, blocking

HEART OF A ROSE

the moonlight shafting down at her feet. He rubbed his knuckles tenderly, but there was nothing tender about the question he barked at her. 'What the hell were you doing out here with him at this time of night?'

Patti's mind went blank. All she wanted was to be swept up in sheltering arms and told that it was all over — that she must forget it ever happened. But Robert's words pierced like a spear, lacerating an already fermenting wound.

'I wasn't with him,' she said wildly. 'I was alone! I needed some air, some space — I love the gardens at night. . .'

'Don't lie to me, Patti.' There was suspicion in his cold voice, and her rage exploded.

'It's not a lie. I'm not a liar. Surely you know that by now?' Her eyes flashed at him and he seemed taken aback at her fury. He stared before replying, very grudgingly,

'Very well. I suppose I must apologise for saying that — '

'Can't you do so with a little better grace?' she snapped. Then she saw his eyes narrow and knew a second's regret, for he was not a man one should anger unnecessarily. But she squared her trembling shoulders, standing defiantly before him. She was in the right, and he must accept the fact.

He said nothing, and she added bitterly, 'As I just said, I came out into the garden and heard footsteps. Jules passed me coming to the glasshouse, so I followed him.'

'Why?'

Patti was taken aback. 'Isn't it obvious? Because I wanted to find out what he was doing here.'

'So you followed him.' Robert's voice was cutting.

'And what were you doing, the two of you? I mean, of course, before *l'amour* took over. . .'

The colour rose in Patti's cheeks. 'That's uncalled for,' she whispered. 'There never was — never could be — anything between Jules and myself. He's Faye's fiancé —— '

'He certainly is not!' Robert's peremptorily snapping interruption made her stop. She stared at him through the shadows, seeing so clearly imprinted on his hostile face the autocratic expression that Faye often complained of.

'Well.' She cleared her throat. 'That's nothing to do with me. Jules came to the glasshouse to steal your plants, Robert.'

'To steal?' Robert's voice softened in disbelief. 'That's a likely story! Why on earth should he do that?'

'Because he can't graft buds properly. . . Oh, Robert — it's *true*.'

An incredulous silence changed her dismay into anger again. 'You don't believe me? As usual. . .' She had the pleasure of seeing Robert look away from her. She frowned, and said wearily, 'I tell you, it *is* true. He was putting the plants into his bag — oh!' There it was, the evidence that could prove her innocence. . . 'Robert, help me find the bag — the Gladstone bag with the plants inside. . .'

She pushed past him, running back into the glasshouse, hands busy on the shelves, but unable to see what she searched for, until Robert retrieved the lantern and came to her side.

'Well?' he asked acidly. 'Where is it, then? This bag you told me about. . .'

Patti searched furiously, but the shelves held nothing save their earthenware pots of plants. And then her foot kicked something in the darkness, close to the ground. Bending, she found it...

'Here it is! Look! Now you *must* believe me...!'

They stared at the bag she held beneath the lantern's dim light. Four potted plants were tightly packed inside it. Four embryo roses... Patti stared triumphantly into Robert's frowning eyes. 'You see?'

Straightening up, he took the bag from her, replaced the pots on the shelves, and snapped the clasp shut before replying grudgingly, 'Yes.' He turned, took her arm in a firm grasp, and hurried her outside, lantern held high to show the way.

Patti halted, facing him. She would not be treated in this high-handed manner any longer. Staring through the shifting shadows, she made out his unfathomable, moody eyes, his jaw set in obstinacy. But the small nerve that pulsed below his cheek was a startling indication of his uncertainty, and this amazed her. However, this terrible situation could not be allowed to continue. If he would not say something, then she would. Anything was better than this sullen distrust between them.

'Robert,' she said, in a shaking voice, 'this is quite ridiculous. I've proved my innocence; or rather, that bag does. So why can't you——?'

He cut across her words, voice low and curt. 'All I can be sure of, Patti, is that Jules was stealing my roses. And——' he paused for a heart-stopping moment, staring at her '—and that you were with him. Helping him, perhaps...'

'But I've told you!' She could not accept that he still suspected her. 'I merely followed him!'

Patti watched the expression of distrust and anger grow even darker on Robert's frowning face, and her consternation grew. Memory stirred sharply, painfully... Grandfather had spoken so often of a family conflict created through the debated ownership of Madame Léonie, and here it was again. Suddenly she knew exactly what Robert was thinking—that she had made use of Jules to come and steal his precious rose grafts...

His rose. Not Grandfather's—and so not hers.

Robert, in his own dictatorial way, was being just as self-opinionated and possessive about Madame Léonie as Grandfather had been. So the conflict endured. And now she was part of it—thrown into an unpleasant quarrel without realising how she had got there.

Patti drew in a deep, strengthening breath and tried to still her churning mind. It would do no good to continue arguing with Robert while he was in this intractable mood. Somehow she must find a solution to the old problem—but in the meantime could she not play upon Robert's recent good humour?

Somehow she managed a casual little laugh. 'Really, Robert, I think you must have had a little too much wine at dinner—you're talking a lot of nonsense...'

But, even as she said the words, she knew they were a mistake.

Robert's hand thrust out, faster than a striking snake, gripping her own and pulling her very close to him. She heard his rapid heartbeat, smelt the fragrance of cigar smoke and his own persuasive masculine smell. She was ensnared, uncertain—even afraid...

Very low, Robert growled, 'I think it's time you and I had a damned good talk, my girl. Come with me.'

'Let me go!' It was impossible to get her hand free. He marched her through the dark garden, pulling her along, thought Patti fearfully, like an errant puppy dog that needed a good whipping. But her pride would not allow her to make any further response, for she, like Robert, was of the Challoner clan, and even though he chose to treat her so unfairly she would not weaken and admit her fear of him.

Silently he hauled her into the house, down the quiet passages and corridors and to his study. Closing the door, he stood with his back to it, glaring down to where she had been unceremoniously dumped in a hard-backed chair beyond his desk. A lamp was burning, giving the room a soft glow. Shadows lay menacingly around the walls. Patti lifted her head and stared defiantly at Robert.

'Now, Patti Nevill, talk to me. . .' The words came from between gritted teeth. 'Tell me all that is in your mind—everything you know about those damned roses in the glasshouses. All about Jules Lacoste. Well? I'm waiting. . .'

Patti found herself staring across the shadowy room, into the eyes of a familiar portrait on the opposite wall. Grandfather Nevill. The old man looked down at her with a half-smile, as if, she thought wildly, he was asking her to stand up for him. She sat a little straighter on her hard chair and turned her head to meet Robert's glowering stare. He still stood by the door, arms crossed over his black dinner-jacket. In the lamplight she thought that he was a threatening shadow, waiting to pounce. . . All around the walls of the study hung prints and other family portraits and photographs. In the dim light they were half-open eyes, staring down, waiting for her next move. Abruptly she knew what she had to do—bring the whole wretched matter out into the open. . . but how would Robert react?

'When I was a child,' she began shakily, 'my grandfather told me the story of Madame Léonie. That he and your great-uncle——'

'Sir Archibald Challoner.' Robert's interruption was a deep growl. Aware of every tone and nuance of his voice, every gleam in his wary eyes, Patti knew with growing dismay that his anger showed no sigh of simmering down.

'Yes, Sir Archibald—Grandfather said they had a— a—well, I suppose one can only call it a difference of opinion. . .'

He snorted abrasively. 'Huh! That's putting it mildly!' Slowly Robert moved away from the door, eyes never leaving her face as he prowled around the desk to fold himself into the chair opposite her. He lit a smaller lamp on the side of the desk, fingers adjusting it until the shadows between them were illumined. Only his set mouth was visible above them. She could not see his eyes.

She was trembling. Robert had become a powerful, menacing creature.

'Go on,' he said curtly, and she watched his mouth become even tighter.

'I don't know—any more. Grandfather only told me of the family conflict, and that—that he was the true owner of Madame Léonie. . .' Her voice died away dispiritedly and her fear grew.

But she had forgotten Robert's unpredictability. She expected rage and vehement denial, not the quiet words that he now spoke. 'Your Grandfather was mistaken, Patti. My great-uncle was the man responsible for the old rose's recovery and development.'

Their eyes suddenly met as Robert pushed aside the lamp, and she gasped at the passion she saw in the dark-chocolate depths. And then, slowly, infinitely gently, he smiled. 'I'm sorry to have to disillusion you. But the fact remains—I am the owner of Madame Léonie de Sange...'

Although the smile stayed on his face, she recognised the challenge and the autocratic dominance. Her mind whirled and for a few seconds she could only stare into the eyes that held hers with such force and intensity. Then without knowing what she did, she allowed all thoughts of Madame Léonie to fade away, for another problem—even more traumatic—was worrying her.

She leaned forward, to perch tensely on the edge of her chair. 'Robert...'

'Well?' His voice was not encouraging, and the smile gradually faded.

Impulsively she sprang up, going around the desk to stand at his side, looking down, wishing the dark eyes would lighten. Breathlessly she asked her foolish question. 'Why did you hit Jules?'

He blinked. She fancied his lips twitched, but his answer was cold. 'Because your call for help sounded real.'

'Yes, but if you truly suspected us both of stealing the roses, then surely all you needed to do was to call the police...?'

Robert shifted impatiently in his chair. 'Great heavens, what a dramatic child you are! Haul you both out of the garden—one under each arm, I dare say—put you in the motor and drive you to Constable Furlong's house? At this time of night? What a pantomime!'

She wouldn't be put off by the growing lightness of his tone. 'Answer me, Robert. You came at Jules like a—well, like a charging buffalo. *Why?*'

The all important question. She held her breath.

And then, out of the tense silence, he growled, 'Why do you think?' and stopped abruptly. When he continued his voice was so quiet that she had to strain to hear. 'Because I couldn't stand the idea of that damned Frenchman pawing you. . .'

Another heart-stopping pause. 'Kissing you.' Robert's mouth snapped shut like a trap as abruptly he rose and for a second stood glowering down into her astonished eyes.

Patti's mind circled, full of impossible thoughts. He was jealous of Jules—why? *Why?* She, having learned the sad fact of his continuing claim to Madame Léonie's ownership, could not be bothered even to think about it any further—again, *why*? What was happening to her, to Robert, to bring them together in this strange and uncomfortable situation?

For a long, stretching moment they stared into each other's eyes, and just as Patti sensed that the heat of their conflict was lessening Robert stepped away from her, his eyes veiled and his voice almost casual, as he said briefly, 'Go to bed, Cousin. Things will have sorted themselves out in the morning. . .'

By the door he swung around, a dark brow winging upwards in mockery. 'Jules will depart—I suppose you'll want to see him off?' Then he smiled, as if to apologise for the tart suggestion, but it was too late.

Patti snatched at her breath, and glared through the soft shadows. 'You're impossible!' she grated, the pain inside her stabbing uncontrollably deep. 'So you still think Jules and I were—were. . .?' Unable to say the hateful words, she turned away.

'I didn't say that.' Robert paced back to her, his face suddenly creased with regret, but Patti's anger flared yet again. She could not take another minute of this constant, exhausting swing of emotions they were forcing upon each other. 'I'm not going to stay here a minute longer!' she cried wildly. 'If you like to think me an accessory to Jules's thieving—as well as his mistress—well, then you must. I don't care! I'm going —I never want to see you again. . .' Her voice had grown shriller as self-control departed, and she hated herself for sounding like a fishwife. She shook with frustration and rage as she tried to push past him.

Robert's hands grabbed hers roughly. 'Stop it! Don't put words into my mouth. Patti—you're hysterical!'

'I'm not! Just angry and hurt that you can be so unfair. . .' Her swimming eyes blazed into his and as she watched, she saw, dismayed even further, how his expression became unrelenting and harsh.

'I see. If that's what you think——'

'I do. I—I hate you, Robert. . .'

She didn't, of course. Even as she said the ridiculous, fateful words, she knew the truth. As Faye had warned, she had fallen in love with Robert. . .

Snatching her hands out of his, she fled from the study, running down the passage, up the stairs and into the safe haven of her bedroom. Locking the door, she flung herself on the bed and allowed the racking sobs to burst forth. It had been a terrible evening.

If Patti slept at all, she was unaware of it. Her head ached, and her body still trembled as she went over and over last night's ghastly scene. And above the pain and the shock, one haunting thought filled her.

Reluctantly, in the small hours of the night, she was forced to confess to herself that she loved Robert Challoner, complicated and autocratic as he was, and so unfairly possessive about the old rose. Yet she knew she wanted him, needed him — longed to step into that guarded mind, sharing his hopes, his fears and dreams. . . Wasn't that love? Sighing, she told herself hopelessly that it must be so. But, of course, she must not allow herself this foolish indulgence of being in love. Clearly Robert was not for her. He thought her fast, a temptation, a thief — a rival claimant to Madame Léonie. . .

It was this last fact that finally enabled Patti to sleep, providing her with a welcome alternative to her yearnings and longings. Idealism, Patti told herself sternly, was far more important than love. She would, from this very moment, put all her energy into resolving Madame Léonie's mystery, and forcing Robert into giving up his dictatorial ownership of the rose.

The morning sun's brilliance woke her at the usual time, despite her troubled and restless night; strangely, she discovered she felt quite herself. She dressed briskly, drawing up a plan of campaign, which was a welcome diversion from the ensnaring images that occasionally made her heart begin to race — recalling Robert's good humour, his gentle sweetness, his tender lovemaking — and went downstairs with a smile fixed upon her stiff face, her traitorous mind harshly controlled with new thoughts of idealism and justice. Grandfather would be proud of her as she righted the wrong done against him.

But, once downstairs, her own troubles receded into the background, for Faye was wailing loudly as she entered the dining-room.

'Patti, I can't bear it! Jules has gone! I didn't see him go, but he looked terrible, so Dora said — black eye, arm in a sling. And that beastly Robert won't explain — simply stalked off when I asked him what had happened, muttering something about Jules proving himself to be no good. . .' Faye sank down heavily on her chair and fixed Patti with glittering eyes. 'Do you know, he actually had the nerve to send Jules off by the milk train, at some ghastly hour this morning! Kendrick was up early to take him to the station. . . and now Mother is unwell. . . Oh, what a perfectly beastly day this is!'

'Lady Challoner, unwell?' Patti ignored her cousin's lamentations. Even her own problems faded into insignificance at this news.

'Yes, she had a bad night. She's been doing too much — all this fuss about the coming house party, I suppose. Well, we'll just have to take it all off her hands — and I do so hate anything to do with household arrangements. . .'

'I'll see what I can do, Faye. Lady Challoner mustn't be worried.'

Directly after a breakfast only made tolerable by Robert's absence — 'He's gone off to see someone in Exeter — let's hope he returns in a better mood,' said Faye spitefully — Patti left her cousin to nurse her grievances by herself, and thankfully headed towards the kitchens to see if she could assume the duties Lady Challoner was forced to drop. And it came to her mind, as she closed the green baize door behind her, that there was much to be said for accepting responsibility, and a concern for other people.

Her fear of encountering Robert grew as the day progressed, and she hoped he would not return until dinnertime, by which time perhaps she would be more in control of herself. . . But, after resting for an hour in the hammocks below the shady cedar as usual, Faye had gone up to her mother's boudoir to see if the invalid was well enough to come down for tea, and Patti had wandered off into the fragrant garden, immersed in her thoughts and quite unprepared to hear the disturbing, mocking voice just behind her, saying, 'Why, Patti — how nice to find you haven't run away after all.'

She swung around, mouth agape, eyes startled, all the old chemistry instantly working anew, and stronger than ever.

Robert had become the gardener again, she saw, arms the colour of mahogany beneath his checked shirt, dark hair gilded with sun-streaks, eyes the colour of melting chocolate, and one large hand brandishing a pair of secateurs. He was looking down at her with a half-smile, a quirk of the lips telling her this was the nearest to an apology that she could expect.

Somehow she found her voice. 'I — I didn't say I was actually running away, Robert. . .'

'You could have fooled me. I very nearly offered you a lift to the station, along with Jules. . .'

Last night she would have been outraged, but now she merely shook her head a little wearily, and stepped away from him.

'Patti. . .' His hand touched her arm and she caught her breath. It wasn't fair, this terrible mastery he had over her, the sweetly sensual effect of his touch upon her body.

Shutting her eyes, she tensed as she suffered the tingling crackle of shared chemistry. Robert's fingers stroked gently, making her blood sing.

'What's up?' he asked lightly. 'Nothing to say? Not like you at all, Cousin Patti — not ill, are you?' His hand left her arm, to trace the gentlest of caressing lines down her pale cheek. Before she could reply, the tone of his voice changed. 'None the worse for our hard words, I trust? Truth will out, you know — and in this case it was for the best. I hope you agree. . .' His arm slid beneath her elbow, propelling her along the path towards the terrace. 'Come and sit down — you look terrible.'

Uncertain whether to laugh or berate his rudeness, she allowed herself to be led to the wrought-iron seat. As before, Robert sat down at an angle to her, so that he could see her face without having to turn aside.

'All my fault — yet again. . .' She was taken aback at the unexpected sudden gentleness of the quiet words, at the plea for forgiveness plainly showing in his watchful eyes. 'Can you forgive me, Patti? I said some terrible things. . .'

'And so did I, Robert. . .'

A capricious breeze stirred the garden and a waft of sweet fragrance melted Patti's unhappy thoughts. A slight smile tugged at her downcast mouth, bringing with it a sense of comfort. At least he'd apologised. But she wouldn't let him get off scot-free. . .

'I haven't forgiven you, not completely,' she murmured wryly. 'You were extremely rude. You shouted at me. You made me feel — '

'Yes?' He was looking at her with a relish that sent all her thoughts flying away.

What a fool she was to try and explain her feelings to this ever changing, complicated, dictatorial man, love him as she did! 'I can't tell you,' she said shortly, turning away to conceal all that she knew must show on her face. 'It's not fair of you to stir things up again. . .'

He leaned forward, taking her hand and smiling

almost absent-mindedly as he looked down at her small fingers. She felt the pressure of his own fingers upon hers, his thumb slowly stroking her knuckles, and again the exquisite sense of shared alchemy sent sparks tingling up her arms.

'You're like a small whirlwind, Patti Nevill,' said Robert sardonically. 'All soft and delightful one minute and then tumbling everything into disruption the next. . .'

Breathless, watching his face and wishing he truly meant this new gentle friendliness, she said huskily, 'Do I disrupt *you* Robert?' and then wished she could recall the foolish words. When would she ever learn? Robert might flirt as much as he liked, but she must never do so.

The truth of it was in his instant response. Her hand was quickly deposited back upon her lap, and his cool voice said disapprovingly, 'Nonsense, Patti, I'm beyond disruption.' He stared at her with a growing impatience, and she knew she had been a fool to let dreams replace her common sense.

CHAPTER EIGHT

LADY CHALLONER, fresh from her rest, came down for tea. 'What a relief, dear child, having you here, to take so much responsibility from my shoulders.' She smiled at Patti with a fondness that settled Patti's uneasy mind, her fear that Robert might have told his mother of their unpleasant scene last night now put at rest.

He joined them on the terrace at teatime, and she saw his mother's eyes register shock at the sight of his shabby clothes. 'Darling—you look like a workman!'

'Exactly what I am, Mother,' said Robert briskly, sitting down beside Faye, 'a working gardener. Jenkins and the boy and I have been in those damned glass-houses for the past two hours. I could drink the well dry. Another cup, if you please. . .'

Patti noticed he took care not to look at her, and her colour rose foolishly as she recalled the chemistry that had sparked between them in those same glasshouses. He drank a second cup of tea with relish before turning his attention to Faye, brooding sulkily beside him. 'You look like the thunderstorm we're going to have if this sultry weather goes on,' he observed sarcastically.

Faye's eyes snapped at him over her teacup. 'Thank you so much, dear brother. Every girl, of course, wishes to look like that!'

Robert stretched out long legs, turned his face towards the sun, and closed his eyes. 'It's the heat,' he said airily. 'Has a bad effect upon people. Hot weather makes emotions run high. I know the feeling, only too well...' On the last word he opened his eyes and looked at Patti, and she saw amusement mingle with something that made her heart beat more rapidly before he turned back towards Faye, who was already answering him angrily.

'Robert, you're utterly heartless! Do you have no feelings other than arrogance and self-importance?'

Patti caught her breath, but Robert appeared in no mood to fight. He looked at his sister lazily. 'I'm a realist, my dear,' he said, as if that explained everything. But while Faye still glared at him, Patti saw a sudden shift of expression on his face which made her tense. 'I, too, have my emotions,' Robert went on, almost flippantly, 'but my saving grace is that I control them...'

Faye growled. 'Just another way of saying you're heartless.'

Suddenly Robert's eyes glinted towards Patti. 'No', he said very quietly. 'Just another way of saying I cover my vulnerability — when I need to.'

Faye attacked again at once, and Patti was able to sit back, thinking over those revealing words, while brother and sister continued their argument.

'What about Jules?' demanded Faye. 'At least you might tell me what the trouble was...'

Robert thought for a second before replying. 'Jules Lacoste,' he said at last, and his voice had grown very hard, 'proved himself to be an out-and-out schemer — if nothing worse. Take my advice and find yourself another admirer.'

Faye's eyes narrowed. 'You have proof of his misdoings?' she asked grimly. Suddenly a note of malice came into her voice, and she glanced briefly across the table at Patti. 'I know he's a flirt—do you mean that things went further than that? Was someone else involved, last night? Are you going to tell me who that "someone" was, Robert?'

'That will do, Faye. . .' her mother's rebuke cut in quickly. 'Your brother has explained to me that Monsieur Lacoste proved himself to be no gentleman and that he had, as a consequence, to request him to leave. I have accepted his explanation, and I think you should do so also. Now—let us change the subject, if you please. . .' Her serene voice slowly charmed the hostility away, and the atmosphere cleared as she continued. 'How nice it will be to see Barbara Latimer again next weekend. I thought she might cheer us all up, Robert—such an old friend, and so full of London's social whirl!'

'Indeed, Mother.' Robert had turned in his chair towards Lady Challoner, and again his expression changed. Patti, painfully aware of his mercurial changes of mood, now saw a remoteness fill his face that she sensed bordered on dislike.

What could it mean? Who was this Barbara Latimer, this old friend? Why did he not enthuse about her coming visit if he had once been fond of her? And exactly *how* fond had that affection been? Her thoughts were fully occupied, and at first she did not hear Faye's mocking words.

'Barbara Latimer! Do you think she'll still reek of wicked French perfume? Last time she was here it took months to get her wretched scent out of the guest room! And Robert—as I recall——' a note of downright wickedness in Faye's voice penetrated Patti's head '—you had a whiff or two of it about you, as well!'

Robert, she noticed, declined to answer the mischievous comment, but his expression was censure enough. Lady Challoner again came to the rescue. 'Don't be naughty, Faye, dear. Barbara moves in the height of London society, and probably her perfume is the latest fashion. . .'

'Thank goodness Stephen is coming with Barbara,' said Faye, suddenly brightening. 'How nice to have another man about the place, and he's always so polite. Robert, you should take lessons. . .'

Patti held her breath, but Robert ignored the teasing comment. Instead, he smiled at his awkward sister. 'So what are you planning to wear while our guests are here, you spoilt child? All your silks and satins, all the latest costumes for walking, for dancing, billiards and croquet, motoring. . .? I shall await your dressmaker's next bill with extreme trepidation!' His deep voice lifted into light-hearted banter. 'Come on, Faye, cheer up, sweetheart — life still goes on, you know! You'll find someone — or something — better than Jules Lacoste to fill your life one of these days!'

'Hmm.' Faye stared at him through her lashes, and Patti saw a twisted smile touch her lips. 'I might just take your advice, Robert — who knows?'

And then Lady Challoner was pondering the distribution of the guest rooms, and the subject changed yet again. 'Barbara likes the blue bedroom, and Stephen always has the turret room — that means Aunt Estelle and Uncle Willie can have the usual double bedroom above the library, and, Robert, dear, your two business friends can go into the west wing. . .'

All was forgotten save the organisation of the coming visits, and Patti sat back, her problems momentarily erased by the warm feeling of being one of this family of hospitable Challoners.

From then on her world seemd occupied entirely with arrangements for the house party, and the village fête which was to take place on the Saturday afternoon. So much to do, thought Patti gladly, only half reproachful at not having time for her own life. Guest rooms to inspect, flowers to arrange, orders to be given daily to cook and staff, menus considered, Lady Challoner's health to be carefully watched over, and Faye's erupting spasms of jealousy to be endured. For Faye kept spitefully accusing Patti of being the possible reason for Jules's shameful banishment. Consequently, Patti's occasional visits to Beth and James, somehow fitted into the busy days, were enjoyable and relaxing.

Only when dinner was over each evening and the summer twilight hung over the garden, increasingly heavy and listless, with the hot June weather continuing, and the threat of thunder growing ever nearer, did Patti find time for her own problems and needs.

Evening was the part of the day she most loved and looked forward to, despite the inevitable introspection it encouraged. No matter what had occurred during the hours of daylight, the bustle of the house seemed to pause as dusk swept in, allowing the atmosphere of serenity and timelessness to surface throughout its echoing rooms and lofty corridors.

After dinner Patti often left Faye and her mother in the drawing-room with their coffee and murmuring exchanges of family talk while she slipped out into the garden to savour the stillness and the renewing solitude.

The roses were in full bloom now, their fragrance

heavy on the humid air, and it was with a sense of mounting excitement that she went towards the yew-sheltered garden, careful to make sure she was not seen. But there were no gardeners about at that time of evening, and she always made certain that Robert was elsewhere — away, dining with business colleagues, or at work in his study, consulting catalogues, answering letters, and writing articles for the many publications which demanded his views upon the growing popularity of the old shrub roses.

Patti knew she was safe out here on such occasions. Safe to wander through the deserted vine pergola, dark now with its green foliage and tiny bunches of white-starred flowers, past the slumbering sundial, and on towards the black yew hedge. And then, once safely inside that magical circle, to breathe in the sweetness of the perfumed roses.

Pink, white and purple, their colours drifted in shadowed pallor, delighting her senses as she stood there, revelling in the beauty of the blossoms, the gentle warmth of the night and her own overflowing joy.

So far removed from the everyday world and its complications, she was startled to sense the approach of another human being. Long before footsteps crunched behind her she turned, alert — her intuition told her whom it must be.

Robert. Of course. It could be no one else, for her lonely enjoyment had abruptly somersaulted into a burst of heart-racing physical pleasure and anticipation.

'Forgive me, I hope I didn't scare you.' Ever the perfect gentleman, he stood at a little distance, smiling and looking strangely humble.

HEART OF A ROSE

Patti smiled nervously. 'Of course not! And. . .' It struck her then that it would be sensible to disarm him with an apology for her presence here, alone, after his previous curt warnings. 'I hope you don't mind my being out here. Alone. At night.' She heard the last words tinged with mockery and wondered if she had gone too far.

But Robert merely cocked an eyebrow and took a step nearer. 'Patti, you're becoming much more sure of yourself. Almost frivolous, I might say.'

She thought she saw a gleam of admiration lighten his deep eyes and was encouraged to say demurely — far more demurely than she felt — 'Why, thank you, Robert. If it *is* a compliment. . .?'

'Stop fishing,' he said crisply. 'You know it is.'

Patti melted slightly at the good humour in his voice. Bending his head down towards her, he added, 'You've become a highly efficient social secretary — my mother is aware of it and grateful. As I am, too. And as for Faye. . .' He paused, and Patti turned away to stare down at the great roseheads lolling in the drowsy half-light. She felt there was a growing danger in this meeting, but knew herself powerless to avoid it. It was almost as if fate was intervening to bring herself and Robert together. . .

Returning her thoughts to Faye, she said bravely, 'I'm afraid I have lost some of Faye's respect, Robert. Some of her trust, too.' She looked up, eyes a little nervous. 'You see, she still suspects me of being involved in Jules's departure.'

Robert seemed unperturbed. She watched his hand reach out to touch a swelling rosebud on the bush beside them. 'These could do with a downpour,' he observed expertly. 'Although, of course, rain will play havoc with their blossoms.' Suddenly his eyes were on her, and she saw a small pulse throbbing restlessly below his tanned cheek. 'Unfortunate, isn't it' he asked very quietly, 'that everything needs a certain disturbance — a certain conflict — to help it develop. . .?'

'Like the pearl in an oyster. Yes, you're right.'

His words made sense, and also revealed a little more of his carefully concealed vulnerability. She had been right — Robert was not merely arrogant and critical, but also a man of strength and integrity. Even his quick tempers, his mercurial moods and his undoubted need to dominate his family could not prevent her from appreciating his more agreeable traits of character. She had to admit that she even respected him now — which made the fact that he still flaunted his ownership of Madame Léonie in front of her an even greater thorn in her flesh than before.

Patti, mind churning, and emotions quickly rising, turned away, as if to put a barrier between herself and this charismatic, enraging man.

A spray of blowsy roses clung to her sleeve as she moved, and she put out her hand to remove the thorns, instinctively changing the subject. 'This is a wonderful year for roses, Robert.' She caressed the exquisite pinky-mauve flowers, conscious that they felt like rich velvet beneath her fingers. 'You must be delighted with the results of all your hard work.'

'I'm — hopeful, Patti. . .' The enigmatic words were just a murmur, and quickly she glanced back at him. His relaxed expression, she saw, mirrored her own — they were talking of roses, but clearly both were thinking of something else. . .

She trembled and then, because she was afraid that, as in the past, this sweet and tantalising moment would end in yet another hateful confrontation, her nerve gave way. She moved quickly aside and then walked rapidly along the path, concentrating on the plethora of flowers filling the shadowy, fragrant beds. And she talked, in order to avoid the danger of that silence that had heralded a new feeling between them — for surely silence was the greatest communication of all?

'Just look at this,' she chattered on, 'so beautiful, especially with those pure white pinks growing beneath; Mrs Sinkins, surely? Mr Sinkins was a workhouse owner, you know, who named them after his wife — so romantic! And the lovely silver lambs' leaves, all around. . . How clever you are, Robert, with your planting.'

A step behind her, his closeness excited her, while the fear of his rejection forced her to keep talking. 'Of course, Miss Clarke herself liked this pale underplanting. Old roses, she said, needed silver and whites to complement their subtle pinks and purples and mauves. But the red roses, like Madame Léonie, needed — needed. . .' She gasped. How could she have let herself ramble on so thoughtlessly? Suddenly his hand was on her arm, burning her with its power. Firmly, yet with great gentleness, he turned her around to face him.

In the blur of the approaching night, he seemed a huge, menacing figure, and Patti's breath flew out of her. It was impossible to resist him, feeling the magic of his presence and loving him as she did. Yet he was her adversary, her feuding cousin who refused to give back Grandfather's rose. . .

She felt the perfume of the flowers, the solitude, the alchemy of the summer night drawing them together, and knew her own frailty was increasing. He stared down as she lifted her face to meet his, and his hand stroked her trembling arm. There was hunger in his dark pools of eyes, and abruptly she sensed that neither of them could any longer deny the desire they both felt so overpoweringly.

Her head was a racing kaleidoscope of images. Madame Léonie, Grandfather, Jules, Robert himself. . . and then his arms closed around her and all the conflicts, the anxieties and the longings melted into a void of sensation and joy.

Clasped firmly against his body, feeling his warmth through her thin gown, sharing the urgency of his passion, Patti delighted in his kisses. His mouth savoured and pleasured hers; his hands spread about her waist, moved slowly down her back, drawing her even closer, until she felt moulded to him.

When at last he released her, she shuddered uncontrollably, aware of his hands still gripping her shoulders. He stared into her swooning eyes. 'I long for you,' he whispered huskily. 'I can't keep away. . .'

A moment of silence spun a trembling thread as Patti laid her face against his chest, unable to speak for the force of her emotions. Robert's heart beat steadily, its quiet regularity slowly bringing her a measure of restored self-control. At last she was able to draw away, newly aware of all the old problems that had them in thrall.

In the gathering darkness Robert stared down at her, his expression impossible to read. His voice was heavy with smothered feeling. 'I think we should go back to the house. . .'

Patti sighed. The moment was over. She was too wise to hope that it might ever come again. For the rest of her life she must live with the memory of Robert's kiss — and the fact that she loved him in vain.

As they turned, retracing their steps down the dark paths, she asked unsteadily. 'What brought you out here, Robert? Not just to kiss me, surely.' And then she wished she had held her tongue. Such a question would surely only make him consider her fast, and yet again the temptation he had already christened her.

But his voice was gentle, and for a moment his fingers caught at hers as he replied, 'You minx! How well you know me! But — to tell you the truth — I came to ask a favour.'

She glanced sideways, bemused, watching his shadowy face looking intently at her. 'What sort of — favour, Robert?'

His voice became brisk. 'I need some of your expertise, Patti. Your knowledge and your secretarial skills.' Turning, he added, 'Would you be willing to do some research for me, cousin?'

'Research?' She sought firmly for her lost poise; he was already businesslike — she must attempt to be the same.

'Into the old roses. You see. . .' If he had been caught up in shared physical passion a moment ago, now he was as deeply caught in his passion for roses. His voice resonated around her mind, full of enthusiasm, and she sensed resentfully that he had already forgotten their embrace.

'You see,' he said as they walked down the flower-laden path, 'I've been asked to contribute a series of articles to an American magazine about developing the old, historical roses. I have the knowledge to do this, but I shall need a bibliography — a list of further reading, of acknowledgements, and so on. Also some help in the actual typewriting of the article... Well, that's where you come in, Patti.' Halting abruptly, he turned and looked at her with the usual autocratic assurance. 'Will you help me?'

And then, just as her mind was registering the usual irritation at such dictatorial habits, he added, endearingly, 'Please, Patti?'

Without considering, she said quickly, 'Goodness, I never thought to hear the great Sir Robert actually say *"please"*...!'

His hand came out of the velvety darkness to stroke her lips, as lightly as the wings of a night-flying moth. 'Such a pretty mouth,' he murmured wryly. 'How can it possibly say such wicked things?'

Patti's heart raced as yet again sparks threatened to ignite between them. Every part of her body longed to feel his touch once more, to taste the sweetness of his kiss — and yet she made no move.

Slowly, and with immense pain, she was learning... It was not easy to banish the sensuality that filled her and to step away, turning to glance down at the flowers, as if he posed no danger, exuded no attraction. Her voice, when she replied, was laudably self-controlled. 'Of course I'll help, Robert. It'll be most interesting to delve back into the books that I read in Miss Clarke's library.'

He gave a sigh of relief. 'Splendid. I thought you might feel that way. And you'll find several published monographs in the family archives too — papers written by the old uncles and cousins who originally found and developed all the roses that now fill the garden...' His voice was quick with enthusiasm again and Patti smiled to herself a little sadly, remembering Madame Léonie and the implacable barrier she presented.

'The roses in Porphyry Court,' she murmured, without considering her words. 'So beautiful. And best of all, of course, the lovely Madame Léonie de Sange...'

In the enveloping darkness the name seemed to resonate between them. Patti held her breath and sensed that Robert, beside her, frowned with instant displeasure. The old conflict, she thought dismally, the ever nagging secret. The grit in the oyster...

Their footsteps paused momentarily, and then quickened as they continued their way back to the house, now, by mutual decision, putting a good pace's distance between them. And then Patti ended the tense silence as the lights of the drawing-room drew near by saying, just a touch too brightly, 'And when do you wish me to start this work, Robert? I might be able to spare an hour tomorrow some time, but of course, now that the house party is so near, your mother's arrangements are bound to keep me rather busy.'

Robert's answer was calm and non-committal, and Patti wondered if he had been as disturbed at the thought of the old rose as she was, and then decided not, for he sounded almost casual as he said slowly, 'That will be splendid. Perhaps after tea? But you mustn't let me overwork you, Patti.'

He took her arm, propelling her on towards the lights of the house, and she shivered, but held her head a little higher and ignored the treacherous longings that seared her.

Behind them the night spread quickly, obliterating all traces of the indigo and turquoise-tinted streaks of approaching sunset. The sky grew blacker, and a faraway growl of thunder reverberated as Patti stepped inside the door.

She shivered again, bade Robert a quiet goodnight, then slipped away quickly, leaving him standing in the dark garden, a huge black figure seeming to merge with the threatening night sky behind him.

CHAPTER NINE

DURING the days that followed, Patti was kept far too busy to think over that evening's happenings. Even when Faye, the following morning, pounced on the early delivery of post on the hall table, saying sharply, 'A French postmark! News of Jules, perhaps. . . I'll make sure Robert tells me. . .' her thoughts had been elsewhere.

Because of the coming house party the house was in uproar, Patti observed with horror and amazement. Was it really necessary to turn out every guest room, take down all the curtains and give everything an extra spring-clean in preparation for the few days' occupation by visitors? A smell of beeswax and drying laundry hung about the passages, and all the maids rushed around with red faces as if they would never be finished in time.

Patti was thankful when Lady Challoner called her to her boudoir one morning to discuss last-minute arrangements. The spacious chamber was airy and cool, shaded from the morning sun by heavily draped floral curtains. Patti's satisfaction increased as she looked discreetly around her. Behind a subtly shaded Japanese screen, the wallpaper was a soft apricot colour, which allowed the classically ornamented frieze above it to stand out. A tall palm in a pot stood on a dark Regency table in the bay window, and another table was covered with silver-framed family photographs.

Patti looked more closely. Was that truly Robert, aged about nine, standing beside a Shetland pony, a seraphic smile upon his lean face? Then Lady Challoner's voice distracted her, and she turned apologetically. 'I beg your pardon?'

Lady Challoner smiled. 'Sit down, my dear. You must be tired—I know how hard you've worked these last few days.'

Gratefully Patti sank into the comfort of a plum-red upholstered Victorian chair and returned the smile. She thought the older woman looked much better. Dressed in a casual light muslin négligé with a Honiton lace collar, and a black velvet ribbon at her throat, Lady Challoner seemed the very epitome of a gracious society lady, sitting at her desk surrounded by all the impedimenta of correspondence and domestic management. Patti had a sudden, curious feeling that she might enjoy such a life herself.

'There! That's the last of my letters for today.' Lady Challoner arose, her négligé whispering across the carpeted floor as she crossed to the window to look out, smiling at Patti as she passed. 'What a lovely day! But there's thunder about, so perhaps it would be as well to cut the flowers before the storm comes, as surely it must. Patti. . .' She turned, looking at Patti enquiringly. 'Have you time to do one other task for me, dear child?'

'But of course, Cousin Enid. What is it?'

'Would you please find Robert and tell him I think it wise to cut the flowers for the house decoration today? Usually Jenkins does it on the Friday morning—but with this threat of bad weather. . .'

'Of course. The roses mustn't be spoilt. . .' Patti felt slightly nervous of relaying such a message to Robert.

Roses, she reminded herself cynically, are not our favourite topic. And then suddenly she wanted to ask Lady Challoner what she knew of this wretched conflict within the family. Impulsively she said, 'My grandfather was a rose grower — like the rest of the family. He — he. . .' Then her words tailed off and she felt foolish and uncertain.

Lady Challoner's cultured voice replied quietly, 'Our entire clan has always been obsessed with roses, my dear. It is the common link between the various branches the world over. Yes, indeed, your grandfather was a very successful grower of roses. . .'

Patti looked up eagerly. 'He used to tell me, when I was small, about his Gallica roses. I saw a picture in an old book of the one rose he loved very dearly. He told me a story about it — he said it was his. . . I have never forgotten what he told me. . .'

But Lady Challoner's eyes grew anxious, her expression abruptly unhappy, and Patti chided herself at once for daring to mention Madame Léonie. Clearly, with mother as with son, this was a forbidden subject.

Hastily, she got to her feet. 'I'll go now, Cousin Enid. I'll give Robert your message at once — in case the weather changes.'

Running down the wide staircase, watched by the portraits of stern-faced Challoners, Patti felt acutely unsettled by Lady Challoner's reaction to her thoughtless words. It seemed that the family mystery had spun endless tendrils everywhere she looked — wretchedly she wondered if it would ever resolve itself, and then thought not. It was shrouded in such harsh secrecy, and she felt in her bones that Robert's dictatorial attitude would never change.

Her steps slowed, and she recalled the conversation she had had with Beth only yesterday, when she'd dropped in at Clematis Cottage for half an hour after tea.

'You've suddenly become very interested—almost obesessed, I might say—with Grandfather's old rose, Patti. Why? What has happened? You were only curious before—or so I remember. . .'

'Yes, Beth. You're right. I never felt like this. But now—well, Robert is so arrogant about his claim to Madame Léonie that I feel bound to try and find out what *really* happened all those years ago. . . I mean, poor Grandfather was cheated out of his rights over the matter. . .'

'I wonder! Have you ever thought that the poor darling simply made the whole thing up? You know how strange he was towards the end of his life.' Beth went on with her knitting and Patti instantly felt irritation grow. Didn't Beth realise how important the matter was?

She heard her voice grow sharp. 'Nonsense! I'm certain Grandfather was the true owner of Madame Léonie. And I shall find out—somehow. . .'

'Yes? And then what will you do? Too late for Grandfather now, Patti, dearest!'

'But not too late to make amends! I shall insist on the truth being made public, when I discover what it is. An apology must be made in the *Rose Growers' Annual*, at the very least——'

'Dear me, what a storm in a teacup! And all over a rose which, I dare say, looks like any other rose!' Beth's voice was full of gentle amusement which made Patti's determination all the greater.

'Beth, it's a matter of principle! Ideals are important.'

Beth's grey eyes suddenly met hers, serene and restraining. 'And so is family unity, Patti. And shared happiness. Can't you see that?'

And for once Beth's wise words had left Patti without an answer.

Now, snatching up her hat from the hall stand before running into the garden to find Robert, Patti felt her longing to clear Grandfather's name grow stronger as the old idealism returned to her, and she dismissed Beth's advice with a supercilious shrug of her shoulders.

She searched the garden without success. Ned was busy with the gardener's boy, Alan, spraying the roses, and could offer no suggestions as to where Robert was. 'Mebbe he's in the furnace room with Mr Thomson, miss — radiators still playing up, so they be... Or down by the cold-frame looking at the new plants he's hoping to find buyers for next week when they gentlemen from London come to visit...'

After ten minutes of futile wandering, Patti grew cross. How thoughtless of Robert to have disappeared like this. The sun beat down relentlessly. She was hot and becoming thirsty. The morning was half over and this afternoon she had promised to attend yet another of Faye's tedious dress fittings; when would the flowers get done? At this rate, never.

In the rose garden she collapsed crossly on one of the stone benches, staring disconsolately around her. The roses were everywhere, climbing up pillars, sprawling over the walls, and standing high, in huge green bushes, all perfectly proportioned in their spacings, the lush underplantings providing a sea of silver, pink, pale blue and white beneath the great swinging sprays. Each bush was covered with a profusion of heavy blooms, touched here and there by a breeze that flirted through the garden. Perfume filled the air.

Slowly her irritation died, and she began remembering Miss Clarke, who had educated her into this continuing passion for roses. Miss Clarke, a horticulturist of advanced views, had had visionary ideas for romantic borders and informal planting. Now, dreamily Patti realised how life had smiled upon her, taking her into Miss Clarke's house and garden, imbuing her with Miss Clarke's own passionate feelings for gardens. . .

Beneath the sizzling noonday sun, the bewitching fragrance crept around her, making the air almost breathless. Patti looked down at the tousled mop heads of the clumps of garden pinks bordering the rosebeds. White and pink, purple, laced with silver. . . Her mind relaxed even further, wandering into forgotten realms of delight.

What had the old herbalists called these lovely flowers? Sops-in-wine. The evocative name banished her last traces of self-pity, and she smiled more freely. Then, a little light-headed from her own thoughts, the fragrance, the brilliance of the sun and the warmth of the stone she sat upon, she felt herself become humbly content. How wonderful to sit in Robert's rose garden. . .

'Patti! What are you doing here? It's much too hot to be sitting in the sun at this time of day. You'd better go indoors at once.'

He stood behind her, his shadow engulfing her with delicious shade and coolness. She twisted her head around, her instinctive smile of welcome fading as she met his dark gaze. Her smile was not returned and flustered, she stood up at once, feeling like a guilty child caught in a wicked act. 'I've been looking for you, Robert,' she said in an aggrieved voice. 'If you hadn't been quite so invisible, I wouldn't have *had* to sit here in the sun waiting for you to appear, would I?'

Aware of every nuance of his behaviour, she was dismayed by the brooding expression filling the deep eyes. Then, almost grudgingly, a glimmer of amusement touched his doubtful face. 'In future I will wear a bell around my neck, so that you can always find me. . .'

She flushed. 'Don't be absurd! Your mother asked me to tell you that she thinks the flowers should be picked at once.'

'Because of the threatening storm? I see.' He looked at her with unfathomable eyes, but now she saw his lips twitching, and a brow flying upwards. 'And so I am to provide you with basket and secateurs and watch you reap havoc among my roses, am I?'

'I promise you I'll be very careful. . .' Her breathing was ragged, her disturbance at his nearness alarming. If she didn't move away she would not be responsible for her actions. . .

'Do you know anything about the language of flowers, Patti?'

'What?' Wide-eyed, she stared. 'I mean — yes, well, of course I do — a very sentimental Victorian idea that each flower symbolises a message, I believe.'

'Quite. Your late employer certainly educated you well. And so you know what the rose symbolises, I presume?'

How could she even think while he looked down at her so intently, dark eyes mysteriously guarded, his skin tanned to a rich brown, and the sensual demands of his presence making her flesh prickle? 'Er—yes, Robert. It means love. . .'

She stopped short, aware of walking into a trap. Blushing hotly, she turned away, desperate to leave. But he moved with her, his hand seeking hers and linking it through the crook of his arm. 'Why are you in such a hurry?' he asked, almost roughly. 'You say you've been looking for me, and then want to run away the moment I'm here—ah, but perhaps, like Mother, you don't find my gardening clothes very attractive?'

'I think. . .' She longed to find witty words, clever repartee that would improve his image of her, but none came. She muttered foolishly, 'I think you are— all right. . .'

'All right? Is that the best you can find to say about me?' He had stopped, was pulling her around to face him, looking down intently into her eyes. Patti felt the sun beating on her back, reflecting on the stones all around, heard her heart pound, and wondered exactly what he meant. His hands held hers, strong and very warm. Panic came as she realised how much she longed to relax in his grasp, but it would not do—he was her enemy, her opponent in the stakes for Grandfather's Madame Léonie.

Pushing her self-control to its limit, she wrenched herself away from him, saying shakily, 'Robert! It's very hot! The sun. . . Must we play games in this heat?'

'Games. . .?' His voice was instantly just a growl and he stepped back from her, nodding coolly. 'Of course. It's far too hot for you to stand about like this. I said you shouldn't be out here. Remiss of me. Come along, back to the house with you.' Briskly he led her down the path, towards the hedge. Patti stumbled along beside him, her head in a whirl, regret mingling with relief.

'But Robert—the flowers! Lady Challoner said——'

He glanced down at her and she saw the familiar mask in position. 'Don't worry,' he said impatiently, deep voice tinged with a note of arrogance, 'Ned shall pick them first thing in the morning. They can stand in water until someone arranges them—Faye, perhaps; she has little else to do. Plenty of time before Friday.'

Patti longed to somehow get rid of this hurtful, impatient mood. 'But. . .' she stuttered with growing despair as she followed him through the garden.

Robert did not even look back at her. 'Indoors with you,' he ordered airily, raising one hand in a casual dismissal. 'I'll see you at luncheon.' He strode off, leaving her bruised and furious. How could she possibly cope with such a man, let alone try and persuade him that he was wrong about Madame Léonie?

She went into the house feeling very downcast. She almost wished she had never come to Porphyry Court, never met Robert Challoner. . .

As Patti had predicted, the afternoon slid along tediously, Faye's bedroom being airless and hot and her temper decidedly on edge as she tried on first one gown and then another.

'You haven't fitted this one properly, Miss Shaw! It falls off me like a country smock! I can't possibly wear it. . .' She spun and twirled, her dull voice grating and complaining until Patti could have slapped her for such bad and inconsiderate behaviour.

When it was her own turn to try on the new, half-finished pale green satin dinner dress which Lady Challoner had insisted on giving her, Patti smiled kindly at poor Miss Shaw, forever on her knees, mouth full of pins and her plain face wearing an expression of constant nervousness. 'You're making it beautifully, Miss Shaw. I shall so enjoy wearing it — this high collar lies very well, don't you think? The lace is lovely. . .'

Miss Shaw removed the pins long enough to smile cautiously and murmur, 'Thank you, miss. And you certainly do look nice. Colour suits your hair, it really does.'

'Green is an unlucky colour.' Faye sounded petulant and unhappy. She pulled off the pale gold woollen coat which Miss Shaw was trying to fit around her, and added roughly, 'Oh, that's enough for this afternoon. Go away and do the alterations, Miss Shaw, it's too hot to try on anything else. . . and make sure the hem shows my feet. It's the new fashion and I intend to wear it.'

Patti sat on the window seat in silence, watching Faye redress her hair after the dressmaker had left the room, arms full of boxes, material and gowns. Faye's face was reflected in the dressing-table mirror and Patti saw from her expression that something had happened to return her to the frustrations of her past. Briefly she wondered if the letter from France had anything to do with Faye's bad mood.

Faye caught her eye and scowled. 'Don't just sit there! You're supposed to be my companion, you know. So come and do my hair for me.'

Perhaps the effect of a hundred gently sweeping brush strokes soothed her. After a while she muttered, 'Sorry. I know I've been horrid. I didn't mean to be — but. . .' Swinging around, she faced Patti. Her colour was high and her green eyes seemed to be sending out sparks. 'Robert is a monster!' she exclaimed. 'He refused to let me see that letter! And I'm sure Jules must have sent me a message. He couldn't just go and never say a word. . .'

Patti felt most uncomfortable. She returned the hairbrush to the dressing-table and persuaded Faye to turn around so that she could neatly coil her blonde hair at the nape of her neck. 'There. You look very elegant, Faye.'

'Don't change the subject!' But Faye was more in control of herself by now. She smiled stiffly before flouncing down on the bed and lay, hands behind neck, staring up at the ceiling. 'Well, if he won't show me the letter, then I'll find it and read it for myself. At least——' she sat up abruptly, staring at Patti with narrowed, determined eyes '—at least—*you* will! Robert told Mother that you're helping him with his old books in the study. . .'

Patti was appalled. 'I am. But I'm not going to read anything he doesn't want me to! And anyway, Jules is nothing to do with me. . .'

'Really?' Faye smirked unpleasantly. 'I don't believe you! Dora said she saw you out in the garden that night, the same time as he was. So what have you to say about *that*?'

Patti swallowed the quick rage which exploded through her. Squaring her shoulders, she said, dangerously quietly, 'I say that Dora is a Nosy Parker and also that you should know better than to listen to servants' gossip!'

'Why, you little brute!' Faye's mouth snapped open and the cats' eyes glittered with fury. She bounced on the bed in anger. 'How dare you? You can't talk to me like that!'

'I can. And I *have*!'

They stared at each other in a hostile silence, until Patti's rueful amusement broke forth in a chuckle. Instantly Faye scowled even deeper. 'What on earth are you laughing about?'

'Us. Fighting like two tabby cats!'

'Tabby? Don't call me a tabby cat—at least let me be an elegant cream Persian.' But Faye was laughing too, and the atmosphere cleared. Settling back on the bed, she regarded Patti through golden lashes. 'You're good for me, Patti. Sorry I shouted and said nasty things. Forgive me?'

'On one condition. . .'

'Oh?' Faye sat up, surprised. 'And that is?'

'That you never again ask me to do anything so cheap and sly as reading your brother's letters.'

Faye's face was a picture of mixed feelings. Clearly she resented being spoken to so sharply, but, just as plainly, she had to accept the truth of Patti's stern words. She sniffed, and then muttered, 'Very well. I suppose it was rather horrid of me. But I do want to know about poor Jules. . .'

Patti crossed to the window-seat and sat down, trying to think what to say. She saw childish uncertainty and hurt in Faye's face, and knew that it would be far better to end her dreams rather than let them linger on indefinitely. She drew in a strengthening breath. 'Jules is a flirt, Faye,' she began tentatively. 'You said so yourself—remember?'

Faye frowned. 'What are you trying to say?'

'That I agree with Robert. You should find another admirer.'

'There you go again!' cried Faye, with new exasperation. 'Trying to part me from Jules! Because you want him yourself, of course—Dora said she saw you go down the garden after him——'

'Stop it, Faye!' Patti felt she could stand no more of these distasteful tantrums and accusations. She walked quickly to the door, turning to look back at Faye before leaving the room. 'If you want to know the real truth, ask Robert. He was there. He knows exactly what I think about Jules Lacoste. . .'

Outside in the gallery she found she was shaking and had to stand still for a while, hand clutching the baluster rail while she fought for control. Memories of Jules were too brutal to brush off. Blindly she stared at the long row of Challoner faces hanging opposite, not seeing the long, thin features, the ruffs, the doublets, the elegant frock coats, but hearing only her own tearing heartbeats, feeling only the hot blood singing in her veins as Jules's arms had enclosed her.

A door opened, closed, somewhere at the end of the gallery, but she was too agitated to register it. Until Robert asked sharply, 'What is it? Are you ill?'

Patti swung around, startled to find him so close to her. 'Go away!' she cried wildly. 'I'm perfectly well! I don't need any help from anyone—certainly not from you.' The words were almost hysterical, holding no meaning, but she screamed them in self-defence, disturbed as she was by the sight and sound of him at a time when she badly needed to regain her composure.

Too late she realised the effect of her outburst. Robert's expression grew very grim. He stepped away from her, and his voice was harsh. 'I'm sorry you find my presence so distressing. I'll leave you at once. If you do need assistance, Cousin Patti, try ringing the bell in your bedroom, and one of the servants will come immediately.' Passing her, he strode down the stairs and did not look back, and Patti, leaning heavily on the baluster, knew that she had damaged their uneasy relationship even further. First this morning's stupid scene, and now this. . .

The converstion at dinner was, naturally enough, of the guests due to arrive on Friday afternoon.

Lady Challoner reminded Faye that last year poor dear Aunt Estelle had gone down with a summer cold the very day she arrived at Porphyry Court. 'And so no doubt, Mother, this year she will come annointed with friar's balsam and wearing her winter underwear, despite this heat!' Faye laughed cheerfully, and then Patti saw a touch of malice cross her face. 'And I wonder what perfume Barbara Latimer will be sporting this year!' She slid a sideways, mischievous glance at her brother, who frowned in answer.

'What an unpleasant child you can be at times, sister mine.' There was a note of annoyance in his deep voice and Patti saw his eyes flash with irritation.

Then Lady Challoner broke in quickly. 'Such nonsense. Sometimes you tease a little too cruelly, Faye, dear. But how nice it will be to have Barbara and Stephen here. I fear we grow a little stodgy in our quiet Devon village — a breath of London air might do us all good!'

'I can't wait to breathe it in for myself, actually,' said Faye with sudden determination. 'London must be so exciting. . .'

'And no doubt Barbara will describe it in great detail. . .' Patti thought Robert's voice was anything but welcoming and wondered again about this obviously exciting and glamorous guest who was coming to stay. She sensed that his mind was occupied with more important things than picking up old friendships; the dark, brooding look remained in his eyes and she saw him watching her as the meal progressed.

She tried very hard to shake off the feeling that he was angry with her, but her customary easiness of mind was deeply affected by that lingering frown.

And yet when Lady Challoner asked, 'Patti, dear child, I do hope you will play for our guests? Your touch is so beautiful,' it was Robert who chipped in dictatorially, saying, 'Of course she will, Mother. We're lucky to have such an excellent pianist in the family.'

She saw him smile briefly at her surprised stare, and was even more astonished when he added, with that mocking quirk of one eyebrow, 'Is there no end to our little cousin's talents, I wonder?'

Patti, bemused by the change of moods, said, a little dazed, 'I shall be delighted to play. But—talents. . .?' She caught a dark gleam in his eyes, and could only shake her head, not knowing how to deal with such a suggestion.

She was very disturbed, and not only because of these mercurial ups and downs—today she sensed an impatient restlessness about him, which alarmed her increasingly. It was almost as if she had done something wrong, and he was picking his time before rebuking her. And then her reflections came to a swift end as he leaned towards her, saying quietly, 'You look very pale, Patti—I suggest a glass of wine to bring the roses back into your cheeks. . .'

She caught her breath. 'Thank you, but no. . .' What did he mean, talking about roses? Was it yet another subtle hint that he had no intention of ever giving way about Madame Léonie? She flinched as he narrowed his eyes, the frown again becoming too obvious for comfort. 'I'm quite well,' she insisted feebly.

'So you said, earlier this afternoon. . .' The words tailed off, but the grimness hung in the air, and Patti knew she must apologise for her rude and panic-stricken outburst.

'Robert, I'm sorry——' she began and then stopped as Faye cut in.

'Patti, you must know the herb I mean? The one that's supposed to be good for hay fever. Perhaps Aunt Estelle should take it to stop her June sniffles!' Faye was smiling and Patti understood that the question was asked more out of need to make apologies for the afternoon scene than to receive information.

Turning from Robert, good-humouredly Patti returned the smile. 'I believe tea, made from eyebright, is the answer——'

And then Robert interrupted once more. 'You're knowledgeable about plants.' He looked at her with a curiosity that chilled her for no good reason. 'Perhaps you should help me in the garden next time Ned has a day off.'

Unsure if he was joking or being unkindly sarcastic, Patti decided to take up the challenge. Meeting his gaze, she said firmly, 'Of course I will, Robert. Nothing will give me more pleasure.'

She saw his gaze deepen and realised it was now his turn to be uncertain. He added, in a more friendly voice, 'I'll lend you my second-best leather gloves, then. We could deadhead the roses together, when they're finished blooming. . .'

The sardonic suggestion made her thoat tighten. If

only he had not made it in such a cutting manner; if only she and Robert could, indeed, work together — friends and companions, in the garden they both loved. . . Her thoughts suddenly became braver and more optimistic, and she was able to say, lightly and in a bright voice that belied her swamping emotions, 'I hope you'll pay me the going rate, Robert. Deadheading in this heat will be quite arduous.'

'Your reward will be what I think you have earned, Patti.' The unexpected seriousness in his words took her breath away.

She stared at him in surprise, and was thankful when Lady Challoner broke the silence between them, saying, very firmly, 'Robert, dear, I do so hope you will arrange to spend some time with Barbara while she is here. You know how very fond of you she has always been — so please don't hide yourself away in the garden *all* the time. . .'

The spell ended; Patti lowered her eyes and Robert looked across the table at his mother. She heard him make some sort of reply, but was not listening. Robert's changes of mood were unsettling, to say the least, and now she could not stop herself thinking about Barbara Latimer.

Barbara and Robert — the names rang through her confused mind like a warning bell. Patti was grateful that Faye began an enthusiastic tirade in which she was not invited to take part about the coming village fête. The rest of the meal passed in a daze, and she began counting the minutes until she could retire to bed.

But when the moment came she was surprised to hear Robert call his sister back as she headed for the stairs with Patti behind her. 'Come into the study, will

you, Faye? Something I need to discuss with you. . .'
Patti, turning, met his eyes with a sense of shock.
There was no friendliness now in their dark depths.
Alone, she went to her room, but could not sleep.

CHAPTER TEN

ONCE family prayers were over, Robert began pacing the dining-room like a caged animal. 'If only I had a telephone!' he muttered. 'This benighted village needs to move with the times! No drainage, no electric power yet — well, I suppose I shall just have to go down to the post office and telegraph.' He slammed out of the room, leaving Faye and Patti exchanging glances of alarm.

Faye sighed. 'Someone once said war makes dogs of men,' she reflected from the sideboard, where she was helping herself to kedgeree, 'but big business also has a lot to answer for.' Returning to the table, she looked keenly at Patti. 'It's that letter,' she confided abruptly. 'From Monsieur Lacoste.'

'Jules's father?' Patti was intrigued.

Faye nodded as she picked up her fork. 'Robert read me bits of it last night. Something's gone badly wrong with the business and Robert needs to speak to his colleagues in London to find out just *how* bad.' She eyed Patti with an uncertain expression, and then blurted out, 'Actually, I think you're involved——'

'Me?' Patti's mouth dropped open. 'In Robert's business? Oh, surely not! It's absolutely nothing to do with me...' Her spoon fell into her porridge. She stared across the table, horror-stricken, suddenly recalling how unpredictable Robert had been yesterday — friendly one moment, almost suspicious the next. Had it all been her fault? But what could she have

179

done to upset him? 'Faye—please tell me what you mean...'

'I'm not sure, but Robert mentioned your name and then shut up like a clam. He looked so horrid that I went to bed in a hurry.' Faye's voice faltered. 'After all, I had enough troubles of my own to think about...'

The plaintive words recalled Patti from her own despairing reflections. 'Jules?' she asked hurriedly. 'Was there a message for you from Jules?'

'Hmm!' Faye snorted and left her breakfast unfinished for a long moment. Then she tossed her head petulantly. 'From all that Monsieur Lacoste said, I gather that dear Jules is not all he pretended to be — "*an absolute bounder*", Robert said last night.' Her voice shook. 'And I believe him now. Yes, I do. I was a fool, I suppose. Well, I know better now.'

Patti watched her cousin blink away a threatening tear and then make a brave attempt at eating her breakfast. Instantly her own troubles melted into the background and impulsively she reached out a hand to touch Faye's arm. 'I'm so sorry,' she said feelingly. 'I know just how you must feel...' And then she bit off the words. But Faye's eyes had softened and her voice was warmer than Patti had heard before as she answered, very quietly, 'So I was right, wasn't I? About the way *you* feel for Robert. Mind you——' she smiled mischievously, quickly regaining her composure '— I can't imagine what you see in him! But I'll do anything I can to help—somehow...'

Patti swallowed the lump in her throat before replying unsteadily. 'Thank you, Faye. Although I don't— really—think anyone can do *anything*. Robert, I'm quite sure, has no feelings for me at all, you see.'

'Hmm.' Faye tightened her lips. 'Well, in the meantime. . .' Faye was recovering fast. She took a slice of toast and buttered it thickly. 'Don't take any notice of all the silly things I said about Robert and the divine Barbara. She's quite awful, and Robert ran a mile the moment she decided to chase him. . .'

Patti smiled, but wondered at the tactlessness of Faye's supposedly heartening words. Her thoughts strayed. Did Barbara intend to renew her pursuit of Robert this coming weekend? Staunchly Patti tried to think of other things. She had enough to deal with now that she knew Robert blamed her for something. What *could* it be? And when would he make the matter clear?

'Excuse me, Miss Nevill. Ned's put the buckets of cut flowers into the flower-room.' Dora's voice pierced Patti's mind an hour later, putting an end to the mixture of bewildering images that occupied her as she went about her morning tasks.

'Thank you, Dora. I'll see to them as soon as I can.'

The flower-room was full of great blowsy roses awaiting her in enamel buckets. And not just roses, but stately lupins, spikes of purple and blue delphiniums, sprays of fragrant orange blossom and great bunches of bright green pittisporum. And yet more roses. . . She looked at the vast array of breathtaking blooms awaiting her arrangement, and set to her task with a sense of mounting pleasure.

This was one way in which she could express all the feelings that churned within her. A duty, to help Lady Challoner, and a small talent of her own which would ease the knotted anxieties within her.

In the atmosphere of beauty, perfume and living

things, a sense of new serenity came to her. By the time all the vases had been filled she knew she had, in some inexplicable way, quietened her fears and recaptured her lost dreams. She could face whatever lay ahead of her with vitality, strength and enduring love.

Lady Challoner was full of compliments. 'How beautifully you've arranged them, Patti, dear. Faye is such a butter-fingers with flowers, and I know she's thankful she won't have to struggle with them this year. Just wait until Robert sees that huge vase of dark red roses — Porphyry Beauty, he calls them. They're my favourites, and the ones he's hoping to find a new market for very soon. Robert is always hybridising new roses, you know... Put them on the piano, will you? Don't they look lovely there, standing out against the pale wall behind them...?'

Glowing from the praise, Patti made her escape, on the pretext that she must change her soiled blouse before luncheon. Once she had done so, however, she slipped out of the house, knowing that she needed a few minutes to herself before the undoubted trauma of encountering Robert over the meal table.

She fled to the wilderness to make the most of its welcoming solitude. The first guests would arrive in time for tea, and after that the days would be crammed with people and social occasions — including the village fête tomorrow.

Restored by the peace of the wild garden, she turned back towards the house, and then halted by a tangle of dog roses climbing high up a silver birch tree. She picked one perfect bloom and held it, examining it. Such purity of shape, the five simple petals blushing pink at their tips and fading inwards to a veined whiteness, the ring of golden stamens, growing tawny as they aged, surrounding the vital dome of the central ovary. She looked into the heart of the pale, fragrant flower, and realised that it was the touchstone of the plant, rich with seeds and fertility. '*The heart of a rose*'.

Grandfather's words rang in her mind. What had he said? The secret of life itself. . . Knowledge came to Patti intuitively and she knew that within every heart, plant or human there was a rich jewel. It varied, being fertility, as in the dog rose, or emotion in a man or woman. It could be fear, pain; it could be hope — or love.

Love, thought Patti, feverishly coming to terms with her new awareness. If only I can find it. If only I can share it — with Robert. It's there, in the rose. . .somewhere.

Twitching her skirt away from a clinging bramble, she turned, smiling to herself, and went quickly back to the house, replenished and renewed. She thought, amused, that she could deal with anything now — even Robert in his worst mood!

There was a hullabaloo of noisy motor engines, horse hoofs and raised voices, filling the quiet afternoon and bringing the servants running into the hall. As Patti ran downstairs, she saw Hodge, the butler, at the open front door, with Dora and Elsie already carrying portmanteaus, dressing cases and leather hat boxes, heading for the staircase.

'Excuse me, miss,' Dora panted as she passed by, lugging huge suitcases in each hand. 'They're here! I'm just taking Miss Latimer's things up to her room.'

Patti joined Faye, waiting just inside the open door

with her mother, and watched the guests as they arrived.

'Dear Aunt Estelle, how good to see you again! And Uncle Willie...' Lady Challoner kissed her relatives with warmth, while Faye's sharp elbow nudged Patti.

'Watch out for Uncle Willie' she whispered. 'He likes comely young gels!' Giggling, she allowed the old man to slap an enthusiastic kiss on her cheek, before saying, 'Uncle Willie, this is Patti Nevill, my long-lost cousin, who lives with us.'

Keen grey eyes assessed Patti's entire body in a practised sweep and then she, in her turn, was subjected to the moist lips. Until a sharp voice behind her said imperiously, 'Willie! Stop that slobbering! Introduce me, if you please!'

Patti liked Aunt Estelle's small, lined face and her vivid blue eyes and thought wryly that Robert was not the only force to be reckoned with in this family. The elderly lady had the same autocratic manner as her nephew, but here it was sugared with even greater charm. 'A Nevill?' demanded Aunt Estelle thoughtfully. 'I remember Ralph—he had two gels; was Elizabeth your elder sister?'

'Beth, Aunt Estelle...' Patti smiled, and was treated to an approving nod before the visitor was swept upstairs, accompanied by maids and butler, carrying the vast amount of luggage which emerged from the carriage at the door. Aunt Estelle's voice drifted down, imperious as ever. 'Thank goodness for the train service; I can't stand these new, smelly, dangerous motor cars...!'

As the voices faded along the gallery, other voices made themselves heard entering the hallway. 'Dear Lady Challoner! How splendid to see you—so good of you to ask us down. Barbara, old thing, come along, here is our hostess waiting to welcome us back to beloved Porphyry Court. . .'

Patti was fascinated by the slender young man who bowed low over Lady Challoner's hand, before being drawn towards her and fondly embraced. 'Stephen! Dear boy! So long since you were last here—nearly a year since we saw you. And here is Barbara. . .'

Slyly, Faye's voice intruded into Patti's thoughts. 'Watch out! She may not want to kiss you, like Uncle Willie, but she has her own way of disturbing everybody!' Aloud, she said flatly, and without a trace of welcome, 'Hello, Barbara. I hope you're quite well?'

Patti watched Barbara Latimer's beautiful face cloud slightly, and although her husky voice sounded friendly as she said lightly, 'Does that mean I look ill, Faye? Hardly the welcome I had hoped for, you naughty thing. . .' Patti knew instinctively that the old friction was still in evidence between the two of them.

Lady Challoner smoothed the awkward moment with her usual composure. 'Faye must have her little joke, Barbara—always making fun of everything! Now, my dear, would you like to go up to your room before tea?'

'Dear Lady Challoner! So thoughtful! The drive down was quite appalling—these country roads are absolute dustbaths! I must wash and change before I can even *consider* tea. . .' Smiling with devastating effect, Barbara Latimer twitched back the skirt of her elegant beige costume and swished upstairs, the billowing dustcoat emitting tiny clouds of dust as she went. Patti, watching with a sense of unwilling fascination, realised that here was a society woman who never stopped her restless pursuit of life and admirers. This grand exit she now saw was merely a suggestion of what was to come later.

Faye led the way into the drawing-room, to await teatime, and muttered gloomily, 'Thank goodness Stephen is here. I don't think I could tolerate things without him. . .' She met Patti's questioning glance and added, 'Aunt Estelle is a termagant, Uncle Willie a lecher, and Barbara a *femme fatale* — only Stephen is remotely normal and therefore likely to be good company.'

Then she grinned. 'If you have any ideas about finding Stephen attractive — stop this minute, cousin! I intend to give him the benefit of my full attention. It's the only way I can possibly pass the time without becoming bored and therefore ill again! Unless, of course ——' her cats' eyes suddenly gleamed brightly '— this unknown Mr Fraser, who's expected by a later train, turns out to be handsome and fascinating!'

Lady Challoner ordered tea to be served in the orangery. Again, Patti was smitten with the scent of the climbing plants, and the airless heat which seemed to sap her strength. Sitting in the shade of a vast palm tree, she realised that although the domed building was not her favourite place it was certainly proving to be a suitable stage for Barbara Latimer's next performance. . .

'Robert — my dear! How too utterly wonderful to see you again!' Barbara, dressed in a voile tea-gown of mingled blue and green floral pattern, rose from her cane chair to glide across the flagged floor, meeting Robert the instant he entered. Her hands, with their long polished nails, were extended in a gesture of intimate affection, and her lovely heart-shaped face was upraised, clearly inviting his kiss.

Patti sat stiffly in her chair, watching the little drama as if in a dream. Robert had changed into his dark suit and looked immaculately elegant. Dark hair, dark eyes, dark clothes — all illuminated by the glowing skin and brilliance of his glance. Numbly, Patti saw him return Barbara's smile, taking her hands and pressing them, while submitting to being kissed on each cheek.

'Barbara, you look your usual lovely self,' he said, his deep voice composed and seemingly warm. 'How good of you to spare the time from your whirlwind life and come and see us down here. I trust you won't find sleepy Moorwood too quiet for you, after the bustle and polish of busy London.'

Patti thought she heard a false note in Robert's pleasant words, and began hoping wildly that he was not as entranced with the guest as he appeared. She wondered if he was putting on one of his acts — but how could she be certain? He was an expert at hiding his feelings, as well she knew. Dismally, she realised the truth would only emerge as the weekend progressed.

Dutifully and discreetly, she helped pass around the plates of cucumber sandwiches and buttered scones, while conversation flowed around her. Only when a pause came did she feel herself being watched by predatory eyes. Turning, she found Barbara looking her way.

'Robert tells me you are a long lost cousin, Miss Nevill.' The drawling, husky voice sounded friendly, but Patti recalled Faye's warning.

'Yes, Miss Latimer, that is so.'

'But how fortunate that you are now *found*! Quite

the happy ending to the story, is it not? Imagine! The little orphan girl coming home to roost in the old family mansion...!'

Robert said quietly, with a note of wry humour that soothed Patti's sinking heart, 'I can't really see Patti roosting anywhere, Barbara. She has the heart of a tiger, not a chicken.'

'But darling, I'm not suggesting she's anything but a veritable *man-eater*!' Barbara's amused tone brought a chuckling response from her listening audience around the orangery, and Patti felt the colour building up in her cheeks. She was thankful when Stephen broke in briskly. 'Come, now, old thing, don't overdo it...'

Patti's quick temper was being kindled. She disliked being made the butt of patronising remarks. Crisply she said, while offering a plate of seed cake to Barbara, 'Man-eating is definitely not one of *my* talents, Miss Latimer.' The emphatic pronoun brought a swift gleam into the dark, hooded eyes. 'I'm just an ordinary female,' Patti continued smoothly. 'My only skills are secretarial.'

'Really? A lady typewriter?' The husky drawl was full of barely concealed triumph. 'You seem out of your element here, Miss Nevill—surely you should be in a gloomy office, wearing dark skirts and lisle stockings? Not here, in this palatial glass edifice, and looking so pretty in that cream lace blouse that sets off your *amazingly* red hair so well! Not dyed, is it, my dear? Oh, but *do* forgive me—in London, you know, we discuss such things quite openly these days...'

Before Patti could snap the angry reply that instantly presented itself, Robert had forestalled her. 'Patti is most efficient in many things, Barbara. She is also well mannered and courteous. I fear your London society brand of humour can hardly be to her country-bred liking. . .'

Patti watched the sloe-black eyes open very wide, and then veil themselves behind long, mascaraed lashes. 'Darling Robert!' murmured Barbara with a pretty pout. 'Always so good at protecting your loved ones! How can I possibly apologise for my naughty lapse? But truly, I was only being complimentary. . . Miss Nevill's hair certainly *is* her crowning glory.' The words seemed sincere, but Patti knew they were meant only to patronise, and make her feel inferior. As if to emphasise this, she saw Barbara languorously raise her left hand to her own gleaming dark hair and pat the elegant coil at the nape of her swan-like neck. Clearly there was an enormous difference between the rough attractions of a country ingénue and and a society lady. . . In that instant Patti knew that she hated Barbara Latimer with all her heart.

And then Lady Challoner was leading the conversation into safer channels, the cake was passed around yet again, and Patti sipped her cooling tea, keeping her eyes down and not wishing to be drawn into any further confrontations with the wretched creature, who was doing her best to win Robert's admiration and approval.

Later, when Robert's voice said, close to her, 'Can you spare an hour in the study, Patti?' she was taken aback and more than a little disturbed. Was this the confrontation she had been awaiting?

'Yes, Robert, of course.' It was easy, under cover of the general conversation, to slip away from the heated orangery into the freshness of the garden. But Patti, glancing back, knew that a pair of dark eyes had watched them leave together.

'You mustn't let Barbara intimidate you.' Robert walked beside her with long, quick strides, and Patti had to run to keep up with him.

'I don't intend to.'

He looked down, suddenly smiling appreciatively. 'I'm sure you don't! When she said you were a man-eater, I don't believe she realised even half the truth of it!'

Patti's apprehension dulled slightly, and she said crisply, 'Actually, I haven't eaten a man for some time, but I wouldn't mind taking a bite out of *her*, given the opportunity. . .!'

'Don't let's turn this party into a circus, Patti; it's going to be involved enough without any further complications.' Robert's voice was abruptly grim and as Patti preceded him into the study her heart sank. Was he about to reveal the mystery that Faye had mentioned — her seeming involvement in his business problems? She looked at him with a knot of anxiety re-forming inside her, but, although he stared back, frowning deeply, he quickly turned away and gestured around the room.

'The books are on the shelves, the family papers in that chest by the fireplace. There's a typewriting machine, if you wish to use it.' His eyes met hers again, and this time his tone was milder.

She thought he looked at her almost as if he wished to add something. But the silence grew until she hastily reorganised her thoughts. 'I'll do my best,' she said unsteadily. 'Is it — is it just a list of suitable reading you want, Robert?'

He put a hand on the door latch, suddenly seeming undecided. 'Whatever you think best,' he told her, almost irritably. 'You know what I'm planning to do. That article. The details. . .'

Patti held her breath, as instinct warned her that this was surely the moment of truth—but no, Robert opened the door, and then, surprisingly, shut it again, turning back to her.

In a rough, cross voice that told her of his own disturbance, he said shortly, 'Patti, I have to talk to you. Later, perhaps. . .' And then he was gone, the door slamming behind him, and she was left alone, her mind in chaos, and emotions in all directions.

'I don't believe it!'

A good hour later, she spoke the words aloud, voice full of amazed consternation. Yet, also, she knew a great surge of triumph. This was what she had been hoping to find! This small scrap of crumpled paper, the slanting writing brown with age—this uncompromising evidence of Madame Léonie's true ownership! *At last.*

After a long pause, she left the open chest and wandered towards the rectangular window. Small leaded lights filtered the rays of fading sunlight, and she stood in the glow of the dusky afternoon sun, trying to put her thoughts into order. The letter—from Grandfather Nevill to his cousin, Sir Archibald Challoner, had been hidden under an album of family photographs. She had almost missed it, thinking it merely rubbish, as she'd turned the pages, smiling at the strange fashions of her Victorian relatives. As it had fallen to the floor, and her eyes had deciphered the writing, she'd caught the words 'Madame Léonie'—then, heart racing, she had put down the album, concentrating instead on the letter.

Grandfather had written in his slanting copperplate script,

The wretched conflict about my rose must end. I am the true and only breeder of Madame Léonie de Sange, as you know. So kindly sign the below-written disclaimer and return it to me. We can then forget the whole distasteful business and try and retrieve what is left of our once happy relationship.

Your affectionate cousin, R.P. Nevill.

Patti stared at the signature and sighed, recalling very vividly the man himself. She forced herself to read on.

I, Archibald Peter Challoner, do renounce forever all claim to the ownership of the Gallica rose, Madame Léonie de Sange.
Signed. . . . .

Sir Archibald, she though uncertainly, and with a hint of unexpected wry amusement, had been a poor scribe. His name was scratched, the letters smudged and completely illegible.

Then a shape passed the window and she looked up and saw Faye running down the path, calling back a laughing remark as she did so. Stephen Latimer puffed behind her, smiling, his pleasant voice full of amusement as he replied.

'Faye, you run like a gazelle, sweetie! Do wait for me—these poor old bones are as stiff as an unopened umbrella!'

And Faye's answer, bright and mischief-laden—
'Stuff and nonsense, Stephen! You sound as old and pompous as Robert's business colleagues who've just arrived. Come on, now, I'll give you a head start if you insist—last one to reach the end of the pergola must pay a forfeit!'

HEART OF A ROSE

Shared laughter and the rapid crunch of feet upon the gravel died into the distance, and the garden became quiet once more. Patti stood by the window, hands unthinkingly trying to smooth out the crumpled bit of paper she held, as if also to wipe away the truth it told.

Why should she feel so confused, all of a sudden? She had hoped beyond all belief that she might find proof of Grandfather's claim to the old rose—and now here it was! But instead of happiness, she felt only a deepening of her previous anxiety—for her understanding of Robert increased, day by day, and she knew now that to show him this forgotten letter could do nothing but deepen the conflict between them.

She could imagine his reaction—the arrogance would grow even stronger, the certainty that she was wrong, despite the proof she held. . .

After an interval of severe soul-searching, Patti arrived at no conclusion. Dully, she finished the list of reading that Robert had asked her to compile and replaced the books on the shelves lining the study. The family papers went back into the chest, but Grandfather's letter burned a hole in her hand. She folded it, and slipped it down her bodice. It would be safe there—safe from prying eyes, and also safe for her to do with it whatever she decided. *When* she had decided. . .

For no reason that she could think of, abruptly her eyes lifted, and she discovered she was looking at a most beautiful print on the wall beside the window. It was a coloured engraving of an old rose, and beneath the elegantly etched flower she read the name of the artist.

P. J. Redouté. Her heart leaped and some of the

awful distress she was suffering died. Here was the picture Robert had mentioned, celebrating the beauty of the roses that Napoleon's wife, Empress Josephine, had grown in her beloved garden at the Château de la Malmaison, in the early eighteen hundreds. There must have been problems, even then, about the true ownership of such roses — yet their beauty had lasted long beyond all memory of such unpleasant human dealings. Was it possible that Madame Léonie, in her new development, would do the same? Would she even be able to heal the long-standing family feud? Only if the families concerned allowed her to do so. . .

Patti's thoughts raced and circled. She heard, in her memory, her own voice speaking proudly to Beth about idealism. She recalled Beth's sensible reply. Turning, she looked again at the Redoubté engraving, as if asking it to help her come to a sure decision. But she was aware only of the beauty and the timelessness of the classic red rose. Redoubté and the lovely, sad Empress Josephine had long ceased to exist. The rose lived on, and it was she, herself, Patti Nevill, who must decide what to do now.

Instinct told her there was a message here — a truth she would do well to consider and then act upon, whatever it might be. Dazed and confused, she went slowly to the door and then, casting a last look around the peaceful room, dimmed the lamp and left it. She badly needed solitude and the healing strength of a night's sleep before she reached a decision. But before that she had to face Robert — and his guests — at the dinner-table.

Steadfastly, Patti went to her room and changed into the exquisite new green gown that Miss Shaw had finished in time for her to wear this evening. The high lace collar covered her throat and the long, tight sleeves fastened snugly. She thought, bleakly, dabbing a touch of Yardley's lavender water on her wrists and, daringly, behind her ears, that Robert would find nothing to look at, covered as she was in the all enveloping satin. No doubt Barbara Latimer would provide a more interesting target for his appreciative eyes. That glowing flesh, thought Patti fiercely, would encapture any man. . . and, from what she already knew of Barbara, plenty of it would be on show this evening.

She was proved right; even her brother Stephen stared as Barbara made her entry into the drawing-room, while Uncle Willie, resplendent in an old-fashioned frockcoat, staggered slightly, putting on his gold-rimmed spectacles with shaking fingers to inspect her more closely.

'I say, old girl — bit near the knuckle, what?' Stephen murmured, but Barbara, swathed in a tight fitting silver-lace gown which fell in a soft fichu around her bare shoulders, revealing the daring line of her cleavage, gave him a glance of withering scorn. 'Don't be obtuse, darling! This is merely Mr Worth's latest creation — fun, don't you think?' She swished the small train around, smiling serenely at her gaping audience. 'Oh — but I *do* hope you don't all think me over-dressed?'

The husky voice was suddenly hesitant. 'Of course, I know you don't dress in the country quite as much as we do in town — but. . .'

The pause was ended by Faye saying savagely, 'We're not exactly peasants, you know, Barbara!'

'Darling! Nothing was further from my mind! I mean, you look absolutely *sweet* in that dear little plain apricot dress. . .'

Patti was wondering when Barbara's attention would alight on her own 'plain' little dress, when Robert appeared, ushering in two strangers, clearly the business colleagues Faye had mentioned earlier.

He made the introductions rapidly. 'My aunt and uncle, Lord and Lady Trehearne. My mother, Lady Challoner. My sister Faye, My cousin, Patricia Nevill. . .' His deep eyes met hers with sudden impact and she felt even more unsettled than before, seeing the hard assurance in them. He continued, unconcerned. 'Miss Barbara and Mr Stephen Latimer. May I present John Curtis and Arnold Fraser, business colleagues of mine, from London?'

Dinner proved to be entirely a showcase for Barbara, who happily held court, claiming the attention of everyone save Patti, who sat in a small, introverted world of her own, longing to escape and counting the minutes until she could politely do so.

As at last Lady Challoner collected eyes, and the ladies arose to leave the men to their port and nuts, Patti's watchful gaze noticed how Robert immediately turned to his friends, engaging them in serious talk, as if he could wait no longer.

His lean face, she thought perceptively, was hard and relentless. He had not appeared at ease at all during the evening, and he had not looked her way as he usually did when she left the room.

She had to stifle her uneasy thoughts and endure another half-hour in the hot drawing-room, listening to Barbara's prattle about the gaiety of London life, and Faye's barbed questions enquiring about the work of the women in the suffragette movement.

'Those poor, silly dears?' said Barbara acidly, clearly put out by the interruption. 'No one takes the slightest notice of them—forever in trouble with the police. Now, what was I saying? Oh, yes, at Henley this year I had the pleasure of being presented to His Majesty — such a charming man! And, although I say it myself, I do believe he found me the same. . .well, we shall see!'

The unspoken suggestion that the King might consider her as a possible candidate for a royal liaison made Aunt Estelle snort irascibly and say loudly that she intended to have an early night.

'Willie, get up,' she ordered. 'It's time we were in bed. Say goodnight now. . .' The old lady turned to Lady Challoner, adding in a voice that clearly did not care that it also reached Barbara's ears, 'The world is not what it was, my dear. I do not care for it very much nowadays. At least we Victorians knew how to behave. . .'

In her quiet bedroom much later, Patti listened to the house settling down for the night. She had seen John Curtis enjoying a last cigar on the terrace, while Robert and Arnold Fraser disappeared into the study, and her hand had immediately flown to her bodice, where Grandfather's crumpled note seemed to be burning into her flesh.

Before she eventually slept, she came to a decision. She must speak to Robert alone, and she must do so very soon. She could not go on with this terrible, threatening scrap of evidence destroying her peace of mind.

CHAPTER ELEVEN

DELIBERATELY, it seemed to Patti, Robert avoided her eyes as, morning prayers ended, they turned their chairs back to the table and went to the sideboard to help themselves from the many hot dishes awaiting them.

Only the younger members of the house party were present, the elder guests and Lady Challoner preferring to breakfast in their rooms. Patti smiled stiffly across the table at Barbara Latimer, and was thankful when Faye and Stephen continued the badinage they had been carrying on since yesterday afternoon. It gave her a chance of sitting quietly and observing Robert.

He immersed himself in conversation with Arnold Fraser and John Curtis, and the three of them appeared to take no notice of their companions at the table. Until Barbara sighed loudly, and said, as if to no one in particular, 'Mornings are so tedious, don't you think? Only the evenings bring enjoyment, I find. . .'

Faye turned away from the chuckling conversation she was having with Stephen, and looked at his sister wickedly. 'Then perhaps you should follow Aunt Estelle's example, Barbara, and spend an extra hour or two upstairs. . .'

Barbara's fine eyes narrowed and Patti was ready for a swift reply which, she felt sure, would effectively silence Faye, when Robert intervened, his voice silkily polite.

'Now, now, ladies! Don't let's spoil a perfectly good breakfast by arguing.' He smiled, very much the head of the family now, no longer the concentrating businessman. Looking around the table, he added, 'Let me suggest how you might spend the morning, Barbara — and Faye — and you, too, Patti. . .' His direct glance drew her back into the circle of the family group, and she felt a glow as she saw the gleam of a smile lighten the dark eyes. 'You will repair to your rooms and spend the next two hours titivating for the village fête this afternoon! Your best hats and prettiest gowns, if you please — the villagers look forward to the Challoner-and-company performance each year, you know!'

As if by magic, the unpleasant atmosphere died, and Faye and Barbara both laughed. Even dour Arnold Fraser, noted Patti, impressed, managed a smile. She thought him a particularly unfriendly and unattractive guest — why on earth had Robert invited him?

But Faye was saying brightly, 'My year would hold no excitement at all if it weren't for the fête! Granny Hext's fortune-telling, and skittling for Tom Brimacombe's pig! To say nothing of the maypole dancing — and rides for the children on my pony, and hoop-la stalls, and — and. . .'

'And the tea tent for the old gossips!' added Robert wryly. 'So you see, my dears, you will have quite an audience to admire all your silks and satins. . .'

'I shall wear my new white gown with the broderie anglaise. And you, Stephen?' Faye grinned mischievously at her neighbour, stolidly eating his kipper. 'You must hang on to your topper, you know — all the village lads will be planning to knock it off with the Aunt Sally balls!'

'As usual, I shall look the very epitome of current fashion. No topper, but my newest straw boater. . .' Stephen's affected voice paused, as, in the middle of filleting his fish, he turned to stare, shocked, at Faye. 'You're not serious, I hope my darling? Horrid little brats! Perhaps I should take my sword stick with me, just in case —!'

Barbara cut in languorously. 'Dear old boy, you will have Robert at your side as protector. . .' Calculated charm softened her voice into a seductive murmur. 'I know he won't allow anything nasty to happen to one of his guests; Robert is always such a *wonderful* host.'

Patti watched the dark, almond-shaped eyes slide an enticing glance at Robert, sitting tall and unruffled at the top of the table. She wondered what she might do if he returned that look — if he showed affection for Barbara — and for that moment her heartbeat slowed. If Robert were to love someone else, then her whole life would mean nothing. Nothing at all.

But his cool voice restored a measure of hope to her dismay. 'And you are always such a flatterer, Barbara. Would it be rude to enquire if the compliment is truly meant, or not?'

Barbara's answering laugh, musical though it was, held, Patti thought, with rising pleasure, a note that made it sound false. 'You naughty man! Always teasing. . .' Suddenly she turned in her chair, eyes flashing maliciously towards Patti, sitting beside her. 'I'm sure you have discovered that same nasty trait in Robert, too, have you not, Miss Nevill? Such a tease. One never knows when he is telling the truth! But perhaps he hasn't bothered to try it on you. . .' Looking away, her smile completed the implication that such a little nobody as this long-lost cousin deserved nothing but the very lowliest of dutiful family attention.

Patti, feeling the quick rage rise inside her, was about to snap back an answer when Robert cut in, forcefully. 'I refute the idea entirely, Barbara. Neither you, nor Patti, has any reason to label me so unpleasantly. Yes, I may tease — just occasionally — but I am no hypocrite.'

He looked away from Barbara, straight into Patti's wide, surprised eyes. She thought he smiled, briefly, just a flash of wry warmth for her alone, but could not be sure. For then the moment was gone, and he was looking back at Faye, asking with concern, 'And how is Mother today? Not unwell again, I hope?'

Faye shook her head casually. 'I said good morning to her before I came down, and she seems well. But the night was so hot — this horrid sultry weather doesn't agree with her, and she thought she would rest in order to be ready for the fête.'

'Yes. If only we could have a really good storm and get this thunder out of the atmosphere.' Impatiently Robert pushed back his chair, and his eyes sought those of Arnold Fraser.

'But not yet Robert!' said Faye cheerfully. 'I can't bear it if the entire afternoon is washed out by rain. And my new dress is stiff with starch — I shall look like a walking ghost if it gets wet!'

Her laughter was infectious, and the rest of the meal passed uneventfully. When everyone went their separate ways, Patti saw Robert and Arnold Fraser, in deep conversation, leaving the room together while John Curtis disappeared into the garden. Although Fraser had not said a word to her since he arrived, she noticed that he turned his head to look in her direction; his eyes, she thought uneasily, were cold and disapproving.

And then she fled towards the kitchen, knowing that Lady Challoner would expect her to make quite sure that all was progressing satisfactorily in her absence. She was kept busy for the rest of the morning, her thoughts filled with mundane matters.

But, when she was dressing for luncheon and adjusting her new pale green straw hat with the silk roses around the crown, Robert's image slid into her mind, dismissing everything else. She gave herself a last critical glance in the long pier-mirror, and thought smugly that she was wise not to try and compete with Barbara Latimer's sophistication. Robert had been so right, she reflected, with a wistful flash of memory; this simple muslin print dress certainly gave her an old-fashioned look, one more in keeping with a homely village féte than the Bond Street magnificence she had first thought of wearing — the gown that Robert had thought so unsuitable for the country. . .

What would he say when he saw her in this avowed favourite? she wondered. Would he even notice her? Once the divine Barbara was clinging to his arm, her perfume enveloping him and her whispering, flirtatious nonsense filling his ears, would he remember her, his unsophisticated, uninteresting and very distant cousin?

Before leaving the room, again Patti tucked Grandfather's letter down her bodice. It contained all the dismaying renewal of the old family conflict that she hated, but she could not leave it hidden in the drawer. She had a strange thought that Madame Léonie deserved better than to be once again forgotten and neglected. Jules's family had rescued her from the deserted château garden; Patti knew with dogged certainty that, now that the truth had been discovered at last, poor Madame Léonie must never again be ignored and lost.

Somehow, she promised herself, the truth must be brought into the open. But not this afternoon—oh, please God, she thought, suddenly wary and full of premonition, let the afternoon be a happy one! For if the threatening thunder storm broke, as surely it must do very soon, she felt instinctively that a similar storm would break in the family. And, she feared, all over poor Madame Léonie...

Luncheon was over and the guests walked slowly through the garden, towards the village green. Soon the afternoon was in full, noisy swing, and Patti's spirits soared as she chatted to Beth and James, who had come to join in the fun.

'Shall we skittle for the pig?' asked Patti enthusiastically. 'Just think Beth—how wonderful if you won a little porker.'

'No, thank you, dearest, my own little porker will soon be keeping me more than busy!'

Beth's good humour brought Patti a renewal of sisterly affection. 'Are you really well?' she asked, her voice unsteady. 'You're not working too hard? What does the doctor say?'

Beth pressed her hands reassuringly. 'Stop fussing, my dear! Everything is going along nicely. James is wonderful and looks after me so well.' Her glance at her smiling, watchful husband was almost more than Patti could bear in her present emotional state. To have a husband who clearly adored you... Then she thought of Robert and sighed. But not for long. Beth must have no added worries; she must not guess that life at Porphyry Court was anything less than easy and uncomplicated. She gripped Beth's hand and changed the subject.

'Let's have our fortunes told! Granny Hext is very gifted, Faye says.'

'You go if you like, dearest.' Firmly Beth disengaged herself. 'I prefer to throw a few gentle hoop-la rings. We'll meet you later for tea.'

She and James disappeared into the crowd of laughing, chattering villagers, and Patti, looking up, suddenly caught a glimpse of Robert escorting Barbara around the various stalls. He was smiling down into Barbara's flirtatious eyes, and Patti felt her stomach knot with wretchedness. Bleakly, she found her way to the tent where Grannie Hext, dressed in outlandish shawls and huge brass earrings, smiled toothlessly at her, laying hands on what was quite clearly, thought Patti, a disguised goldfish bowl.

'Sit down, maid. Cross the gypsy's palm with silver. Now let's see what the crystal do say. . .'

Patti scored Granny's hand with a shilling and then sat back, a little apprehensive, despite her outward calm. When the old woman began muttering about a loving country upbringing, Patti sat up straighter. 'An ole man with a passion — a story o' some kind? Like a fairy-story, on'y real. . .'

'Granny, you're a wizard! Tell me more!'

Faded eyes searched Patti's. 'This story, m'dear, rules yer life, so it does. An' gives 'ee heartache along the way. But now, what else can I see? A tall man. Strong. Big. Oooh, mighty powerful — but hard. Like what they do say, eh?' Granny grinned at her over the crystal. 'Tall, dark an' 'andsome! But you can't just take his love, see, maid; no, you gotta give...that's what love is. Loving is giving. Not taking. An' now — well, look, the crystal's gone cloudy. No more, lovie, not today...' Granny's eyes grew keen. 'Worth more'n that shilling, eh, maid?'

Offering her thanks and an extra coin, Patti left the tent, squinting into the suddenly brilliant sunshine, her feet hardly touching the ground. Granny's words rang in her ears and she was still smiling beatifically when she bumped into Faye. Green eyes gleamed wickedly. 'Had your fortune told?'

'Yes!' enthused Patti. 'What an amazing old woman! Told me so much that I *know* is true...'

Faye snorted derisively. 'A lot of rubbish, more like! She's well known for making money out of her so-called gift.' Faye paused, searching Patti's startled eyes. 'Didn't you know that her granddaughter is your sister Beth's maid? Cissie feeds all the local tittle-tattle to Gran! That's how the famous gift works! Oh, but have I disappointed you, Patti? Too bad!'

Patti watched Faye's pale eyebrows arch sardonically before she turned briskly away, calling back to Stephen as she did so. As Patti went towards the tea tent, her thoughts jostled uncomfortably. Tall, dark and handsome; a fairy-story that would bring heartache — had Cissie known all that? Was it rubbish? Or a flash of true inspiration? Would she ever know? But, despite her uncertainty, one small bit of Granny's wisdom remained, dominating her mind; love was giving, not taking. Patti knew that that, at least, was right.

Saturday night dinner was the *pièce de résistance* of the house party programme and Patti dressed very carefully, knowing that all the gowns worn by the ladies this evening would be elaborate and expensive. When she joined the others in the drawing-room for sherry before dinner, she saw she had been right. Lady Challoner wore an indigo velvet gown of great elegance that subtly emphasised her pale skin and beautiful bone-structure, while Aunt Estelle surely outdid them all in her old-fashioned but magnificently boned and corsetted sway-back dress of black brocade, with glittering jet at ears and throat that made Barbara Latimer's sparkling diamonds look tawdry and cheap.

Patti's own lavender-coloured dress was the one she had first worn to Porphyry Court; in her earlier days she had considered it the last word in smartness, but now, seeing Barbara Latimer sweeping into the room in her lustrous cream silk gown rich with gorgeous draperies, she knew she must look very much the long-lost country cousin beside such ravishing splendour.

But Robert, apparently, did not share her opinion; he came to her quietly, without drawing attention to himself, and said, in a low voice that only she could hear, 'You look lovely, Patti.'

The unexpected words throbbed through her mind, and for a second she was too surprised to answer. Quickly he went on, dark brow winging upwards and eyes dancing. 'Did you enjoy the fête? I saw you heading for Granny Hext's tent — I trust she foretold a happy future for you, little cousin?'

Incensed by the hateful reminder that he had seen her while he was with Barbara, and by what she took to be near-mockery in his words, she asked snappily, 'Are you making fun of me, Robert?'

Abruptly his expression changed to extreme soberness. 'I would never do that, Patti.' His eyes searched hers and she had the extraordinary thought that he understood her dismay.

She bit her lip, taken aback. 'I'm sorry.' She bowed her head to avoid that raking gaze. 'It's just that—well, I was told things that seemed to be true. Until Faye said——'

'Ah!' His voice deepened into even greater intensity, and Patti looked up in surprise. 'So little sister has deflated all your dreams, has she? I fear Faye is a realist, like me—it's a heavy burden to bear Patti.'

She thought she saw an unexpectedly wistful expression in his dark eyes, and longed wildly to reassure him. 'But sometimes, Robert, dreams *do* come true. . .' If only she could let out her pent-up feelings—tell him he was part of those dreams, confide in him her confusion about Madame Léonie. . .

He looked down at her without speaking, and she realised how tangled his own emotions had become. She wished she dared to put a hand on his arm, but knew she could not take the risk. This was a shared, extraordinary moment, and she must not spoil it. But knowledge had come to her—in his hesitant, deep eyes she saw the conflict that he kept to himself so closely. Faye had spoken about it—the business problem Arnold Fraser had revealed, and her part in it, whatever that might be. Clearly Robert knew something that she did not. And he knew, also, that soon he must disclose it. A new warmth began to disperse some of Patti's old uneasiness, for the understanding that now filled her was of Robert's reluctance to heap more trouble upon her head. He had some sort of feeling for her, hidden though it still was—a feeling, Patti sensed sagely, that went far deeper than the first attraction for a chit of a girl who proved to be a 'temptation' as he had so scornfully called her.

But here, in the intimate corner of the room where they stood together, unnoticed by the chatting group around the fireplace, she felt a new maturity enclosing her. And was able to say calmly, and without disclosing the throb of emotion that raged within her, 'Dreams are able to balance reality, Robert — have you ever considered that?'

She hoped fervently for an answer that would prove their further understanding of one another, for he still looked at her with a softness she had never seen before. But then Barbara's tinkling laugh exploded through the quiet hum of general conversation, and abruptly Robert's mood changed. He stepped back, frowning, and saying harshly, 'For you, perhaps, Patti; but not, I fear, for me.'

And then, from across the room, Patti saw Lady Challoner signalling to him that it was time to go in to dinner. He bowed stiffly before going over to Barbara to offer her his arm. Patti, aware of her suddenly swimming eyes, accepted John Curtis's presence beside her with searing disappointment, and hardly knew how she responded to his polite and friendly remarks during the ensuing meal.

Back in the drawing-room after dinner, with Patti feeling exhausted from the effort of trying to keep up a brave and social appearance despite her raging distress, Lady Challoner requested her to play for them.

She was glad of the opportunity to have some solitude; and, although Faye and Stephen and Barbara impolitely talked all through her performance, she felt easier of mind as she ended her first piece. Robert and his unkind words were never far from her thoughts, and so, as she began to play again, her choice of piece naturally fell on the Chopin mazurka which he had requested before.

As if she had known it would happen, Robert, Arnold Fraser and John Curtis entered the room as she played. She was aware of Fraser going to the fireplace, where Lady Challoner and Aunt Estelle sat, and then felt her senses tingle; Robert was coming to stand in the bow of the piano, looking at her, sharing the music with her, the old chemistry reaching out to make her heart beat faster, her fingers play with more expertise than ever before.

When she finished, spontaneous clapping sounded from down the room, and Barbara's lazy drawl said, indelicately, 'Bravo! You'd make a fortune on the halls, my dear.'

Patti ignored the suggestion, for Robert was looking at her very intently. He smiled, and she saw unexpected pride fill his face for a moment. 'Thank you,' he said quietly, and then looked towards the vase of red roses that Lady Challoner had said were his new products.

She followed his glance as he told her, 'You've arranged them beautifully, Patti. Curtis, who is a potential customer of mine, has already commented on them; in fact he's given me a very large order — and all due to your talent in exhibiting them so splendidly...'

Patti discovered a lump in her throat. She said huskily, 'I'm so glad...'

Robert's eyes deepened and his voice fell a tone. He leaned a little nearer, so that she felt the warmth of his breath, as he said slowly, and hesitantly, 'You and I together, Patti — with our combined love of roses —

surely, we should be able to—to...' Abruptly he stopped, but she thought she read the question in his searching glance.

'Mend our differences, Robert? Oh, but how I wish we could...' Her cheeks were warm and she knew her heart was in her smile.

For a long, wonderful moment they looked at each other and then, with terrible dismay, she saw the return of his familiar frown and narrowed eyes. 'Patti,' he said harshly, stepping away and looking over his shoulder, as if in a hurry to be gone, 'there are things we have to discuss. But not now. I must attend to my guests.'

Alone, Patti watched him pass among them, offering a word here, a humorous comment there, leaving his aunt and uncle, his mother, his sister and his London friends smiling and amiably nodding as he finally offered his excuses to withdraw.

Once he and Arnold Fraser had left the room it was some time before Patti felt controlled enough to rejoin the rest of the company, who spent the remainder of the evening playing whist, or—in Barbara's, Faye's and Stephen's case—going to the billiard-room to play a noisy, competitive game that seemed to last for ever.

At last the house was quiet. Aunt Estelle and Uncle Willie had gone upstairs to bed and Lady Challoner had soon followed them. Patti fancied that Barbara, too, declaring herself quite exhausted and making one of her grand exits, had disappeared to her room. Where Faye, Stephen and John Curtis were, she had no idea and cared even less.

A small but insistent voice in her head urged her to go to Robert's study to see if she could find him alone, for surely Mr Fraser must also have retired by now. It was very nearly midnight, and Patti knew she could not sleep yet.

Grandfather's letter pressed uncomfortably inside her bodice. It seemed to be demanding to be taken out and shown to Robert—and she knew she could stand the suspense no longer. Gathering her strength, Patti went down the dark passage towards his study. A gleam of light filtered through the crack between door and floorboard. So he was still there—she listened for a few seconds and then, hearing no sound, knocked a little uncertainly

'Come in.' Robert's voice was quick and low.

She entered, closing the door and looking around her. At first she saw only Robert sitting in the chair behind his desk, face lit by the lamp on the bookcase, the immediate circle of papers spread about his desk visible in the arc of light glowing down from the smaller lamp.

'Robert?' she said, her voice unnaturally high and agitated.

He rose, frowning at her. 'What is it, Patti?' She had hoped for a warmer reception, and the cool tone of his response momentarily dismayed her. But then she felt again the pressure of the scrap of paper inside her gown, and resolution grew stronger.

'Robert, I have to speak to you about—about a certain matter which—which concerns us both, and which——'

There was a clearing of a throat in the darkness which hung beyond the glow of the lamp. 'If I am at all *de trop*,' said the nasal voice of Arnold Fraser, 'I will be glad to leave you, Challoner.'

Patti nearly jumped out of her skin. Turning, she

stared into the shadows. Her distress was clear, and Fraser added, with a suspicion of wry amusement, 'I fear I have startled you, Miss Nevill. I apologise. Allow me to withdraw.' Scraping back his chair, he emerged into the lamplight, stockily built, heavily bearded, and cold-eyed.

Patti was embarrassed. 'No, no!' she said wildly, stepping back towards the door. 'I had no idea! I mean. . .'

Robert moved very fast. She had forgotten how swiftly he could do so; there one moment, beside her the next. His hand gripped her arm and led her back into the brilliance of the desk light. 'Sit down, Patti,' he ordered heavily. 'And you, too, Fraser. I have a feeling that what Miss Nevill wishes to discuss may well involve you as well as me. . .' He paused, and by the impatient, slightly grating tone of his voice Patti recognised that he was in no mood to waste time or energy on the niceties, either of speech or action. 'Well, Patti? We're waiting. . .'

She took a last, hopeless look into his unfathomable eyes and bowed her head. This was not the way she had imagined the conversation would go. Her voice, when finally she managed to speak, was low. 'It's about—about roses. . .'

'Quite. And what have you to tell us—about roses?' Robert sounded almost sarcastic. He added quickly, 'Fraser is also a grower. We speak the same language, have the same troubles. And his visit here this weekend is due to a problem that involves us both. So speak freely, Patti, whatever it is that you are trying to say. . .'

She felt Fraser's gaze upon her face, sensed the critical manner in which they awaited her revelation.

And knew instantly that nothing would make her speak of Grandfather and Madame Léonie while Fraser was here, so cold, so impatiently awaiting that intimate little story which involved only the family.

It was with great surprise, therefore, that she heard herself recounting not Grandfather's story, but an even older tale. 'It's about the Empress Josephine! Napoleon's wife. Just a story I read. . .'

Her voice tailed away, and Robert said stonily, holding her eyes with his, 'You mentioned it before. That day we were in the glasshouse. . .'

Patti felt the colour rising in her cheeks. 'Yes. Well. . .' She took a quick breath and launched herself into feverish story-telling. 'Well, Josephine loved roses, as you do. As I do. And she discovered this wonderful painter, called Pierre-Joseph Redoubté; he had huge, grotesque hands — the hands of a navvy, they said — but he shared her love of roses, and — and when she was ill — the very night before she died, in fact — he came to her room and offered to paint her roses for her. . .'

Patti's voice died. Neither man spoke nor intimated in any way that they were interested in what she was telling them. She went on, a little wildly, 'And, according to the story, poor Josephine smiled at him and croaked — because her throat hurt so much, you see — "Please do paint them. But don't come too near, for you may catch my complaint." And — and she died the same night. . .'

Silence met the end of the story. She swallowed, to ease the tightness in her throat, and kept her eyes on Robert's hands, clasped on the desk in the circle of lamplight, big, and well scrubbed, but with slight earth stains around the base of his nails and across the knuckles. She had felt them in many moods — hard, on her arms and shoulders; gentle, stroking her hair, caressing her cheek, spanning her waist, spread about her back, stroking her, forcing her body to mould into his. . .

With infinite difficulty, she brought her thoughts back to this moment. The silence held and she was still looking at Robert's hands. Big, but not grotesque, like poor Redoubté's. . .

'I think,' Robert said quietly, 'that it is time for us all to retire. It's been a trying day. . .' Rising, he came around the desk to lean down and take her hands. Pointedly, over his shoulder, as he drew her up from her chair, he said 'Goodnight, Fraser. We'll talk again tomorrow, when, I hope, we'll clear up the matter for good. . .'

Patti understood exactly what he meant. She and Robert were, at last, about to have the confrontation which she sensed could end only in even more hostility. She tensed, and took several deep breaths while Fraser bid her goodnight and left the room.

Alone together, they looked at each other as Robert returned to stand beside his chair. Patti said forlornly, 'I'm sorry. I don't know why I said all that—I should have gone when I saw he was here. . .'

She was surprised at Robert's next words. 'Come and look at this,' he said and, lifting the lamp, carried it to the far wall of the study, where he stood looking at the picture Patti had admired when she was here alone.

Looking up at the immaculate engraving of Pierre-Joseph's work, she read the small print beneath the rose. 'Souvenir de la Malmaison,' she whispered unsteadily. 'Josephine's rose.'

Robert said heavily, 'Indeed; Josephine's rose. And now you are going to tell me about another rose, Patti

Nevill; the one called Madame Léonie. The rose that is a sport of Josephine's. Madame Léonie, which belongs to *me*.'

Strong hands turned her so that she was forced to face him. His eyes were deep and seemed to contain a flicker of fire that increased her dismay. Patti shivered, seeking to find the courage to challenge those egotistical words.

'Your rose?' she whispered at last. 'I don't think so. That's why I came here — to show you this...' She drew Grandfather's letter from the front of her gown and handed it across the space that divided them.

Robert read it, his expression blank. Slowly he began to pace the room, finally halting beneath the portrait of his uncle, Sir Archibald. Something caught at Patti's mind, and she looked behind her. Yes, as she had sensed, she stood directly beneath Grandfather's portrait... The fact sent a shaft of strength through her and she raised her head defiantly.

At last Robert looked at her. He let the scrap of crumpled paper fall on to his desk as he said disdainfully, 'I fear this so-called claim to ownership doesn't impress me in the least. No matter what you think——' abruptly his lip curled '— and no matter to what ends you have gone to find it, it means nothing at all.'

She could not stand such scorn and arrogance. Words threw themselves from her lips. 'Of course it does! It means what I've always believed — that Madame Léonie belongs to the Nevills! To *my* family, Robert...'

He gave her a hard, narrowed stare, and, with angry despair, she watched his lips set in a rigid line. 'No, Patti. That is quite incorrect. The rose is *mine* — and mine alone.'

CHAPTER TWELVE

THEY glared at each other in what, to Patti, seemed the greatest show of hostility that had ever been engendered between them. Then Robert returned to his chair behind the desk and looked at her briefly, as he ordered, 'Sit down, Patti.'

Haughtily, hating his arrogance, she obeyed, and watched him glance down at the scrap of paper he had thrown away so contemptuously. Then he leaned back in his chair, putting his elbows on the desk, arching his powerful fingers, and staring coldly at her from behind them.

'I have several things to tell you. . .' His voice was flat and she realised painfully that his very harshness concealed as much raging emotion as she herself felt. She nodded grudgingly, and he went on, 'First of all, you must know that Arnold Fraser came down this weekend especially to tell me of the unpleasant rumour being generated throughout the rose-growing world, and which will no doubt soon reach the newspapers.' Abruptly he stopped, meeting her apprehensive, startled eyes. 'The rumour is one which concerns you, Patti. . .'

'What on earth are you talking about, Robert?'

He frowned and inspected his fingernails. 'You won't deny that you were the late Miss Clarke's confidante? In fact, not only her secretary, but her nearest — I might almost say, her only — friend?'

'She had no family.' Patti was reeling, trying

wretchedly to recall forgotten facts which seemed to have no relevance to Robert's set face and accusatory words. 'Yes, I suppose we were quite close — she was very kind to me. . .'

'So you would agree that you could be the only possible source of the story which Miss Clarke's last published article has proclaimed to the world?'

Patti swallowed tightly. 'Robert, I have no idea what you are talking about!'

'I think you do.' His eyes darkened, visibly raging now, although his voice remained steady. He rose to pace the floor in the familiar restlessness. Stopping, he glared down at her. 'You told her about Madame Léonie, didn't you Patti?'

'Oh!' Patti's hands flew to her face as she remembered Miss Clarke's last few weeks. Ill, exhausted and depressed, the old lady had pleaded for entertainment of all sorts to distract her. Trying to please her, Patti had read well-loved books, played gramophone records, sung childish songs they both remembered, and then, racking her brains as the requests continued, even told Miss Clarke Grandfather's romantic tale of his beloved old rose. She had, indeed, told her about Madame Léonie de Sange, the sport of a rose that Empress Josephine of Malmaison had once loved. . .

Now she stared up at Robert, and said shakily, 'I did. But it never entered my mind that she would tell anyone else. She was so ill, you see. . .'

'But apparently not too ill to want to write yet another article.' Clearly Robert was furious. 'Surely you saw it? Saw her notes? Sent it to the magazine?'

'No.' Patti jumped up. The need to explain and clear herself was all-important. She turned to Robert, who halted his pacing and now stood staring down at her.

'Miss Clarke gave me an afternoon off—I remember now! And when I returned, the maid said she had been so much better, she had been writing. . .but I never imagined—I mean, she was so ill. How could she have possibly have found the strength to write another article?'

Robert dismissed the question angrily. 'Yet plainly she did. And now it is published and the story is out.' His eyes searched hers furiously. 'Are you certain you didn't know? But you knew where to look for this ridiculous scrap of letter, didn't you? In fact, ever since you arrived here I daresay you have been trying to find evidence of your Grandfather's totally incorrect story about Madame Léonie! I suppose that's why you came . . .why you appeared so pleasant and friendly, so—so. . .'

She saw his lips close uncompromisingly and felt her own anger grow almost uncontrollable. 'So *tempting*, were you about to say, Robert?' she demanded, her voice deep with passion. 'How dare you accuse me like this? I've done nothing wrong at all—but now I'm certainly going to use Grandfather's letter to right the wrong you and your beastly Challoner uncle have allowed to continue for all these years! I shall publicly demand an apology from you! I shall. . .' And then, watching his eyes, her furious words died away.

He was smiling, an unpleasant, hurtful smile that made her pause before finding the courage to ask, 'Why are you looking like that Robert?'

Thoughtfully, he moved one hand towards the gold chain that swung across his waistcoat. Following the movement, she saw his fingers bring out a gold hunter from a concealed pocket, and slowly separate something else that hung beside it. He brought the bronze medallion up for her to see, saying very quietly, and with plain triumph in his deep, rich voice, 'That letter, with its unsigned disclaimer——'

She jumped in instantly. 'But it *is* signed! Your uncle——'

'Nonsense. That scribble? No one could ever prove that was Archibald's signature. But this, Patti—this medal, which he won when Madame Léonie was exhibited in 1892—*does* prove ownership, and was left to me. So I think you'll have to agree, my dear, that my claim is infinitely stronger than yours. . .'

Unable to bear the tone of victorious condescension in his words, Patti snatched the medal from his hand and stared at it, frantically seeking a way out of the problem. She held it nearer the lamp, reading the worn, engraved words with difficulty. '"Madame Léonie de Sange, winner of the Rose of the Year Award, London, 1892."' Suddenly her eyes sparkled. 'But this doesn't say to *whom* it was awarded! The medal belongs to Madame Léonie—your Uncle Archibald doesn't even get a mention.'

Robert took it from her hands with great deliberation and stared, in his turn, at the engraved words. Then he looked up into her eyes. 'You're right. But neither does it proclaim Grandfather Nevill as the winner. . .'

For a long, stretching moment they stared at each other challengingly. Then Patti's eyes dropped and she stepped away, unable to stand the tension of his nearness any longer.

'We're letting it happen all over again,' she said numbly, looking up at the two portraits on opposite sides of the study. 'Grandfather and Uncle Archibald, fighting their battles — and now, you and I, Robert, doing just the same. It goes on and on. . .'

Suddenly there was a movement and Robert was at her side. He grabbed her hands and pulled her close to him, until her head tilted back and she was forced to stare up into his passionate eyes.

'But it needn't, Patti,' he said between gritted teeth. 'You have no interest in the business — *my* business. What do you care that your foolishness has ruined my business? All you want is to be able to fulfil the foolish, romantic dreams with which that silly old man filled your impressionable head. You only want to call Madame Léonie *yours*. . . Why can't you let the matter drop? Adopt another rose, if you must!' Abruptly, his passion disappeared. He smiled, a quirk of his mouth, and let her hands go, as he added wryly, 'Did you know that roses are nearly always called after real people?'

Patti let out her breath in a long, silent gust, staring at him with wide eyes. His mood of near-violence had stimulated rather than frightened her. She began to long for him to touch her again, to look at her once more with that same, exciting passion. . . Unsteadily, she murmured, 'I never thought, but yes, I suppose it would be quite an honour, to leave one's name to posterity. . .'

She watched him pace away, as if to distance himself from her. 'Quite!' His voice held a note of amusement now. 'And considering that Madame Léonie was in fact a wicked but beautiful courtesan in Napoleon's court, leaving her name to posterity as she did was an honour indeed!'

'A courtesan? Oh. . .' Patti laughed away the instinctive embarrassment that coloured her cheeks. 'And did Grandfather and Great-Uncle Archibald know her?'

she asked, trying to keep Robert talking. She guessed that he, too, was now trying to suppress his deep-felt emotions and bring the situation back to normality.

'I fancy she was a little before their time,' he replied, with a twinkle in his eyes.

Patti was slowly feeling more relaxed. Robert's rage had been enlightening and she was beginning to realise that he would never give up his claim to the old rose. And yet she knew that, in his heart of hearts, he had no more desire to keep the conflict going than she had herself. Somehow, between them, they must find a resolution. . .

She wandered around the room, until she came to the Redoubté engraving on the wall. Looking up at it, she mused quietly, 'Poor Madame Léonie. I don't suppose she ever imagined that one day she would cause such a terrible rift in the family that loved her so well — and tried so hard to keep her name alive.' Turning, she looked over her shoulder at Robert, who stood pensively watching her every movement.

Behind him, Great-Uncle Archibald stared out of his portrait, challenging Grandfather on the opposite wall. Patti trembled. 'Robert,' she whispered plaintively, 'what are we going to do?'

He didn't answer for a while and she watched, hopelessly, as his eyes grew deep and hard, his shoulders slowly more square as he spread his muscular body in a defiant stance. When he spoke at last, his voice was as musical as ever, but the message was clear. 'That, my dear Patti, is for you to decide,' he said slowly. 'While you continue to challenge me about the old rose, I fear there is nothing that can be done to solve the problem. And, in the meantime. . .' He took a step towards her and instinctively she drew back, for his gaze narrowed and she knew anger had returned. 'In the meantime, Patti Nevill, you have ruined my business.'

'How can I have done?' she cried nervously.

'You've blackened my reputation,' he told her grimly, standing only a few inches away and glaring at her with such ferocity that she shrank back. 'Who will ever believe now that I, personally — one of the famous feuding Challoners you've told the world about — can ever be trusted to breed another rose, once such a stigma is attached to my name?'

Patti winced. To hear the truth put in such uncompromising words was more painful than she could bear. Suddenly it came to her that he was right and that she was indeed to blame. She bit her lip and tried to avoid his searing gaze. 'I didn't mean. . .' she whispered miserably. 'Oh, Robert, surely you must know that I had no intention. . .'

But he wasn't listening. He was pacing again, up and down, backwards and forwards, until abruptly he halted by the desk, reached down, rummaging among some papers, and picked up a letter which he thrust beneath her nose. 'Read this,' he ordered harshly and she could do no more than stare down at the slanting writing, not understanding a word of what the paper contained.

Numbly she shook her head. 'I — can't. . .' Tears threatened and she wished with all her throbbing heart that she could run. But her legs refused to move, because he was looking at her in a way that almost paralysed her.

Silence built up between them, powerful as never before, menacing and potentially dangerous. As if to emphasise the fact, a rumble of thunder murmured in the far distance of the night. Robert's piercing gaze never wavered, searching her pale face with a cold clarity that she found infinitely more disturbing than his familiar outbursts of raging anger.

'Read it, Patti,' he gritted and moved restlessly from behind the desk to the window, where he stopped and looked back at her. Abruptly he took a step nearer, and then halted.

'Robert?' she whispered, and there was a huskiness in her voice, a fading of all her resolution, as desperately she tried to balance things in her exhausted and confused mind. 'Robert?' she said again, but got no further.

He was so close that she could smell the fumes of cigar smoke and wine on his warm, rapid breath. Longingly, she looked at his lips, tightly compressed, as if restraining the passion that she knew lurked behind them. She stared into his eyes, dark chocolate-brown, lit by an inner, compelling fire that caught at hers, ensnaring them in a gaze that excited her, made her traitorous body tremble, disturbing the even tenor of her breath, making the blood race through her veins. . .

He said something—short, monosyllabic, fierce—which she did not quite hear. All she knew was that their passion shared a common deepness, that the past had entangled them in a web of deceit which was now compounded by fatal attraction.

And then, even as she watched and waited, longing, but still with the small voice of distrust whispering at the back of her mind, he drew away from her. His eyes narrowed, became pools of unfathomable moodiness, reflecting her own suspicion.

'There's something else,' he muttered, flinging himself back into the pacing routine. 'Jules. . .'

The name split the charged atmosphere and she sank into the chair beside her. What now? She trembled. Surely she had suffered enough punishment this evening? Was there yet another accusation to be meted out? It took a little while and an immense search for courage before she could face Robert and say, in a steady voice, 'And what about Jules?'

He had sat down opposite her. Now he threw the letter across the desk, his forcefulness making her pick it up and look, once more, at the slanting writing covering the paper.

Patti could make no sense of it, until she saw the one word. Again, that name. Jules. Abruptly his sly, prurient smile was there in front of her closed eyes. His grasping hands, and — until this moment forgotten — his threat to get his revenge.

'I can't read it,' she muttered, turning away her head. 'Tell me — if you must. . .'

Numbly she saw Robert's powerful, suntanned hand retrieve the letter and smooth it out on the blotter in front of him. He looked away from her pale face, and began to read, in a hard unemotional voice.

'"My son, Jules, agrees with me that we no longer wish to continue our business connection, as clearly, according to the reports we have heard, you, Robert, are guilty of cultivating a rose of which you are not the true owner. Furthermore. . ."'

Robert paused, lifting his head to meet Patti's eyes, his own deep with bitter distrust.

'Furthermore, I understand that your cousin, Miss Patricia Nevill, who we believe is the source of this information, will undoubtedly bear witness for us, if required, as to the validity of this accusation".'

Again, Robert paused. Then he added, putting down the letter, 'Signed, Edouard Lacoste.'

Silence. Patti's world reeled about her and she had no words with which to deny this most upsetting of all accusations. She stared at Robert, saw the bruised shadows below his eyes, and thought dully that his lean face had a harder set to it than she had ever seen before. She sensed the pain within him, and almost wished she could die. Idealism over Madame Léonie was one thing; betrayal was another.

Helplessly she shook her head, as she searched for some grain of truth that he would believe — for a forgotten fact that might, miraculously, save the day. Nothing came. Remorse deepened. She had ruined Robert's reputation and his business. Worse, she had forced him to believe she had withheld her love from him.

Again that growl of thunder — nearer this time — making her head jerk, her eyes widen, and the knot of misery tighten within her. And then, out of that fear and tension generated between them, a strange new energy was unexpectedly born — like the lightning that flickered weirdly beyond the uncurtained window.

Suddenly Patti was able to get up, to look at him very directly, and say, in a steady voice that she hardly recognised as her own, 'I acknowledge that I am guilty of telling Miss Clarke about Madame Léonie, and I'm sorry Robert, more sorry than I can possibly say — but I will not admit to this! This. . .' She stared scornfully at Monsieur Lacoste's letter on the desk. 'This disgusting untruth! Surely you know enough about me,

Robert, to understand the sort of woman I am? Foolish, without doubt, at times—but never unfaithful to you. Never. *Never...*'

Her voice broke and she turned, hurrying to the door, only one thought in her tormented mind: to escape, to think things through, to decide what to do next. *To get away from Robert.*

But halfway through the entrance to the study, she stopped, turned, and met his bleak eyes staring through the hazy lamplight. 'I'll prove it,' she whispered fiercely. 'Somehow I'll prove that Jules is telling a terrible lie.'

Sitting on her bed, eyes staring blindly at the scarlet poppy pattern of the wallpaper on the opposite wall, Patti slowly emerged from the bewildering mêlée of thoughts, regrets and guilt that filled her mind, and knew at last what she must do.

Two things, both difficult, but necessary. Somehow she must find the strength to carry them through, must make herself sufficiently humble to do them with sincerity and telling force. Even as her plans crystallised, she moved, going out of her door and down the darkened gallery towards Faye's room.

Her firm but subdued tap was answered almost at once. Faye, in an ivory woollen wrapper, hair braided and falling over one shoulder, looked at her in surprise. 'Whatever is it?'

'I must talk to you, Faye—please may I come in? You're not in bed yet?'

'No. I was thinking. Making plans...' Faye's guarded expression gave way to understanding. 'Come in, of course...'

Inside the pretty room, with its soft lamplight and

warm, feminine ambience, Patti was able to speak more easily. Thankful that she had a friend in whom to confide, she told Faye all that had passed between her and Robert in the last hour. 'So, you see, I have to go to France, to the Lacoste rosery,' she ended, eyes pleading for understanding and help. 'I must meet Jules—make him take back that wicked lie. As if I really *would* side with him against Robert. . .' Suddenly a sob shook her body and great weakness overcame her. Faye's hands touched her comfortingly.

'Cheer up, Patti. *I* know you love Robert, and I'm quite sure he does too, but he's so obstinate he won't admit it!' Faye's voice was tender. Then it grew crisp. 'Never mind, we'll clear it all up.'

'We, Faye?' Patti dried her eyes.

'Yes.' Faye began wandering around the room and Patti was so reminded of Robert's angry pacings that her misery subsided a little. Faye swung around, excitement making her cats' eyes gleam. 'We'll go to France together!' she said enthusiastically. 'Elsie can come—I suppose we must take her as a sop to conformity! Oh, what fun it will be! I'll organise the train tickets and the boat. . . We'll go as soon as all our guests have gone home.' She plumped herself down on the chair by the fireplace and smiled wickedly at Patti. 'What a bore this party has been! Won't it be lovely to have the divine Barbara and that weak-chinned Stephen out of the way? Such tedious people. . .'

'But I thought you and Stephen. . .'

'Certainly not!' Faye's smile switched off. 'He's only been a brief amusement—and I'm tired of that already. Paris will be much more interesting!' She jumped to her feet. 'Go to bed now, Patti, and stop worrying.

Dream of telling that awful Jules exactly what you think of him—if you don't I will!'

Patti nodded, exhausted by the maelstrom of emotions that the evening had brought with it. She smiled wearily but fondly at Faye. 'Thank you. You're being so good to me.'

Faye's thin face grew sharp, her eyes suddenly ashine with a softer light. 'I'm only trying to repay all that *you've* done for me—goodnight, Patti, dear. Sleep well. And don't worry!'

Returning to her own room, Patti reached the doorway just as a snarl of far-away thunder echoed down the long, dark gallery. Her childish fear of storms flared and her heart raced. But she slipped into her room, undressed, and went to bed with her mind still clear about the next hurdle to jump—Arnold Fraser...

She found him in the rose garden, directly after breakfast—a rotund, dark-clad figure immersed in the morning newspaper. Patti approached him silently, pausing first to pick a small, perfect cream-coloured bud rising from shiny green leaves on the wall nearby. Holding it to her nose, and smiling persuasively, she presented herself in front of the seat he occupied and held out the offering, saying lightly, 'The Glory rose, for your buttonhole, Mr Fraser—cream, to match your smart hat!'

Robert's remark that she was a temptation, with all its attributes, came to mind—yes, she was being flirtatious at this moment; she would do anything to remove the slur she had caused to be cast upon Robert's reputation. On awakening early this morning, she discovered the decision was irrevocably made.

'Mr Fraser, I have a great favour to ask of you.' Smiling as bewitchingly as she knew how, she watched the little man rise to his feet, bow, and then gesture her to the seat he had just vacated. Laboriously he re-settled himself beside her.

Granny Hext's words rang through her mind. 'Loving is giving. Not taking.' Her confidence grew, and she looked into Arnold Fraser's steady eyes without further doubt.

'Delighted to help, if I can, Miss Nevill.' He pulled his panama a little deeper over the unblinking gaze and listened in silence to her words. They stumbled at first but became clearer as her courage grew. 'You see, Mr Fraser, I have realised at last that it doesn't really matter *who* owns Madame Léonie — her continued existence is all important. And so — and so. . .' Clearing her throat, she took a deep, sustaining breath. Even now, with her mind resolutely made up, it was still hard to give in. . .

'And so, Mr Fraser, this favour I mentioned — well, it's simply to take a message to London when you return and ask the editor of *The Times* — or whichever paper you think best — to publish what I have written.'

Arnold Fraser's eyes never left her face. 'And what exactly is that message, Miss Nevill? If I am to act upon your behalf, I think I should approve the text of it.'

'Of course. Well.' Patti pulled from her pocket the letter she had spent a good hour composing before she got up this morning. Her writing was small and straight. The words rose to meet her very plainly, and her voice, as she read them, remained even despite her unsteady emotions. 'I, Patricia Nevill,' she read to the silent man beside her, 'wish to correct the story I related to Miss Edith Clarke, whose article about the ownership of the Gallica rose, Madame Léonie de Sange, I have just been told about. Although at the time I thought my grandfather, Ralph Nevill, to be the true owner of the rose, new evidence——' her voice trembled, but only for a second '—new evidence has come my way, making me reverse that decision. Now I believe Madame Léonie was, indeed, the property of my grandfather's cousin, Sir Archibald Challoner. I regret all the trouble that my inadvertent mistake has caused. And I apologise——' she stopped to swallow a lump that suddenly came into her throat '—particularly to my cousin, Sir Robert Challoner...' Her voice tailed off and she was thankful that Arnold Fraser said nothing. They sat in silence for a few moments, during which she managed to slowly regain her self-control. Then, slowly, he rose to his feet. Suddenly, he smiled down at her, touching the rosebud in his buttonhole and bending his head to sniff the glorious fragrance.

'Miss Nevill,' he said slowly, in his unemotional voice, 'allow me to say how impressed I am with your courage and honesty.'

Astonished, Patti watched him shaking his head very ponderously, as he added, 'Values so sadly lacking in today's changing world, I fear...' As she gaped at him, he lifted one hand from her lap, touched dry lips to it, and bowed, and she knew she would remember, for the rest of her life, the smile upon his plain and stolid face. 'I envy the man for whom you are doing this courageous thing, Miss Nevill.'

'Why, th-thank you, Mr Fraser.' A sudden sense of release began to flow through her and, as she watched him slowly walk back towards the house, she told herself she had, as Beth said, been a fool to make such a storm in a teacup.

What did the ownership of a rose, however old and precious, matter, where loved ones were concerned?

After luncheon, Barbara retired to her room to rest, Stephen joined Robert on a tour of the garden, Mr Fraser and John Curtis departed to catch the afternoon train back to town, the elder guests disappeared, and Faye and Patti — as usual — repaired to the hammocks in the shade. 'Well?' asked Faye curiously. 'I saw you go in search of that old stick Fraser — what happened?'

Patti leaned back, staring up through the sun-dappled leaves. 'Quite a lot, actually. And he's not as dry as we thought.'

'Go on! Don't leave me hanging in the air!'

'He's agreed to — well, to help me do something that I should have done long ago. To give up something.'

'Give up?' Faye snorted disapprovingly. 'That sounds most defeatist! I'm disappointed in you, Patti.'

Patti smiled a secret smile to herself. 'Don't be — because what I'm really doing is taking a most positive step forward. . .' She sat up with a jerk and the hammock nearly tipped her out. She stared at Faye with eyes suddenly brilliant with new thoughts. 'Yes! You see, I've actually overcome some of my stupid, childish beliefs. . .'

'That's better,' said Faye. 'Sounds as if you've struck a blow for personal freedom. . .'

Patti blinked. 'Whatever does that mean?'

'It means,' Faye answered crisply, with an authoritative ring to her voice, 'that you have had the courage of your convictions. You have acted upon them, which is splendid. We should all do that! Think of the wonderful Pankhursts and their determination!' Her face lit up with enthusiasm. She smiled radiantly at Patti. 'And I've decided to make my own personal bid for freedom, too! I'm going to leave home! I want to do something more with my life than just read novels and arrange flowers — which I do very badly! I want to learn, to study, to meet new people. . . Just think, Patti, what I will be able to do in London. . .'

A silence enclosed them, only the concerted song of the bees plundering nectar from a vast lime tree near by gently breaking it. Patti looked into Faye's shining eyes and thought abruptly, Goodness, what a lot Porphyry Court has to answer for. Here's Faye, changing from her dull chrysalis into a brave new butterfly — and me, forever learning lessons that will, with any luck, perhaps make me new, too. . .

Impatiently Faye said, 'Well? Don't go all dreamy on me! What do you think?'

Patti smiled warmly. 'You're right, Faye. Life is for living.'

'Splendid! So you won't be too surprised when I take off for London one day, will you?'

'But you can't do that. . .'

'Why not? You've just agreed. . .'

'But Faye, what about Robert? And your mother?'

Faye was on her feet by now, dancing ahead, out of the shadow of the cedar into the brilliant sunshine and the cloying heat of the humid afternoon. Fanning herself with her hat, she looked back over her shoulder and grinned wickedly. 'Don't be silly, Patti — they won't mind me going. I mean, you'll be here, won't you?' Then she raced towards the house, leaving Patti alone to consider the true import of her last words.

* * *

They played sardines after dinner, trying to ignore the thunderstorm which lurked in the near distance. Faye hid in the wine cellar, laughing loudly when Stephen found her, and then leading him a mischievous dance around the kitchen passages. Then it was Barbara's turn to hide, and she chose to go out into the orangery. Patti, with instinctive awareness, found her there, crouched behind the biggest palm tree, hidden by shadows.

'Do go away, can't you, little long-lost cousin?' she snapped crossly. 'Surely you know the rules of the game? A girl *never* finds another girl — that's no fun at all. . .' Turning her back, the curve of her shoulder a seductive and subtle invitation, she retreated further into the darkness, leaving Patti smarting from the dislike in her voice.

As Patti retreated, ready to leave the orangery, she heard footsteps approaching and backed away. She saw Robert pause on the threshold, big, heavy and disturbing. She had avoided him all day, and even over dinner their eyes had only met briefly, and with no sense of companionship. Now he was here — but he was looking for Barbara. Her heart sank in wretchedness.

For a large man he moved fast and silently. A bittersweetness invaded her misery as she recalled other times when he had proved his ability to do this. Now he stood, staring into the shadows that loomed around the huge potted palm trees and the furniture that filled the dark spaces between.

Then Barbara laughed — husky, inviting, secretive. Patti held her breath, found herself filled with hatred. She watched, mesmerised, while Robert prowled a few steps nearer the concealing palm. Barbara's voice whispered through the silence, tempting, provocative. Patti, stunned with disbelief, watched as he turned towards her. Then the two faint shapes came together, melting into one with the shadows that loomed around the palm tree, and Patti was unable to bear what she instinctively knew was an embrace between lovers of old, newly attracted. . .

She fled then, running with agonised speed out of the orangery into the darkness of the garden. As she crossed the lawn, a sudden wind arose, murmuring between the trees, whispering through shrubs and plants. Looking up, she saw clouds racing across a moody sky, hiding the dark blue arc of infinity. Clouds, bearing storms and conflict, making sleepy birds fly for cover, battering garden flowers, warning of worse to come. . .

A faint rumble of thunder rolled around the enraged sky. Not too near, but definitely there — a reminder of conflicting forces. Nature and life, thought Patti wildly, are not so different, after all.

By the time she had reached the house the storm had taken a step nearer. Thunder now seemed to roar from all quarters and she saw the first forked flash of lightning illuminate the dark garden. Her old, childish terror returned and, picking up her skirt, she ran, filled with mindless fright.

The house was an oasis of light and safety, but still her fear persisted. Reaching the passage leading to the drawing-room, she trembled, and, when a door opened suddenly beside her, gasped in fright. Familiar arms caught her as she swayed and she closed her eyes, unable to resist the temptation of resting against that strong chest, hearing the steady and reassuring beat of his well-beloved heart. She stared into searching brown eyes and said, with a touch of near-hysteria, 'But you were in the orangery—you were with Barbara a minute ago...'

Robert frowned. 'I was—trying to persuade the silly girl to come back into the house. This storm's going to break at any moment. Why are you in such a state of panic, Patti?'

'I—I don't like thunder. I never have...' She felt very foolish. 'But—but you, and Barbara, in the orangery...'

Robert's arms released her and his frown grew very stiff. 'I've told you,' he said tightly. They stared at each other in tense silence for a long moment, before he added, 'You do have the very oddest notions at times, Patti...' and she saw his mouth quirk at the corner. Her heart expanded, thinking he had forgiven her suspicions, and she was almost convincing herself that her recent certainty about that embrace with Barbara had been a mistake, when he continued, his voice deep and becoming increasingly full of disapproval. 'Yes, extremely odd—Faye's just told me about your latest plan. Apparently you intend to go to Paris together and see Jules Lacoste.'

Despite the rising inflexion of obvious impatience, Patti found the strength to mutter, 'Yes, we do. Why are you so cross about it?'

Robert's reply was not the one she had expected. 'I'm angry because you planned it without my consent. Of course, I'm coming with you,' he said heavily, in a voice that she recognised instantly as patriarchal, arrogant and final.

CHAPTER THIRTEEN

PATTI lay in a tight ball of misery in her bed, trying in vain to ignore the storm that now filled the night. But lightning streaked into her room and thunder roared so menacingly all around that she got up, trembling and tense, wondering wearily how much longer she could stand the assault.

Pacing beside the curtained window, robe clutched around her, she thought she heard a sound outside her room. And then again — the passage floor creaked. She flew to the door, opened it a crack, and stared out into the shadows. A small light wavered along just beyond her door, held by an invisible hand. Briefly Patti wondered if Lady Challoner had been taken ill; she was deliberating whether she should go and find out when a door at the far end of the gallery opened, emitting a hazy glow of lamplight, the light moving down the passage halted, and Barbara Latimer's voice murmured inaudibly. The door shut, both lights disappeared, and Patti was left staring, unnerved by what she had seen, and by the misery of her subsequent thoughts.

Back in bed, she pulled the covers tightly around her throat, and closed her eyes. Now it was easy to put her fear of the storm behind her, for an even greater panic filled her. Had it been Robert, going to Barbara's room? Was he, even now, holding her in his arms? Kissing her, as he had done in the orangery? *Loving Barbara. . .?*

Patti's thoughts were legion. Robert and Barbara were old friends, and Barbara had hinted, more than once, of something warmer than mere friendship still existing between them. And yet Robert had been angry when Patti had so foolishly said she had seen him with Barbara in the orangery... His quick excuse did little now to ease her misery, remembering.

But even such wretchedness could not entirely stop sleep from claiming her. Once, in her restless, troubled state, she thought she felt someone close to her — a reassuring presence, a touch upon her hands as she tossed and turned between disturbed sleep and frightened half-consciousness.

By the time she was fully awake at dawn, though, only the same old shadows met her eyes, furniture touched by the pearly grey light slowly replacing the awful blackness of night. No human form looked down from the bedside; no warm hand reached out to touch her relaxed, rosy body, stirring beneath the linen sheets.

She lay still for a while, remembering. Robert had been angry with her last night. She had imagined him with Barbara, and yet now she could have sworn he had been here, during the storm...

Patti sighed, told herself wretchedly that she was far too worked up for her own good, and feebly set about preparing for the day ahead.

She knew there was much to be done. The house guests would all be leaving, and she must supervise the tidying of their rooms. And then she had to explain to Lady Challoner that she wished to go to Paris — if she could be spared.

But she had reckoned without Faye, who came running down the gallery behind her as she headed for the staircase. 'It's all arranged!' said Faye gaily. 'I've told Mother and she doesn't mind us going. And Robert knows. . .' She stopped abruptly, staring at Patti's straight face. 'What's wrong?'

'From what he said to me last night, he's taking *us* to France. We're not going by ourselves. . .' Patti's voice was weak.

'And a good thing, too. Why shouldn't he come and help out? That's what men are for! It'll save us having to take Elsie, and he'll be there to stop Jules from being too nasty when you meet him face to face!' Faye danced ahead, and Patti descended the stairs more decorously, wondering just how this trip to France would end. She felt distinctly nervous about Robert and Jules having yet another confrontation — and all because of her. . .

Her entrance into the dining-room was unnoticed. Barbara and Stephen, already down, were asking Robert about the damage the storm had caused to the garden.

'Disastrous,' said Robert bleakly. 'A tree fell on the wall beside the first glasshouse. It's completely shattered.'

Patti was unable to stop her exclamation of dismay. 'Madame Léonie?' she gasped.

Robert's grim eyes met hers. 'Ruined,' he said curtly, before turning aside to greet his aunt and uncle, and question them politely about their night's sleep.

All Patti's new-found courage seemed to die within her as she realised what Robert's one word truly meant. Madame Léonie — *ruined*. Were the grafted buds sliced about by the cut glass? Were they destroyed completely? She could have wept, but suddenly heard Robert saying her name, and turned to look at him as everyone found their chairs and prepared to kneel for family prayers.

'How did you sleep, Patti? Do you feel more rested?' She nodded dully, before slipping down on to her knees. What a strange thing to ask, she thought, when they both knew that it was Madame Léonie's demise that filled their grieving minds.

The guests left once breakfast was finished, and Patti joined Lady Challoner and Faye in the hall. Robert appeared at the last minute, changed into his shabby gardening clothes, which brought a frown to his mother's face, and a provocative drawl from Barbara.

'Darling, what a handsome peasant you make!'

Aunt Estelle and Uncle Willie were the first to leave, the ancient dowager pecking Faye and then Patti on their cheeks. 'You're good gels,' she told them fondly. 'Come and stay in London soon—our house in Belgravia is empty and dull, and Willie and I could do with some young company.' She glanced over her shoulder as she swept out of the front door. 'Willie! Come along! We must not miss our train. . .'

Smothered in furs, despite the July sunshine, and smelling strongly of camphorated oil, Aunt Estelle climbed into the creaking carriage, ordering the placing of her numerous pieces of luggage as she did so. Uncle Willie took the opportunity to slip an arm around Patti's waist as he embraced her.

'Gad, what I'd give to be forty years younger. . .!'

His kiss was enthusiastic and, coupled with his words, made Patti blush bright red; her colour grew even brighter when she met Robert's eyes as he assisted his uncle into the carriage, and then stepped back to stand beside her waving the old couple farewell.

Barbara was waiting impatiently beside Stephen's very modern limousine — 'my car magnificent', as he proudly called it. She wore the simple but elegant calf-length beige coat and matching dress she had arrived in. Lace frothed at her throat, and a light cream dustcoat enveloped the smart ensemble. Tying a chiffon scarf over her large-crowned beige hat, she slid into the passenger seat, tightly clutching Robert's proffered hand. 'Don't we go well together?' she joked, nodding at the gleaming cream paintwork of the car, her eyes seeking his.

But Patti thought Robert's reply sounded a trifle impatient. 'Indeed you do, but you'll both be covered in white dust before you've gone a mile out of the village!'

Barbara pouted. 'Darling, you're a proper old grouch today — not a bit like you *used* to be. . .' She opened her arms wide in an invitation for him to embrace her. 'Say you'll miss me. Just a teensy-weensy bit. . .?'

As Robert smiled enigmatically, leaning forward to kiss not her offered lips but her cheek, Patti saw Barbara glance at her across his shoulder. The dark doe eyes were cold and filled with hostility.

Then suddenly Faye and Stephen were laughing together, the waiting groom obligingly cranked the engine, which fired at the first twist of the handle, and in a cloud of smoke the beautiful limousine slid away, Stephen, in his checked motoring coat, waving and Barbara throwing kisses back towards Robert.

Lady Challoner sighed as she turned back into the

hall. 'I do hope they enjoyed themselves. So lovely to have guests. . .'

Robert, beside Patti, threw her a rapid sideways glance of gleaming cynicism. 'But even more delightful when they leave!' His eyes twinkled, and she was dumbfounded. Did that mean his feelings for the divine Barbara were purely platonic? But before she could think any further he had gripped her hand and was leading her down the drive towards the vine pergola, and the distant, looming yew hedge. 'Come with me, Patti. Something I want to show you

Her thoughts took wing. She recalled him saying the same words earlier in their friendship; then they had resulted in an emotional confrontation in the glasshouse. Obediently, she let him lead her, realising just how much she had changed since that day in late May. Now, over two months later, she knew she was less wilful, more disciplined — but still full of a passion that threatened to break out and engulf her.

They passed through the cool archway of the hedge where Robert had asked if she had missed him, and she sensed that he, too, remembered. And then they were in the sun again, and Patti put a hand to her mouth despairingly as she saw the first shattered glasshouse, just beyond the rose garden.

The old apple tree in the orchard, outside the wall, had been struck by lightning and had smashed through the brickwork of the wall, falling directly along the length of the glasshouse roof, breaking the glass and ending up lodged obliquely down both sides of the slatted shelfing within.

Robert's hand tightened its grip, and his voice throbbed with feeling as he said, 'Careful where you tread. Ned and Alan have cleared away most of the mess, but broken glass can be treacherous. This way, Patti...'

They stood inside the ruin, twisted iron framework towering above them and a broken radiator lying on its side in a pool of stained water. Patti could hardly bear to look around her for fear of seeing further destruction. Her mind raced with memories of the healthy embryo roses, so green and sturdy, and reluctantly she forced herself to glance down at the broken shelves.

Shards of earthenware lay everywhere and, among them, small torn brown stems, with drying roots still clinging to clumps of the soil that had nurtured them. A great sorrow and disappointment surged inside her, too powerful to be controlled. She gave a choked cry, then turned away from the awful scene of destruction and lost hopes.

Immediately Robert's arms closed around her and she was drawn near to him, her wet cheeks resting against his green jacket. The thick tweed was rough and smelt of smoke and the countryside, allied to his own, very masculine smell. It mopped up her tears, finally giving her the ability to free herself, to smile rather waterily, and look up into his concerned face.

'Th-thank you,' she stuttered. 'It was just that I felt—well, *you* know, don't you? No more Madame Léonie...'

Robert's arms were strong about her. She felt their warmth, but, even as she spoke the last trembling words, instinctively she knew that now the embrace must end. The old rose, mourn her as they both did, was still a barrier between them.

His arms dropped, and she stepped away, swaying a little because of the pain of their rejection. He stood looking down at her, and she saw an expression of agonised indecision in his deep eyes.

'Yes,' he muttered, almost between his teeth. 'Madame Léonie again — and I *do* know how you feel, Patti, because I feel the same. The pride of ownership. The certainty that fills me. . .and yet. . .'

Suddenly his lips twisted, and his voice grew less harsh. 'And yet is this all you can think of, Patti? That Madame Léonie is *your* rose — is that what still fills your idealistic, stubborn little mind? Even now, when you and I are so close — so comfortable together — like this?'

Knowledge came to her like a gift, and one that she could hardly bring herself to believe; he, like her, wanted to forget Madame Léonie, to forget everything except the fact that they were here together. . .

Lost in the haunting appeal in his dark, rich eyes, in the sculptured planes of his lean face, and the very nearness of him, Patti was on the brink of giving herself. She longed to do so. And then, when she was about to move back into his arms, remembrance captured her mind. Robert had been in Barbara's room last night. And he still thought of Madame Léonie as his! How could she possibly trust him? Indeed, his very charm was suspicious. . .

Pausing, she searched his eyes, and in that instant knew she had lost whatever it was he offered her. Robert stepped away, his face set into the familir mask of mockery that made her heart contract with pain.

'No answer?' he asked her wryly. 'But I hardly expected one — we'll never resolve our differences, I fear. However, my little weeping nymph, no need to look quite so miserable — this should cheer you up a bit. Come over here and see this. . .'

Almost roughly, he put an arm around her, leading her over the cluttered earthen floor to the end of the glasshouse, where one small section of shelving remained miraculously intact.

A ring of excitement vibrated in his deep voice. 'I was wrong about Madame Léonie being completely wiped out,' he told her. 'Look Patti—just one plant left. And it's actually in bloom. . .'

One frail little rose stood, secure and undamaged, in its brown clay pot. Somehow it had escaped the rain of broken glass, falling branches and storm debris that surrounded it.

Patti stared, disbelieving. Then a great lightness of spirit and pleasure bore her up, out of the hopelessness and pain that the scene of destruction had brought with it.

'Madame Léonie!' she whispered, and bent to examine the flower that she feared had gone for ever.

The sport of the old Gallica rose stood upright on its young, healthy stem, warm red, velvety petals in a double layer that lay flat and open, revealing the circle of thick golden stamens at its heart.

She sniffed delicately and the rich, heady perfume almost intoxicated her. A little light-headed, wavering between tears and laughter, she smiled. 'There it is!' she murmured ecstatically. 'The golden heart of the rose that Grandfather told me about! The mystery—the secret of life itself. . .'

Silence stretched around them; she, Madame Léonie and Robert, caught together in an old enchantment that would, surely, never part them again. Patti could not tear her gaze away from the ancient and beautiful blossom. She had dreamed of it, waited for it so long—and then, abruptly, with a stab of erupting pain, she

HEART OF A ROSE

recalled that she had changed her mind about Grandfather's claim to its ownership. Smile dying, she wondered with dismay if she had, after all, done the right thing. . .

Then Robert's voice penetrted her confusion, so gentle and vibrant that she was recalled at once to the moment and the fact that, as Beth had so wisely told her, love was more important than idealism.

'Well,' he said, with just a tinge of lazy mockery in the words, 'now the mystery has revealed itself to you, Patti, tell me. . .' She turned to face him.

A wry half-smile softened the suntanned angles of his cheekbones, and his eyes were steady pools of narrowed, intent darkness. He went on, 'You've learned the secret, you say. What is it, then — this all-important secret that you've been chasing since your childhood? Please tell me. . .'

'Love, Robert. Just — love.' Her answer was simple and instinctive. Watching his searching eyes, she smiled, waiting for the reciprocal words she so longed to hear. At the very least, she expected understanding — perhaps even a hint of warmth that would let her go on hoping — but, as she watched, slowly the depths of his eyes grew turbulent, his mouth set grimly in a rigid line, and he said, almost roughly, 'Clearly love is something you find simple to indulge in. I fear I cannot share that ease. . .'

They looked at each other, the echoes of his words ringing painfully around them. Patti felt her heart grow small and withered. Her hands flew to her breast as if to shield the gift she had just offered him.

But, with the silence, realisation came to balance her swimming emotions. She sensed the terrible struggle going on in his own racing mind, knew that the past still held him in his grip, knew too that he suspected her, just as she held him in distrust.

Madame Léonie was a symbol of love; but somehow they could not share her. Again, Patti's confusion grew. Perhaps she had been gullible and foolish to relinquish her dream for the old rose... Perhaps she had demeaned herself by letting Robert see how much she yearned for him

The fateful moment died. The old magic they had created for each other sparked into darkness. Patti watched Robert turn and stride across the debris-littered floor, pausing only as he reached the doorway. His glance back at her was controlled but she thought a dying fire still gleamed in the depths of his gaze. 'I'm sorry,' he said shortly, 'but there's a lot to be done. And no doubt you, too, are busy.'

Patti inclined her head, blinking furiously at the unshed tears that pricked so hotly behind her lids. 'Of course,' she replied with a touch of arrogance. 'Don't let me detain you, Robert.' She passed him without looking up, but was aware of his tension, of the question lurking in his eyes. 'Thank you for showing me — ' her voice was uneven ' — Madame Léonie.'

Safely past, she paused, forcing her mind back into mundane things. She looked down the row of three glasshouses, and saw with relief that the final building had escaped all danger.

'A good thing that one, at least, is saved.' She nodded towards it, trying to return their stormy relationship to easier depths. 'Have you anything valuable there?' Glancing back, she was startled by the abrupt expression of concentration on Robert's face, and by the vehemence of his reply.

'Yes.' One terse word. She waited for an explanation, but none came. Again, that hard line of a mouth, the continued torment in his eyes.

Patti sighed. 'I had better go now. So much to do. . .' The words dragged out of her, and quickly she turned away and left him. She felt him watching as she went, and even the joy of having at last seen the glory of Madame Léonie in bloom could not stop her misery as she set about the duties awaiting her in the house.

The visit to Paris was arranged for the following week, but not without further complications. Robert, in his usual dictatorial manner, had demurred about Patti accompanying Faye and himself. 'There's no need for her to come. I can deal with Edouard and Jules without her presence. . .'

'Nonsense, Robert!' Faye's voice was determined. 'I need a travelling companion — stop being so horrid! Patti is coming and that's that. . .'

On the Monday morning of their departure, Patti and Faye watched their luggage being piled into the carriage while awaiting Robert's arrival. He came down from Lady Challoner's boudoir two stairs at a time, looking very much the man of business in his dark, pin-stripe suit with a pearl pin in the smart, shiny tie. His manner to both girls was smooth and polite, but masterful, and Patti sighed, knowing he resented her forced appearance in the carriage. To him this trip was merely a humdrum routine, she thought crossly, avoiding his cool gaze as he seated himself opposite them. Had he any idea what it meant to her?

During the last week she had had time to think things through. No doubt Robert was still hostile about Madame Léonie. . . A smile touched her tight lips then; it would do him no harm at all to have to await the outcome of her conversation with Arnold Fraser... Then the smile died. Of course, he still distrusted her over that wretched business of Jules, and Monsieur Lacoste's letter.

Faye heard her sigh, and said brightly, 'Cheer up! We're not going to a funeral, you know! And you do look nice in that new linen suit—sea-green, isn't it? I've changed my mind about colours being lucky or unlucky now; I just *know* everything is going to turn out well—for all of us!' She smiled at Patti reassuringly, and then added, with an imp of mischief in the words, 'I bet all the Frenchmen will be looking at you in that lovely flowery hat...!'

Robert cleared his throat grimly, and Faye shut up, but nudged Patti with her elbow first, hissing *sotto voce*, 'Don't take any notice of him! Let's just enjoy ourselves!'

The Cornish Riviera express bore them away through the glorious August day with its clean, crisp air. Faye chattered on, pointing out the various landmarks as they steamed out of the little town of Newton Abbot to follow the broad sweep of the River Teign until it flowed into the sea at its mouth, and then turned northeast, running along the coast before turning inland and heading for Exeter.

Privately, Patti thought Faye to be in very high spirits. Not a word of ill health, whether real or assumed, for weeks now. An uncomfortable thought came to her—was Faye glad to be renewing her old friendship with Jules? Surely not. Patti shuddered in anticipation as her own meeting with the beastly man edged nearer.

But at Paddington Faye's exuberance was explained.

They had just emerged from the station, and Patti was calling up a motor-cab to take them across London to Victoria, when Patti realised Faye had disappeared. She turned anxiously, looking around through the crowds, but could see not a trace of Faye in her smart brown costume. Robert turned away from the waiting cab. 'Come along,' he said impatiently. 'Where's Faye?'

'I'm not sure — I can't see her...'

He smothered an oath. 'Wretched girl! Why can't she behave herself?' And then, as a porter approached, holding out a folded piece of paper, he turned to him and frowned. 'What on earth's this?'

'Lady said to give it to you, guv...' The man retreated, touching his cap, and Robert unfolded the shabby note, read it, and then grimly clenched it in his powerful fist.

'What is it? What did it say?' Patti was scared at his expression.

Robert's eyes met hers with a clash. He scowled and his voice was deeper than she had ever heard. 'Faye has the audacity to send me a cheeky note to say she's not coming to Paris with us. She's decided instead to go and stay with Aunt Estelle...' His words were full of disbelief.

'Is that all?' Patti could have laughed with relief, but her lightness of heart soon died.

Robert glowered angrily. '*All*?' he thundered. 'Faye turning herself loose in London, with only a dithery old woman and a foolish old man to look after her? I won't have it!'

Patti held her breath and remained silent while he turned away and paced up and down the pavement, all his anger and frustration clear to see. And slowly the comic potential of the situation hit her; she began to smile. When Robert paused at her side, she was actually laughing.

He frowned fiercely. 'Nothing to laugh at, Patti! Now I'll have to take you back to Porphyry Court — all my arrangements will have to be remade. . . Damn the girl!' He looked suspiciously at Patti's smiling face. 'I suppose I have you to thank for this — no doubt you whetted her appetite about living in London. . .'

Patti regarded him calmly and thoughtfully before answering. 'Yes, Robert,' she said slowly. 'I suppose I did. And it can only be a good thing. Why should Faye not lead the interesting, busy life that you yourself do? Women are coming into their own these days, you know. . . Surely you would be the last to deny us a few rights and pleasures?'

The provocative question seemed to astonish him. For a moment he just stood glaring at her, and then, as she watched, she saw reason assert itself. He sighed, as if relinquishing his anger grudgingly, but a small smile touched his lips. 'I see. So you're sisters together in this brave new world. . .' The smile grew a little broader. 'And so what do you suggest we do, cousin? Of course, you have a plan already prepared. . .'

His cynicism only made her own smile grow. 'No, cousin, no plan made. But yours still holds good, surely? We go to Paris as arranged.'

He exploded once again. 'Do you realise the sitution we're in? No chaperon! I'll have to hire a maid for you. . .'

'Nonsense, Robert,' she said quickly. 'Life is not nearly so stuffy as you seem to think! We are cousins, after all — and I trust you to look after me. Plese don't let us change any thing. I mean, we both know we need to visit the Lacostes, don't we?'

She saw, by the surprise in his eyes, that she had scored a point. Reluctantly, he nodded, and helped her into the cab. Her confidence grew. Now he had learned that she was as independently minded as his sister. She had a feeling that it would make their shared journey a lot easier than she had at first anticipated.

But, even so, at times during the lengthy journey the atmosphere between them was occasionally highly charged. . .

'If Faye hadn't sprung this change of plan on me so late I could have organised things much better,' grumbled Robert as he and Patti entered the new electrically powered lift at the hotel in Dover where they were spending the night before embarking on the steamer bound for Calais next morning.

Clearly anger was not far away. Patti swayed as the lift jolted to a halt at the third floor and felt his hand instantly supporting her. She guessed that his temper was not really directed at Faye, but at this unconventional situation. Cousins of opposite sexes travelling unaccompanied, even in these enlightened Edwardian days, must necessarily attract unwanted speculation and gossip. Abruptly, his concern touched her deeply, and she smiled up at him. 'Don't worry! Everything is all right, Robert. And we shall be in Paris in time for dinner tomorrow evening. . .' She saw the suspicion of a smile lighten his set face and added encouragingly, 'I'm so excited! I've never been to Paris before!'

Half teasingly, and with only a hint of the old annoyance, he said gruffly, 'Well, let's hope we meet no one we know. The very last thing I want is to compromise you, my dear.'

Suddenly Patti's lightness of mood darkened. 'My dear'. Fond though the term was, it froze her heart, for plainly Robert had stepped back into the safety of his patriarchal role, and even in her darkest moments she had not imagined he would find it necessary to do that.

Dismay brought quick temper and before she knew what she was saying she snapped back at him, 'If you're so worried you'd better buy me a ring and we'll pretend we're married. . .'

And then she wished she could take the foolish words back. His face darkened and he said distastefully, 'Don't be ridiculous.' He left her then so that she could enter the room and close the door behind her, recalling only the look of mingled emotions on his face as he turned and strode down the corridor.

The rest of the evening was a disaster, Patti thought unhappily. They dined in the hotel restaurant and then Robert escorted her upstairs when she was ready to retire. He looked strained and tired, and for the first time she realised the great pressure he must be under; she had not truly considered what it was to lose one's reputation, and the idea of his suffering made her regret the snappy comment she had made earlier.

At her door, impulsively she turned and laid a hand upon his arm. 'Robert, I'm so sorry—I spoke without thinking. I was cross—but it was childish. Hurtful. And I realise now that you were only thinking of me. . .'

Robert's hand slowly covered hers. He looked into her eyes and nodded, as if in acceptance of her apology. Quietly he said, 'That was it, of course, Patti. I mean, I am your cousin — your guardian, almost. . .'

She felt the light in her eyes die and slipped her hand away from his at once. Hateful words! Her cousin! Her guardian! And she longed for him to be her lover. . . The truth swamped her, suddenly and without any mercy. Never mind her suspicions of Barbara, never mind how dictatorial he was, never mind anything; she wanted him. She loved him.

But somehow she lifted her head and smiled into his dark, veiled eyes, as she murmured, with a touch of the irrepressible humour that always leavened even the blackest of hour, 'And so goodnight, dear guardian. . .'

She heard the soft words linger, with their echo of sensual suggestion, waited for his reaction, closed her eyes and hoped, wondering what he would choose to do.

As she might have expected, she thought wryly, his choice was the strong-minded one. 'Goodnight, dear cousin.' He bent, brushed her cheeks with his lips, and then left her.

Patti, alone in the big twin-bedded room that should also have accommodated Faye, undressed in a state of deep speculation. This visit to Paris, full of conflict as it undoubtedly was, would give Robert and herself time in which to get to know each other truly. 'Almost,' she muttered, brushing out her hair, 'as if we were married.' And then blushed into the mirror, aghast at the way her thoughts were running on.

She fancied things were a little easier between them next day, Robert taking pains to make the journey as comfortable as possible, and pointing out places of interest as they went. During the morning there was time to visit Dover Castle before they embarked on the boat. The luncheon was good, and the crossing to Calais so smooth that Patti could hardly believe she was actually steaming through the English Channel.

A noisy train with a fussy siren rattled them down to Paris and the hotel where Robert had booked rooms by telegraph for the night.

'I expect you're tired,' he said, ushering her into yet another twin-bedded room. 'We'll have an early dinner and then ——'

'And then we'll go out on the town!' Patti cut in brightly. She laughed up into his surprised eyes. 'Please, Robert? This *is* Paris, you know — surely you don't expect me to go to bed early, like a naughty child? I want to walk up the Champs-Elysées — look at the Seine by moonlight — visit the Louvre. . .'

Robert's patriarchal expression, which had been with him all day, softened abruptly. 'And dance the night away, I suppose? And then oversleep so that we arrive late at the Lacoste rosery tomorrow. . .' He sounded amused, but the name Lacoste put an abrupt end to Patti's euphoria.

What would tomorrow bring? Suddenly she realised just how much she was dreading this meeting with Jules, especially as Robert would be grimly watching every expression on her face, and possibly misinterpreting every word she said. . .

'Oh, damn tomorrow!' she burst out, astonished at her own temerity. 'Don't let's think about tomorrow, Robert.' She stepped nearer, looking up at him with pleading eyes. 'Let's just enjoy ourselves tonight. . .' The words themselves were harmless, but abruptly the full implication of what she had said raced through her, bringing shame and regret. She coloured, drew back, and said hastily, 'I mean——'

'I know exactly what you mean, Patti.' His gaze revealed the truth of his words, and her cheeks grew crimson. His voice dropped unsteadily. 'And I share your longing to do something about it. But. . .' Abruptly he stopped, lifted his hand as if to caress her, and then let it drop to his side. Harshly he said, 'We're here on business, remember? It's not just a pleasure trip.' His voice had grown bitter and Patti saw the old hunger in his eyes. 'We both need to be at our best tomorrow. A good night's sleep will ensure that.'

Patti's shame fled beneath a veneer of brittle anger. 'Just as you like,' she said, with a snap in her uneven voice. 'And please don't think I was trying to—to seduce you. I've changed quite a lot, you know, since you last told me I was a "temptation".'

Robert's eyes were hollow pools, his face a mask of tension. He nodded grimly, and said between set teeth, 'How dare you throw things back at me. . .? Goodnight, Cousin Patti.'

Patti watched his broad back striding down the passage through a mist of frustrated tears. '*Goodnight, Robert*,' she called after him, and, stepping back into her bedroom, slammed the door behind her.

CHAPTER FOURTEEN

ALL that Patti could think about next morning was the coming meeting with Jules and his father. She and Robert breakfasted in silence, their tense non-communication continuing as they prepared to leave the hotel and go to the Roseraie du Val where the two Lacostes awaited them. Then a pageboy's piping voice summoned Robert to the desk in the foyer, and there stood Jules, as boyish and attractive as ever, his smile warm and friendly, as though nothing untoward had ever happened between the three of them.

'Ah! The lovely Patti! And Robert. . .'

Patti felt Robert's grim gaze upon her as she smiled tightly, allowing Jules to kiss her hand. She said, with chilly politenes, 'Good morning, Monsieur Lacoste,' and then coloured deeply as he murmured, with quiet intimacy,

'No, no! *Jules*, please. . .!' Inclining her head to hide the mounting blush, she deliberately avoided his gaze, instinctively knowing that it would be suggestive and unpleasant. Instead, she glanced aside at Robert, meeting his eyes and seeing in them a certain grudging appreciation of her controlled behaviour. At once her confidence began to return.

It was easy, then, to stand beside them as Jules said brashly that he had brought his new motor car in which to drive them to the rosery. 'A new American model, quite the newest thing—wait till you see it,' he boasted. 'Your old Daimler can't hold a candle to it!'

They drove away from the hotel in the gleaming motor, which Patti thought privately really quite vulgar, passing through suburbs until they reached the quiet edge of countryside where the rosery stood, its several hectares of land stretching away into trees and fields. Patti had been assessing the situation as Jules hooted and screeched his way past trams and horse-drawn traffic—so far, she thought with relief, so good. Athough seeming to be friendly, Jules had already shown himself to be very much the villain of the piece—and Robert's approval of the way she had reacted to the sly greeting had definitely helped to improve her peace of mind.

But when she sat down in Edouard Lacoste's hot, dusty little office in the cobbled courtyard at the rosery entrance, and saw his shrewd green eyes staring at her across a table littered with papers, spikes of bills and old catalogues, her heart sank. If his son was a deceiver, it was clear that old Monsieur Lacoste was a realist.

And it was also clear that he held Robert in great affection because of their long-standing relationship. She watched as the two men shook hands and embraced, and her dismay grew. The cutting-off of such a friendship, in addition to the end of their business connection, must surely embitter Robert's whole life—and it was all due to her. . . She sat on the edge of the chair Monsieur Lacoste indicated and saw the three men eyeing each other speculatively before Robert ended the silence by saying brusquely, in fluent French, 'Well, Edouard, this is a sad meeting. Your letter was totally unexpected—and hit me hard. . .'

The older man nodded slowly, folding work-worn hands on the table. He looked at Robert without answering and then turned his brooding gaze on Patti. Bravely she met his eyes, but did not smile. He must not think her the temptress she was sure Jules had described her to be. When he spoke, it was to her, and not, as she had expected, to Robert.

'I have looked forward to meeting you, Miss Nevill. Jules has told me about you. . .'

Patti felt a shiver run down her spine. *What* has he told you, I wonder? she thought wretchedly.

'Words can paint pictures, certainly,' Edouard Lacoste continued in his slow, hoarse voice, 'but only the real person can convey the truth.'

Patti blinked with surprise. She had expected accusations, not wisdom. Hesitantly, she smiled, abruptly aware of a certain respect for this old man, who so clearly loved Robert, and was inclined to justice rather than hearsay. 'And is there a great difference, Monsieur Lacoste,' she asked impulsively, 'between Jules's word-picture of me and what you see here?'

The lined, sun-burned face unexpectedly returned her smile. Green eyes gleamed and Patti saw the charm that youthful Edouard had once possessed, and which he had passed on to Jules.

'I see a charming English lady, Miss Nevill. And I sense a personality which does not quite fit in with Jules's description of you — or of your behaviour. . .'

Patti snatched a quick breath. Here it was, then — the story which Jules had woven around them both. Did his father really think she had been on his son's side? That she had betrayed Robert?

Jules broke in, voice annoyed and dark. 'Papa, why do you say that? I am your son! I do not tell lies.'

Patti's rage swooped her up too fast for thought, and she found words erupting from her mouth. 'Nonsense!

Not only are you a liar, but a thief as well—clearly you did not tell your father about stealing the grafted plants of Madame Léonie...or of kissing me because you tried to force me to be your accomplice. Or how unkind you were to poor Faye. How can you pretend to be so innocent, when you have caused such terrible trouble all around...?'

She stopped as abruptly as she had begun, running out of both breath and words, and sitting on the edge of her chair, glaring at Jules's frowning face.

Silence lengthened in the small, airless room, until a bee droned at the blotchy window, and Patti looked down at the floor, ashamed of her emotional outburst. Beth's reproving voice rang in her ears...'When did you ever not say exactly what you felt? And always at the wrong moment...!' Now she dared not lift her head to meet Robert's eyes for fear of seeing in them an even greater disapproval than that which he already felt for her.

It was Edouard Lacoste's sudden throaty chuckle that ended the silence and made Patti look up to meet his shrewd eyes, narrowed as laughter creased the leathery skin beside them. 'Bravo, Miss Nevill!' he said, as the laughter ceased. 'We have the truth, I think now.' Swiftly turning, he looked at Robert. 'Your cousin has a will of her own, eh, Robert? Not what we men are used to—but the world changes fast and our quiet little women become...what is the new word? Liberated? Whatever that means...'

'It means giving us something of a shock, Edouard—I entirely agree with you.' Robert's voice was rich with amusement, and, glancing at him, Patti met his eyes; smiling, they were full of a direct affection that made her heart beat faster. Then he was speaking again, the smile gone, a note of firm resolution hardening his voice. 'Painful although it is to make trouble between old friends, the truth is exactly as Miss Nevill — Patti — has just told you. I fear Jules has behaved less than honestly——'

'Not true, Papa.' Jules's angry words were raw and edgy.

Edouard silenced him imperiously. 'Enough!' he banged a fist on the table. 'I know you, my son, know how your mind works. You want fame, but dislike the hard work it entails——'

'But Papa, I swear that——'

Edouard Lacoste growled, deep in his throat. 'No more, Jules. Just leave us, if you please. We will put things right better without you here.'

The furious blue gaze swept the room. Patti saw Robert eye Jules with controlled distaste. She herself outstared him before he flung open the door, striding out without another word. The door slammed shut, the dust arose, and then silence again settled in the quiet room. Only now, thought Patti, with immense relief, a different silence — one filled with friendship and co-operation.

She met Edouard's searching gaze with confidence. 'You believe me?' she asked, and then went on, as the old man nodded, 'So please, Monsieur Lacoste — please reconsider your plans about Robert's business — he's done nothing wrong. It was me who behaved so stupidly. . .'

Again that chuckle, stopping her, making her catch her breath, while he turned to Robert, saying between more wheezes and chuckles, 'Liberated, you said? More like a small earthquake breaking out, I think. *Eh bien*, but you have a handful here, *mon brave*! Too much for you, perhaps?'

Robert looked at Patti before answering, and she thought his eyes searched her innermost hopes and fears. He smiled, a generous, amused smile that gentled his lean face. 'Yes, a handful indeed, Edouard,' he mused. 'But not impossible to tame. She has her moments of wonderful tenderness...and I believe we are — at last — beginning to understand each other...' His voice dropped away with the last words, and in his deep eyes Patti saw an acceptance that made her gasp.

Her thoughts were uncontrollable. What did he mean? Had he forgiven her? Was Madame Léonie forgotten? Were they friends again? Her pulse raced — perhaps more than friends?

But Edouard was speaking again. Crisply he said, 'I see how things are between you, Robert. That is good. And now to the other matter — the old rose. And our business connection...'

Patti heard Robert's tone grow wary as he explained the storm damage which had destroyed his embryo rose plants. 'Only one is left,' he finished bleakly. 'Of course, I can start again — more buds, more grafting — but as you know, Edouard, it will take five to ten years to re-establish the rose as a commercial product...'

'And our own attempts here at grafting were useless. That foolish boy! I should never have left it all to him, but I grow old and one must give youth a chance... Well, things change all the time, Robert, we both know it. Perhaps it is time for little Madame Léonie de Sange to rest in peace...' Sadly he shook his head. 'Other roses are being bred — you yourself, *mon ami*, have several beauties on the way up, as I know —

maybe one will prove even more enchanting than the old Gallica.'

His eyes strayed to Patti, who had gasped aloud as he pronounced what she took to be Madame Léonie's death sentence. 'You are sad, Miss Nevill, but do not be. You are young! The world lies before you—and you have done a fine thing, coming here and helping Robert and I to settle our differences.'

She grasped at the straw offered in his last word. 'So you're not going to break off your business connection? And his reputation will remain unharmed? Oh, dear Monsieur Lacoste, that's wonderful——!'

Robert interrupted, a note of surprise deepening his voice. 'But Edouard, in your letter you clearly said——'

The old man held up a callused hand. 'Forget the letter, *mon brave*. Jules persuaded me—I should have known better. Besides, I have heard a little tale today, buzzing around the rosery like that old bee in the window...' His eyes gleamed with secret delight. 'No, no, we will waste no time in talking of it. Instead, let us go into the salon and drink a glass of champagne to celebrate our renewed friendship and business. No doubt the truth will reach you eventually. Now...' Rising, he came around the table, extending his arm towards Patti. 'Miss Nevill, may I have the honour of inviting you into my house to drink to our shared future?'

Patti sighed happily. She got up, put her hand upon his dusty black serge sleeve and, bowing her head demurely, allowed him to lead her from the untidy little office.

* * *

The Veuve Clicquot was deliciously cool and extremely heartening. By the time Patti's glass had been refilled by a twinkling Edouard, she felt as if she were walking on air. But eventually Robert's hand was beneath her elbow, and they went out into the brilliant heat of the courtyard to make their adieus.

Patti, about to open her parasol, saw Jules standing by his motor, polishing the gleaming chrome. He came over the cobbles, smile not quite disguising the dislike in his eyes. 'I will get even with you, Miss Patti,' he muttered. 'Indeed I will. . .'

And then, abruptly, she could no longer control her contempt for him. Wine, sunshine and the relief that the morning's discussions had brought mingled together in a heady brew of explosive action. She pushed him, laughing with delight as she did so, and suddenly remembering a childish epithet which seemed entirely to suit his behaviour. 'You're a horrid pig, Jules Lacoste! Yes, that's what you are—*un cochon*. . .'

Taken by surprise, Jules lost his balance and fell against the body of his car. A huge dent appeared as swiftly he righted himself. French obscenities mingled with Patti's continued laughter, and Robert pulled her away with strong, restraining hands.

'Get into the cab,' he ordered, words stern, but voice bubbling with suppressed mirth. 'You've done enough this morning to last a lifetime, Patti—I think we'll beat a swift retreat before another Nevill eruption occurs. . .'

Edouard Lacoste's hearty laughter followed them as the cab drove away and Patti turned to wave back. The last thing she saw, before leaving the courtyard, was the angry expression on Jules's face as he rushed into the office, hand reaching for the earpiece of the telephone on the wall by the door.

Patti hardly dared to look at Robert as they left the rosery behind them, but when his arm encircled her waist and he said between deep chuckles of amusement, 'Clearly, even the Pankhurst ladies would find it hard to compete with you, Cousin Patti—what a little tiger in lamb's clothing you truly are!' her uneasiness left her. His chuckles grew into peals of loud, unrestrained laughter and he pulled her close, hugging her to his side and kissing her abruptly blushing cheek. 'I shall never forget the look of amazement on Jules's face. . .' he said, when finally the laughter ended. He smiled down into Patti's eyes. 'Thank heavens you're on my side—you make a truly ferocious enemy!

Patti leaned against him, revelling in their closeness and in the enjoyment his smile revealed. 'Serve Jules right,' she murmured happily. 'He deserved all he got.'

Robert nodded, and became solemn. 'He always was a devious chap—even as a child. I never trusted him. Not since the day I caught him kicking one of my dogs. That's a long time ago, but. . .'

Patti began fitting pieces of puzzle together. 'That's why I thought you seemed suspicious of him when first I saw you with him.'

Robert's arm around her tightened. 'That was because he treated you to one of his false smiles and you smiled back!' he teased.

Patti turned her radiant face to him, and forgot about Jules. 'How very nice you can be when you want to, Robert,' she murmured mischievously. 'I do hope this good mood will last—I'm keeping my fingers crossed that you won't lose your temper with me before we get back to Porphyry Court. . .'

And then, suddenly, she realised that she had no need to return there; Faye was in London, and she, as Faye's companion, no longer had a situation to go back to... But, as swiftly as the thought had come, she put it from her. I won't think about that yet...

They had luncheon at a small restaurant overlooking the Seine, eating outside on the balcony, watching the gleaming river dance along beside them. Patti ate lobster salad and drank a dry white wine and thought she had never been so happy.

'And now,' said Robert lazily, as he escorted her out into the sunny afternoon street, 'I have a special treat for you, Miss Nevill.' He cocked an eyebrow at her, and slid a firm hand under her elbow. 'I hope you're not too light-headed after that excellent Chablis to enjoy a little journey into the past?'

Abruptly, Patti's floating mind focused more sharply. 'The past? What do you mean?'

'Wait and see!' Robert's mocking smile filled her dreamy thoughts, and she was content then to sit close to him in another cab while he gave directions to the driver to take them to the Château of la Malmaison. 'Where the Empress Josephine herself lived,' murmured Patti ecstatically, as she heard the famous name. 'Oh, Robert, you couldn't have thought of anything nicer.'

He sat down beside her. 'What, better than shopping in the Champs-Elysées?' he asked teasingly. Then he added, seriously, 'You deserve a treat, little cousin. Life hasn't been exactly easy for you lately, I know. We'll go and see the museum that's recently been opened.'

* * *

The curving drive to the château passed through lush green parkland; here and there Patti caught the distant glint of the afternoon sun on spectacular waterfalls. But it was the enclosed rose garden that touched her heart.

She and Robert wandered along paths laden with fragrant bushes, the scent of many blooms lying heavily on the warm, breathless air. 'Rose Gallica.' Robert halted beside a bush covered with a profusion of elegant scarlet flowers. 'The red rose of Lancaster, originally grown by the Ancient Greeks. Smell it, Patti, and you'll understand just how it started an industry in conserves and similar concoctions that still goes on today. . .'

Their eyes met as Patti lifted her head. 'Poor Madame Léonie's ancestress,' she mused sadly.

Robert nodded. 'We should be thankful that at least the true Gallica lives,' he said shortly.

'And now, please may I see Josephine's house?' Patti asked, sensibly banishing Madame Léonie's demise from her mind. 'Can it possibly be as beautiful as this garden, I wonder?'

Robert took her hand in his. 'Come and see,' he invited.

The entrance to the château was through a veranda and vestibule, ornamented with busts of the Imperial family, and Patti stared hard, unimpressed. 'Napoleon wasn't *nearly* as handsome as I thought,' she complained.

'Handsome is as handsome does,' Robert chuckled. 'I doubt if Josephine shared your disappointment! Let's look at the reception rooms — or would you rather go up to the first floor and see the Empress's private appartments?'

'Her own rooms?' Patti was full of deep and tender feelings. To actually experience something of the life Josephine had lived, here, in this haunted and lovely place, was almost too much to bear. But once she entered the gracious, elegantly-decorated chambers, a great happiness swept through her. 'I'm *sure* Josephine loved this place,' she told Robert earnestly, staring at the huge scarlet and gold ornamental bed, draped with gold embroidered cream curtains, and crowned by the proud sculpture of the Imperial Eagle. And then there were the intimate, personal possessions of the late Empress—a muslin gown, frail and wonderful, a tiny slipper, pictures Josephine had loved, things she had touched and used every day...

'It all has such a serene feel to it, just like the rose garden; and she died in such pain—oh, Robert...' Patti turned away, blinking hard, ashamed at the surge of emotion which threatened to overflow.

But he understood. His arms enclosed her in a quiet corner of the large bed-chamber, and a white linen handkerchief was discreetly pressed into her hand. 'Cheer up,' he said softly, hiding her from the curious stares of the other visitors. 'What a soft-hearted little goose you are!'

The affection in his deep, low voice made her smile rather waterily, but she was able then to regain her poise. 'I'm not a—a goose. But I *am* soft-hearted. I'm sorry...'

'Don't apologise.' He pressed her hand as they retraced their steps down the great stone staircase. 'And don't ever change...'

'And now we must go back to the hotel and have dinner. It's been a long, exciting day.' Robert's voice was gentle as they drove back through the suburbs, and Patti knew that his thoughts were centred entirely upon her well-being. She felt like a princess, her every whim pandered to—indeed, she was so sure of his regard for her that she dared now to ask the question that had had been nagging her since they left England.

'Robert—have you forgiven me? For still claiming Madame Léonie as Grandfather's property?'

She watched his lean face grow pensive and sensed him trying to come to a decision. She was tempted then to turn the balance of his thoughts by revealing the truth of what she had done—but he spoke before she had quite made up her mind to do so.

'If I must be honest, Patti——' his eyes caught at hers, a glint of the old arrogance lighting them '—and nothing else will satisfy you, I know—then I have to say no. No, I have not entirely forgiven you for clinging to your Grandfather's fairy-story. You see, it's not true! I think, in wanting to still believe it, you are being obstinate and romantic and—well——' a brief smile lit his face '— just being Patti Nevill, if you see what I mean. . .' He fingered the medal hanging from his watch chain.

Patti nodded. She was not disappointed; indeed, rather the reverse. She had known that Robert was not a man to change his allegiance and she was proud of the fact. But still she probed. 'But you do agree that it wasn't my fault naughty Miss Clarke decided to publish the story?'

'I do. I absolve you from that bit.' Again the flash of affection in his smile before it abruptly faded. 'But it seems that we are still on opposite sides, Patti.'

She wondered how much further she dared go. 'You

mean you still think of Madame Léonie as a Challoner rose?' she asked innocently.

'Of course! Certainly not a *Nevill* rose. . .' The old pride sharpened his face and his voice, and Patti turned away, looking out of the window of the cab to prevent him seeing the approval which filled her.

Her thoughts wandered a little; how extraordinary that she could now think of Grandfather's story as a mere fantasy, after all those early years of passionate idealism! But she had not met Robert then, had not known that love could be stronger than ideals. . .

'What are you thinking about?' he demanded, and she looked back, recognising vulnerability in his deep eyes and the expression hovering over his mouth. She knew that he needed her, and yet still had doubts that he really trusted her. Wisdom came, joyous and uplifting. Very soon he would know the truth. Very soon all would be well.

And in the meantime it was enjoyable to tease him — just a little. To get her own back, in the nicest possible way, for all the times he, in his turn, had teased her. . .

Her smile was full of mischief, but her eyes glowed warmly. 'Wait and see,' she taunted, using his own words. Then she reached for his hand, touching it shyly. 'I'll tell you later, Robert. When I've had a rest, when I've changed my gown, when we've had dinner. . .'

'Is that a promise?' His eyes were hungry and a thrill spread through her. Silently she nodded, anticipating the moment when, indeed, the truth could be told when there would be no more conflict between them. And then the cab stopped, and it was time again to enter the bustling world, shattering her dreams and hopes for the time being.

The top-hatted commissionaire outside their hotel opened the cab door with a flourish and a smile upon his thin face. 'Good evening, milady.'

Patti imagined she had misheard and smiled an acknowledgement. But once inside the foyer, it became clear that she and Robert were the attention of all eyes. 'Why are they staring at us?' she whispered to Robert, and he smiled wryly back at her.

'It's your hat,' he answered, very low. 'Faye did warn you, you know. . .'

But the diminutive pageboy hid a smirk behind his gloved hand, a passing waiter glanced back at a colleague with a knowing grin, and the manager himself came out from behind the reception desk to welcome their return.

'Good evening, Sir Robert — Lady Challoner. . .' His bow was subservient. 'We had no idea of the good news, until your friend telephoned this morning to tell us. Of course, we have immediately prepared the bridal suite for you.' He twirled the waxed end of his moustache and lowered pale eyes as he waved them towards the waiting lift.

Robert stopped in mid-stride. 'What are you talking about? *Bridal suite*?'

Patti gasped, instinctively knowing that this must be Jules's work, his sly way of getting his revenge, of embarrassing her. Robert's deep voice was growling at the manager. 'I fear some sort of joke has been played on you, Monsieur Pascal. There has been no wedding. And there's certainly no need for the bridal suite! We'll have our old rooms, if you please.'

'But, Sir Robert, they have been occupied. The hotel is very full — and the gentleman who spoke to me was extremely convincing. . .'

'He would be.' Robert was very angry. He glared down into the manager's wondering eyes. 'The whole thing is a mistake. Kindly find us two other rooms. *Separate* rooms. . .' His emphasis on the adjective rolled around the foyer, creating a little buzz of subdued mirth. Patti raised her head defiantly. The joke had gone too far — she and Robert did not deserve the prurient glances and sniggering that was going on. Damn Jules and his nasty mind! With her hand on Robert's arm, proudly she stepped into the lift, her face expressionless and her back very straight.

The manager flew back to the desk, still arguing volubly, and then returned, having conveniently discovered he had, after all, one vacant bedroom for the night. He handed the keys to the grinning liftman, while Robert said angrily to Patti, 'I fear you'll have to sleep in the damned bridal suite after all. . .' His voice rose in a crescendo of rage. 'That bastard, Jules! He must have telephoned. . . I've a good mind to go back to the rosery and teach him a lesson! He should be horsewhipped, if not something much worse. . .'

Patti tried to calm him down by saying in English, so that the liftman would not understand, 'It's just a stupid and rather distasteful joke, Robert.' And then, foolishly, she tried to embellish the awkward situation. 'Are you telling me you don't want to share the bridal suite with me. . .?' Instantly she knew she had gone too far.

Robert stared at her, exasperation written plain on his cross face. 'Don't you start, too, Patti,' he said between his teeth. 'I've had enough of practical jokes for today!'

'But — but that *wasn't* a joke. . .' Her voice was

muffled as she quickly turned aside, staring at the lift floor. 'I love you, Robert. I—I want you. . .'

She gave a gasp of dismay, even as the words left her lips. She'd done it again! Said the wrong thing at the wrong moment. . . The lift groaned, jerked and then stopped. Robert grabbed her hand without looking at her, and strode rapidly down the passage, followed by the liftman with the keys. Patti was shown into the bridal suite, where she immediately shut the door behind her, and listened to Robert's heavy footsteps fading away as he was conducted to his own room, somewhere in the labyrinthine depths of the hotel.

Once her head had stopped spinning with regret and shame at her reckless and ill-timed declaration of love, slowly she recovered herself. She looked around the ornately decorated bedroom with interest, gloomily aware of how much pleasure the plush surroundings must give to a newly married couple, already floating high on a cloud of romantic love. . .

The shining glass chandelier swayed slightly in the evening breeze that touched the thick pink brocade curtains. A Turkish carpet, rich with scarlets, peacock-blues and golden tones, felt like spongy moss as she moved across the room. Small gilt gas-fittings on the walls provided intimate pools of glowing light, and the bed. . .

Patti stood beside it, her heart starting to race. Such a bed! A handsome oak four-poster, its end carved with nude figures coupling in astonishingly intricate positions that raised her ignorant eyebrows very high, festooned with curtains of billowy muslin, all delicately embroidered with pink bows, and caught back in thick swaths by matching, gold-tasselled velvet bands.

She sat down nervously on a mattress that lured her down into its inviting depths. Her thoughts swelled suddenly with sensuous longings, and she had to force herself back into a more decorous frame of mind. Determination came winging with new hopes; all was not lost yet. She still had one card left up her sleeve — would it prove to be the trump that might, even now, win the vital prize of Robert's love and trust?

Her eyes gleamed as she left the bed to prepare for the evening that lay ahead — for her last chance to clear herself in his eyes and persuade him that he need have no more fears about either her honesty, her fidelity — or her abiding love for him.

She went down the sweeping staircase knowing that she had done her best to please him. The new emerald-green silk gown fitted sleekly about her small bosom, the modest neckline heavily swathed with creamy guipure lace which matched the cascade falling about her wrists from tight sleeves. Her eighteen-inch waist swelled discreetly into curving hips over which the shining silk fell in luxurious folds, forming a small train that whispered with every step she took. She had dressed her hair high over a small transformation, and decorated its auburn richness with a single osprey feather mounted on a comb, the dyed feather exactly matching the green of her gown.

When she met Robert, awaiting her at the foot of the staircase, she knew, by his awed and approving expression, that she looked as beautiful as she had wished herself to be.

He offered her his arm, and she smiled up into his melting eyes, her mind reeling with pleasure. He was looking at her, she thought, as if he could eat her. . . She felt his gaze sweep rapidly from her face to the toes of her small satin shoes, peeping from below the green gown.

Then they were on her face again. As they entered the palatial hotel dining-room and she was shown to a table in a discreetly shaded corner, she became aware of the hunger in his eyes. Rosy happiness suffused her body and she smiled radiantly at him as he seated himself opposite her, so wonderfully charismatic and handsome in his black tailcoat and pristine white linen.

She waited until the *maître d'hôtel* had retired and then could restrain herself no longer. 'Robert,' she murmured, her heart almost too full to speak, 'what I said in the lift — about — about — loving you. . .' Pausing, she looked deep into his eyes and then, incredulous and almost destroyed by pain, saw them grow abruptly guarded and wary.

With controlled hands, Robert spread a napkin across his knees. 'Ah, yes,' he said crisply, and in those two words Patti heard his rejection of her offered love. 'Ah yes' meant he had become the patriarch again. The guardian. Lowering her head and blinking hard, she guessed, raging biterly, that he would doubtless call her 'my dear' in a minute. . .

'My dear Patti,' he said, sounding avuncular and only slightly amused. 'I know how carried away you can easily be — by people, by situations, by your own ——' he paused and she thought his voice was unsteady, but only for a moment '— your unruly emotions.' He hurried on. 'We'll say no more about the matter. Just a slip of the tongue after that wine, I dare say. Now. . .' He picked up the gold-rimmed menu. 'Do you favour the frogs' legs in cream and wine, or good old *sole à la bonne femme*?'

* * *

Dinner, despite the excellence of food, wine and service, was the worst experience of Patti's entire life. Somehow she and Robert conversed, but merely on a very superficial level; the weather, the atmospheric noise and flavour of Parisian streets in late summer. The journey back to England tomorrow. The autumnal work awaiting Robert at Porphyry Court...

By the time the lengthy meal was over Patti was exhausted. The wonderful moment she had been longing for had never come. What was the point now, she asked herself wretchedly, of playing a trump card when the other player had clearly opted out of the game? She had no heart to do anything, save retire upstairs and weep alone in the silence of the disgustingly plush bedroom...

When Robert bade her goodnight, a flicker of belated awareness returned to her numbed wits, and she suddenly realised how he, too, suffered: shadows bruising the flesh around his eyes, set lips; a muscle that twitched below his cheek. For a second she was possessed by the urge to fling herself into his arms and cry, 'Don't be so silly, Robert! Please just love me!' but she had learned a hard lesson recently. Instead, she smiled wearily. 'Goodnight, Robert.'

'Patti...' There was an urgency in his voice that made her stop on the threshold of her room, making her senses tingle, her heart leap anew. But then he said, in his usual tight voice, 'I hope you sleep well. Goodnight, Patti.'

Closing the door behind her, she leaned against it and at last allowed herself to give way to the misery that swamped every other thought in her distraught mind.

* * *

Spent with passion, cheeks still wet from tears, eventually she undressed and clambered into the huge, opulent bed. Never in her whole life had she felt so alone in the world—alone and rejected. Her thoughts rose and fell like a switchback. Impossible now to return to Porphyry Court with Robert; he had made it abundantly clear that he did not—could not?—love her. She must find a new situation, make a new life for herself, become used to the idea that Robert might well marry the horrible, divine Barbara—and, also, she had lost Madame Léonie. . .

She fell asleep long before any decision about her future had been made, and then awoke abruptly. A noise, intruding into her mishmash dreams. A quiet, yet persistent, tapping on the door. . .

Half asleep still, she slipped out of bed, pulling a wrapper around her, and stumbled to the door. Was it a fire? A message from England? Lady Challoner, unwell again, perhaps? Beth's baby. . .?

A familiar figure stood, dark and bulky, in the shadows of the corridor. Patti's hazy mind cleared instantly. 'Robert!'

She stared at him, saw his eyes linger on her disarrayed clothing, and quickly stepped back. 'What is it?' she asked unevenly.

Entering the room, he closed the door behind him and stood there, for a stretching moment, staring at her. Patti's heart hammered; her senses sung. Quickly, he went to the nearest gas jet and lit it before turning to her again. In the small, cosy glow, they looked at each other very intently. Patti thought he seemed in some way different from the stern, falsely jolly man she had only recently dined with. His deep eyes were hesitant, his voice almost tentative as he searched her startled eyes.

'What can I say, Patti?'

'I—I don't know, Robert. What do you *want* to say?'

'Just that I love you. . .'

He led her towards the bed, and drew her down on to it, relaxed now, at ease, and beset with laughter that made her whisper anxiously, 'Hush! Someone will hear!'

He moved—that fast, lithe action that had always taken her by surprise—and she was in his arms, his lips just a breath away from hers. 'If they do, they won't mind.' Delicately, he kissed the tip of her nose, her fluttering eyelids, her brow and the side of her face, pausing only to whisper mockingly, 'We *are* in the bridal suite, you know!' and then continued kissing his way down to her chin, her throat, and finally the warm flesh that hid beneath the prim white silk nightdress.

Vaguely Patti wondered if she had died in the night and woken up in Heaven—but Robert's lips and hands were awakening sensuous feelings that surely had no place anywhere but here on earth. . .

Somehow she freed herself from his caressing hands, his ardent mouth, and pulled away to sit, straight and breathless, at the far side of the vast bed.

'Explain!' she demanded, wide-eyed. 'Please explain! I mean—well, why? Now? All of a sudden. . .'

Robert sighed, and lazily spread his length down the bed, regarding her with hooded, dancing eyes. 'How typically Nevill,' he said affectionately. 'In the middle of the greatest love scene of the decade, suddenly you have to ask questions!' Reaching for her hand, he kissed its palm and held it to his heart. She watched his face grow serious. 'Very well, I'll tell you. Because there is a reason. . .' He looked deep into her eyes. 'You didn't tell me what you had done,' he accused gravely. 'That apology in the paper. Your disclaimer to the ownership of Madame Léonie. . .'

'Oh!' Patti's free hand flew to her mouth, and a radiant smile spread across her face. 'The editor printed it? So dear Mr Fraser did as I asked. . .'

Robert's face was full of curiosity, but she merely laughed. 'I was going to tell you, but——' she faltered, remembering '—but everything went wrong this evening, didn't it?'

He nodded. 'My fault—again. And I was so furious with myself after dinner that I had to walk the streets for an hour or so to cool down. Then I took a look at the English newspapers before coming to bed, and there it was. And then I knew what I had to do. And here I am. . .'

His warm fingers curled protectively around her hand, and he pleaded, with a strangely humble tone to the quiet words, 'Can you ever forgive me? For not allowing myself to trust you? You see, sweetheart, it took your unselfish act of giving up Madame Léonie to make me realise just how self-centred and proud and— yes!—so damned foolish I've been. Patti. . .?'

'Yes, Robert?'

'*Can* you love me? As I truly love you?

'Oh, yes, Robert! Very easily indeed! Let me show you. . .'

He kissed her then with a thoroughness and expertise that once again forged the old magic between them, sending great waves of love and desire through her. When he whispered unsteadily, 'Darling! Darling! Oh, God, how I love you!' she could only murmur foolish words of delight and answering passion.

But Robert would not allow her abandon to carry them beyond the limits of his own firmly embedded sense of morality. 'No,' he whispered, as she sought to persuade him, 'not yet, my darling. But soon, I promise you. Very soon.'

'Don't go,' she pleaded. 'Don't go!'

Disentangling her clinging arms, reluctantly he left her there in the great bed, settling himself on the nearby *chaise-longue*, a reassuring shadow close to her, but not close enough for disturbance.

Before she slept, she heard him murmur lovingly, and with a hint of fond amusement, 'Remember the storm, sweetheart? This isn't the first time I've spent the night with you — and it certainly won't be the last.'

Patti's sleepy eyes opened wide. 'But — but I thought you were with Barbara. . .'

He laughed. 'Only because she swore there was a mouse hiding under her bed! I didn't stay long, I can tell you — not when I knew you needed me. I went straight to your room; you were sleeping then, but I stayed beside you. . .'

She smiled lovingly. 'How good you are to me, dear Robert.' Her voice fell into a sensuous murmur. 'Oh, my love, must you stay so far away. . .?'

Sleep claimed her then, and she fell into a delicious, dreaming state of joy, in which he was close beside her, and the magic they made went on — and on. . .

On their return to Porphyry Court, Patti was happy to spend time trying to explain Faye's plans to a slightly bemused Lady Challoner and then visiting Beth and

James at Clematis Cottage. Here her emotions could no longer restrain themselves—she burst out radiantly, 'Isn't it just wonderful? Robert and I are in love! Oh, everything is so marvellous. . .'

'Dearest, I *am* pleased! But. . .' Beth's smile faded. 'But what about Madame Léonie?'

'Oh, I've given up all thoughts of *that*!' remarked Patti dismissively. 'Love is so much more important than silly old childish ideals. . .'

Beth's lips twitched. 'I see. And so you and Robert are actually engaged, dearest?'

'Well—not yet. I mean, of course we *will* be—I suppose. . .'

'Patti,' said Beth severely, 'what you mean is that naughty Cousin Robert hasn't popped the question yet; well, you must *make* him do so. . .'

Deadheading the overblown roses with Robert one late August afternoon, Patti removed the borrowed leather glove from her left hand and looked anxiously at her ringless third finger.

Beth's comments echoed in her mind and she stared at Robert. She was very confused as to his intentions . . .certainly he seemed very fond of her, was most attentive, and thoroughly delightful, but he had said nothing about actually *marrying her*. . .

A dreadful thought edged into Patti's mind, to be instantly banished, and then slowly and uneasily reconsidered. Could it be that he was, after all, just a charming philanderer, a man who delighted in kisses and embraces, but stopped short of a definite commitment? Was he merely treating her as the temptation he had once called her? Did he have no plan at all to propose to her?

'Robert!' She gasped out his name, and at once he looked at her.

'What is it, sweetheart?'

'We do — love each other — don't we?'

'Indeed we do, my darling.' His smile was reassuring, but still her fear remained.

Taking a huge breath, Patti whispered unevenly, 'But — but you haven't — well — proposed to me. Not yet. . .'

There was a pause that went on for ever. Robert took her hand, smiling down at it as if with secret amusement. His eyes met hers, deep and unreadable. 'Mmm! We must do something about it, Patti — one of these days. Now what do you think of my new plan to sign a contract with John Curtis for the sole sale to him of the Porphyry Beauty roses?'

Sighing, and acknowledging the diversion, she nodded, thankful at least that he now considered her a part of his business. But her confidence was lowered. She wondered still whether his intentions were as honourable as she had first thought.

And then, two days later, he sought her out as she went rather drearily about her indoor duties for Lady Challoner.

'I wish to make an appointment with you, Patti — it's important.' His face was alive with pleasure, his eyes so rich and full that instinctively she brightened.

'An appointment, Robert — what on earth do you mean?'

He grasped her hands and held them to his heart. 'I've been waiting, you see — but the time is very near now. Dear, delightful, adorable Miss Nevill. . .shall we say Saturday of this week at — let me see — would ten-thirty in the morning suit you?'

'What for?' She was astounded, but excited.

He pulled her towards her and slowly kissed her mouth. 'To propose, of course...' His smile grew. 'Did you think I was never going to? Well, come and keep this appointment on Saturday...'

'Saturday morning!' Despite her joy, a faint disappointment intruded. 'But isn't the evening more appropriate? In the moonlight? With owls hooting and the honeysuckle smelling wonderful?'

'Not for the proposal I have in mind,' he said firmly, then added teasingly, 'Take it or leave it, my darling!'

She grabbed at his hands. 'I'll take it! Whenever you say!'

'Good. Then we'll meet in glasshouse number three at half-past ten on Saturday morning.' Meeting her surprised eyes, he added wryly, 'This is quite ridiculous, Patti!'

'But so romantic...' Adoration lit her face.

Robert grinned. 'And being so romantically minded, you will, of course, dress accordingly...'

'Only if you will too!'

He pulled her very close and kissed her parted lips again. 'It's a deal, then, my lovely...'

Dressing for a proposal? How foolish! Patti's fingers were all thumbs as she did up the small pearl buttons of her pale cotton print dress — the dress Robert liked so much. How on earth would she ever deal with a wedding, if she felt so nervous already? She tied the chiffon veil untidily around the old straw hat as she ran downstairs and out into the sunlit garden, her mind a jumble of thoughts and images. Why on earth had Robert insisted on proposing in a glasshouse? And why the *third* glasshouse?

HEART OF A ROSE

Wearing his green lovat jacket and the old, shabby checked shirt, he awaited her, saying nothing as she approached, but smiling tenderly and leading her into the hot glasshouse.

Patti savoured the sensual atmosphere. An earthy, moist fragrance. Warmth. And a familiar tingle through her senses, bringing anticipatory delight. . .

The shelves were full of small plants in earthenware pots, all of them, Patti noticed, once she had come down to earth again, thriving roses. For a second, as her eyes ran the gamut of the shelving on both sides of the house, she felt a stab of disappointment. No Madame Léonie here.

But Robert's hand was firm about hers. He stopped at the end of the shelving, and looked down into her wondering eyes. 'This is my new rose,' he said crisply, but there was a depth of feeling in his low voice that made her catch her breath. 'The plant is healthy, well established and almost eight years old, which means it's safely on the road to commercial production.' He paused, and then smiled teasingly. 'I've given it a sex—she's a female rose—but as yet she has no name. And I've been waiting for her to bloom before I brought you here to see her. . .'

'She's—beautiful. . .' Bewildered, Patti looked carefully at the fragile white blossom that his tender fingers turned up for her inspection. Golden stamens frilled around a central heart. . . Patti swallowed the sudden tightness in her throat.

'The heart of a rose. . .' She murmured the mysterious words to herself. But it was a mystery no longer, for here *they* were—she and Robert—with their love declared. . . She turned her glowing face towards

Robert. 'And what is this gorgeous new rose to be called?' she enquired unsteadily.

Robert's arms folded around her, his darkly luminous eyes staring deep into hers. 'Lady Challoner, I hope,' he answered very slowly, and humbly. 'She's to be *your* rose, darling Patti — if you will accept her. I hope she will replace your beloved but lost Madame Léonie. Certainly, she will ensure you a niche in the future history of the rose — just like the Empress Josephine!' A fond, teasing smile crinkled the sunburned skin beside his dark eyes, and he caressed her cheek with a large, gentle forefinger. 'I've tried to make you the most romantic proposal that anyone could ever conjure up — is it enough, my darling? My heart, my name, and my new rose?'

'Oh, yes, yes! Of course it is!' Patti was bubbling with happiness. Throwing her arms around his neck, she pulled his head down towards her own. 'I accept, darling Robert! But how *wonderful* to be called Lady Challoner, and have a rose named after me, and to marry you, and — and——'

'Patti,' Robert cut in autocratically, but with dancing eyes and a tender quirk to his mouth, 'for heaven's sake, stop chattering! And I can't possibly kiss you properly in that damned hat. . .'

Slowly, carefully, he began to untie the chiffon veil beneath her chin, but, as her hat fell to the ground, Patti was in no state to notice its descent.

MILLS & BOON

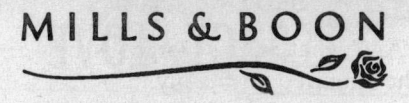

CHRISTMAS KISSES...

...THE GIFT OF LOVE

Four exciting new Romances to melt your heart this Christmas from some of our most popular authors.

ROMANTIC NOTIONS — Roz Denny
TAHITIAN WEDDING — Angela Devine
UNGOVERNED PASSION — Sarah Holland
IN THE MARKET — Day Leclaire

Available November 1993   *Special Price only £6.99*

*Available from W. H. Smith, John Menzies, Martins, Forbuoys, most supermarkets and other paperback stockists.
Also available from Mills & Boon Reader Service, FREEPOST, PO Box 236, Thornton Road, Croydon, Surrey CR9 9EL. (UK Postage & Packing free)*

LEGACY of LOVE

Coming next month

DEBT OF HONOUR
Gail Mallin

Cumbria 1793

Sophie Fleming knew that she had an indulgent guardian in her Uncle Thomas, after all, at 20 and an heiress, she might have been expected to be married long since. It was flattering to receive the attentions of Sir Pelham Stanton, but Sophie wasn't quite sure what she thought of him. She definitely knew what she thought of Kirk Thorburn! He was rude and abrupt and completely lacking in manners! He was also the most exciting man she had ever seen, and clearly there was very bad feeling between Kirk and Pelham. Caught in the middle, not aware of how long standing the feud was, how could Sophie know which man to believe?

DEVIL-MAY-DARE
Mary Nichols

Regency

Jack Bellingham knew something peculiar was going on, and it seemed that Lydia Wenthorpe was at the centre of the intrigue. He had enough to do trying to trace the owners of a cache of jewels he had found when fighting in the French wars, but when it seemed that Lydia also might be after the jewels, Jack was determined to find out exactly what she was up to!

Lydia, in fear of being discovered, found herself torn between wanting Jack near her, yet as far away as she could send him. There seemed no answer to her dilemma...

LEGACY of LOVE

Coming next month

STARDUST AND WHIRLWINDS
Pamela Litton

Texas 1873

In the dusty town of Santa Angela, the only law was the gun, and Amelia Cummings' no-good husband had died by it, leaving her with a debt-ridden mercantile business. Gunslinger Ross Tanner seemed anxious for her to leave, but she wasn't ready to give up just yet.

To Ross, Amelia appeared to be made of stronger stuff than her husband. Still, the frontier was no place for a lady, and she needed someone to protect her from the dangerous men the harsh land seemed to breed. Someone besides himself. Because as far as the widow Cummings was concerned, he was the most dangerous of all.

AUTUMN ROSE
Louisa Rawlings

France 1672

Years spent cloistered in Normandy had done little to temper the spirited Amalie de Saint-Hillaire. While travelling to her father's château, she had flirted shamelessly with handsome Jean-Marc Beaunoir, never dreaming the rogue was on his way to the very same destination.

What had begun as a playful seduction had turned into something far more serious than Jean-Marc had intended. The young architect marvelled as Amalie blossomed with each forbidden caress, but the past had taught him that love could not bridge the barriers of class. Had destiny made them prisoners of a love that could never be?

FOUR HISTORICAL ROMANCES & TWO FREE GIFTS!

LEGACY OF LOVE

Witness the fight for love and honour, and experience the tradition and splendour of the past for FREE! We will send you FOUR Legacy of Love romances PLUS a cuddly teddy and a mystery gift. Then, if you choose, go on to enjoy FOUR exciting Legacy of Love romances for only £2.50 each! Return the coupon below today to:-
Mills & Boon Reader Service, FREEPOST, PO Box 236, Croydon, Surrey CR9 9EL

NO STAMP REQUIRED

Please rush me FOUR FREE *Legacy of Love* romances and TWO FREE gifts! Please also reserve me a Reader Service subscription, which means I can look forward to receiving FOUR brand new *Legacy of Love* romances for only £10.00 every month, postage and packing FREE. If I choose not to subscribe, I shall write to you within 10 days and still keep my FREE books and gifts. I may cancel or suspend my subscription at any time. I am over 18 years. Please write in BLOCK CAPITALS.

*Ms/Mrs/Miss/Mr*_____ EP61M

Address _____

_____

_____ *Postcode* _____

Signature _____

Offer closes 31st March 1994. The right is reserved to refuse an application and change the terms of this offer. One application per household. Overseas readers please write for details. Offer not valid to current Legacy of Love subscribers. Offer valid in UK and Eire only. Southern Africa write to IBS, Private Bag, X3010, Randburg, 2125, South Africa. You may be mailed with offers from other reputable companies as a result of this application. Please tick box if you would prefer not to receive such offers. ☐

mps MAILING PREFERENCE SERVICE